The House on Creek Road

Caron Todd

TORONTO • NEW YORK • LONDON
AMSTERDAM • PARIS • SYDNEY • HAMBURG
STOCKHOLM • ATHENS • TOKYO • MILAN • MADRID
PRAGUE • WARSAW • BUDAPEST • AUCKLAND

ISBN 0-373-71159-X

THE HOUSE ON CREEK ROAD

This edition published by arrangement with Harlequin Books S.A.

Visit us at www.eHarlequin.com

Printed in U.S.A.

Despite the dull browns and grays of late fall, the farm looked beautiful

Liz pulled over, as far off the road as she could get. If she parked in the field that was already bumper-to-bumper with cars her escape route might be cut off by people arriving later. She pulled down the sun visor for one last check of her appearance. The view in the small rectangular mirror wasn't reassuring.

Pretending not to notice the curious faces that had turned her way, Liz lifted a monster salad bowl from the back seat. She could sense anxiety in the air, and restrained excitement, as if people were waiting to see the queen or Santa Claus at the end of a long parade and thought someone might get in their line of vision. Was she the source of all that feeling or had it just been too long between parties?

There was a barrier between herself and the people who'd come to welcome her, and she didn't know how to cross it. She didn't *want* to cross it.

Dear Reader,

I decided to come home to my own province for my second novel. You tend to think of somewhere else, anywhere else, as being a more romantic setting than the place where you live, but it struck me a while ago that the history, geography and population of Manitoba are so varied I could write for the next twenty years without leaving these borders and find a different background for each story. "Three Creeks" is the original, discarded name of a town near mine. It was satisfying to rescue it and give it to my fictitious town.

In *The House on Creek Road* Elizabeth Robb (a cousin of Susannah Robb from *Into the Badland*—Harlequin Superromance #1053) returns to Three Creeks to help her grandmother sort through a lifetime's worth of belongings before selling the family farm. She has mixed feelings about spending time in this rural area dominated by her family and by an incident she can't forget. Her grandmother's new neighbor, Jack McKinnon, catches her eye and her imagination right away, but he has a secret that might hurt them both if he can't keep it hidden.

So many people helped with this book, answering questions and telling stories about rural life, explaining the mysteries of old houses, describing what Jack might be doing with computers and how Liz might make children's books. Writing a book to deadline for the first time had its challenges. My thanks to Superromance editor Laura Shin whose humor and skill and confidence-building I so appreciate, and to my husband, who, when I was discouraged by the things I don't like about small-town life, took me for coffee in an old, tin-ceilinged building in a beautiful, peaceful town not far away, reminding me of the things I like best.

Sincerely,

Caron Todd

P.S. I'd love to her from readers. Please write to me at
P.O. Box 20045, Brandon, MB, R7A 6Y8 or ctodd@prairie.ca.

To my grandmother, who always won at double solitaire.

CHAPTER ONE

"ANYTHING?"

His new partner shook his head. "You never know with these old houses. Nooks and crannies everywhere. Did you get into his files?"

"Nope."

"We could take the laptop with us."

"Just to let him know we were here? No, thanks." A suggestion like that made him wonder. Was this guy dumber or more reckless than he looked, or was it a test? They'd been working together for a week, but they might as well have been standing at opposite ends of the morning bus for all they'd got to know each other. "Anyway, a laptop's too easy to lose. Not a good place to store something really valuable."

"Maybe he destroyed it, just like he said."

"Never."

"You're sure?"

"I know him."

There was a short silence. "We can look again."

"Right. And when he gets home, he can give us a hand."

The little guy from town, sniffing and gurgling as usual, came down the stairs from the second floor. "He's supposed to see an implement dealer in Brandon next

Friday. It's a couple of hours both ways, never mind looking at equipment.''

As hard as it was to believe, the farm seemed to be the real thing. ''Friday it is. We'll have all day. If it's here, we'll find it.''

A POOL OF MURKY LIGHT CUT A FEW feet of gravel road out of the darkness. Liz reached over the steering wheel and wiped her already damp sleeve through the condensation clouding the windshield. Trembling beads of water stood on the glass, then slid, in little zigzagging streams, to the bottom. In seconds, the fog began to form again. She cracked open the window. Crisp cold air, full of the smells of fallen leaves and field fires, flowed into the car.

She must have taken the wrong road. Some people might have an internal compass, but she didn't. North was wherever she was pointing, west and east were always changing places. The turnoff had felt right, though. Her body had seemed to tell her to turn, as if her cells remembered the way even if she didn't. Since then, not a single landmark. Just miles of bush and empty fields, and the odd furry thing darting in front of the car, evidently sure where *it* was going. So much for cells.

Liz glanced at the clock on the dash. Two hours since she'd left the lights of the city behind. It felt like ten. If Susannah had been navigating, they'd be warm in their grandmother's kitchen by now. They had planned to come together, one last visit for old times' sake, after Susannah had finished her season's digging for bones and Liz her new children's book. But Sue had looked up from her fossils long enough to fall in love with the man digging beside her, and instead of coming home to Three Creeks with her cousin, she'd gone off to the Gobi Desert with her new husband. It wasn't old times without Sue.

"Now, what's this?" Liz slowed almost to a stop. A few dots of light to her left suggested a house set far back from the road. She could just make out a scraggly grove of bur oaks. It was the Ramsey place! She'd done it, after all. Five minutes stood between her and a gallon of tea.

No need to worry about fogged windows now—she could drive this last section of road blindfolded. A clear view and five minutes of October night air might be safer, though. Liz held one finger on the switch that had seen so much action over the past couple of hours, and the driver's window hummed all the way down. Above it, she heard another sound. She turned to look. A car was coming right at her.

Her stomach lurched. She wrenched the steering wheel to the right, and floored the gas pedal. Her car surged forward and sideways. The rear tires bit into loose gravel and the back end began to skid. Just a little, then sharply. She heard herself swearing softly even before she saw the deer. On the side of the road. Deep in the ditch. Everywhere.

They bolted. All but one. Sides heaving, knees locked. At the last moment, it leapt away, the white of its raised tail flashing once before it disappeared. The car slid past the place where the deer had stood and came to a jolting stop when it met a rock at the crest of the ditch.

Liz sat, trembling, her hands clutching the steering wheel. Where was the other car? It had come out of nowhere. No headlights. No horn. She fumbled for the recessed door handle. Cold air hit her legs when she stepped out of the car, and her heels sank into soft gravel. Heels. They'd seemed just right in Vancouver.

"Is anybody there?" Rustling noises came from the ditch. Small, slinking noises. Liz moved closer to the middle of the road, to the smooth track where tires had worn away the gravel. "Hello?"

She walked a short distance on legs that still wobbled, reluctant to go further than her car's headlights reached. She peered along the road and into the ditches on either side, trying to distinguish in the shades of darkness, shrubs from rocks from empty space. There would be a glint from metal or glass, if a car had crashed. A smell of burning rubber, or the sound of an engine still running. The other driver must have gone. The new neighbor, maybe, the pumpkin farmer who'd bought the Ramsey place last year.

Everyone was all right, then. That was the main thing. Even the deer was all right. She had been so sure it would die, that it would come through the windshield, sharp hooves flailing at her head, and she would die, too. There were always deer on the roads in fall. They wandered from field to field, grazing on stubble and hay bales, gorging themselves before winter. She had forgotten.

The car door was wide open, and at last the windshield was completely clear. Liz buckled up, then eased her foot onto the gas pedal. The wheels turned, and there was a skin-crawling scrape of metal against rock as the car ground forward. A glitch in her happy ending. She'd never damaged a car before, not enough to notice, anyway. Had she got the extra insurance? Twelve dollars for peace of mind, the clerk at the rental desk had said. She must have got it. Still, they'd be angry.

At jogging pace, she drove until she came to a bend where the road curved to follow the largest of the three creeks. For anyone reading a map, it was still Creek Road from here on in, but locally it had always been known as Robb's Road. It was narrow, darkened by Manitoba maples that filled the ditches and nearly met overhead. When they were children, it had seemed like part of their own land. They'd walked or ridden their bikes or horses right down the middle, surprised, and a little indignant, if cars came along raising dust and expecting space.

The woods thinned, and the house came into view. Her grandmother had made sure she couldn't miss it: two stories of light glowed through the maples and elms in the yard, tall narrow windows and a wide front entrance beckoning. As she turned into the driveway something emerged from the lilac bushes, a large, slow-moving shape that divided into two as it drew nearer. Black labs. There had always been black labs at Grandma's, quiet dignified dogs who kept a careful eye on visitors. If they knew you, their dignity fell away and they brought sticks and fallen crab apples for you to throw. These two didn't know Liz. They trotted just ahead of the car, out of the way, but watching.

"This is so weird," she whispered. An odd, disjointed feeling had come over her, as if there were a fold in time, as if the past and present occupied the same space. She could see herself at five, at ten, at fifteen…all coming up the driveway with her now, all greeted by the dogs. Like the *Twilight Zone.* That couldn't be good. The *Twilight Zone* never had a happy ending.

The driveway was empty. Relief mixed with disappointment. She'd half expected her entire family to be waiting, arms outstretched. Not that it would have been as big a group as it used to be. The family wasn't replacing itself with its old gusto, and not everyone chose to farm and live along Robb's Road these days. Even her parents had retired to White Rock, just an hour south of her apartment, close enough for Sunday dinners.

Liz lifted her overnight bag from the passenger seat. There were two larger cases in the trunk, filled with clothes and presents and sketches to show her grandmother, but she'd leave them until morning. Now all she had to do was get safely past the dogs. She pushed open the car door. "Hey there, big fellas."

"Bella! Dora!" The dogs pricked up their ears and bounded toward a small figure on the veranda, by the side door. "Elizabeth, you're not afraid of the dogs, are you?"

"Grandma!" Liz hurried to the house. She let her bag drop to the ground and gently wrapped her arms around her grandmother. Bella and Dora stood quietly, reserving judgment. "Of course I'm not scared."

"They're Flora's granddaughters." Eleanor's voice was muffled by Liz's shoulder. "You remember how friendly she was. By tomorrow they'll think they've known you forever. Now, come in—you're shivering. Didn't the heater work?"

"It was the fan. I had to leave the window open to see. Then your new neighbor came crashing out of his driveway without headlights and nearly ran me off the road—" Her grandmother gave an anxious exclamation. Liz wished she hadn't said anything. "I'm completely fine. Nothing to worry about."

Just inside the door, she stopped. A man sat at the

kitchen table drinking tea, a stranger with unblinking silver eyes. He put down his cup and stood, one hand outstretched. ''Jack McKinnon. The neighbor.''

His voice was warm and medium-deep. Now that she was closer to him, she could see that his eyes were light gray, not silver. They looked watchful. Like the dogs, suspending judgment. She smiled, but his expression didn't relax. ''The car was going the other way, toward the highway, so I suppose it couldn't have been you.''

He lifted her overnight bag onto a chair. ''You think it came from my driveway, though?''

''It must have. Nothing else intersects with the road there. I hope it wasn't somebody causing you trouble.''

''Boys up to no good on a Friday night,'' Eleanor said. ''They'll settle down once hockey starts.'' She exclaimed when Liz gave a sudden shiver. ''You're chilled to the bone! No wonder, with your sleeve so wet. Let's get you out of this coat.'' She pulled while Liz shrugged her way out of the sleeves. Jack McKinnon took the coat and hung it on one of a series of hooks by the door.

Eleanor patted an armchair beside the woodstove. ''Come sit by the fire.'' She shook out a crocheted afghan that had been folded over the back of the chair, multicolored squares edged with black. ''Wrap that around you, and we'll get a hot drink into you. I should have told you to stay in the city overnight, or to take the bus out. You're not used to country driving anymore.''

Liz pulled the afghan up to her chin. The wool was itchy, but it was warm enough to be worth it. ''Please don't worry, Grandma. Why don't you sit down? You and Mr. McKinnon.''

''Can I help, Eleanor?''

''If you'd just bring over a cup of tea? Clear, unless she's changed her ways.''

The neighbor appeared in front of Liz, holding out a cup three-quarters full of a liquid so dark she couldn't see the pattern at the bottom. Eleanor liked her tea strong. No loose leaves, no added flavors, no subtle blending of green and black, just plain tea strong enough to stain the cup and your teeth and keep you up half the night. Liz handled the cup carefully. It was the special-occasion Spode. She hadn't seen it since all the hullabaloo after her marriage.

She pulled her mind away from the memory. Her grandmother and Jack McKinnon bustled around together, arranging two more chairs and a small table near the stove, bringing cups and cream and sugar. Eleanor had hardly changed since her last visit to Vancouver. She looked a little smaller, a little thinner, but her short white hair was still permed into gentle curls, and she wore the style of dress she always had: knee-length, belted, three-quarter sleeves. She sewed them herself, apparently from the same pattern each time. This one was cornflower blue, one of her best colors. The kitchen was the same as it had always been, too. Nothing seemed moved or worn or different in any way, as if the room had been turned off when Liz left fifteen years ago, and had just been turned back on now.

One thing was different. The neighbor. Liz never would have expected to find such a perfect man in her grandmother's kitchen. He was just the right height, tall, but not so tall that you'd get a stiff neck looking up at him. He moved almost gracefully, handling the china with long, narrow fingers, the fingers of a surgeon or a violinist, strong but precise in their movements—

Enough of that. At her age, hovering near the brink of her mid-thirties, it was time to stop idealizing every man she met. Past time.

"Did you want the pie and dessert plates by the fire, too, Eleanor?"

"If there's room on that little table..."

So who was he, if not a graceful violinist or a neurosurgeon in hiding? Liz tried to limit herself to observable fact. He wore blue jeans and a high-necked navy fleece top, open at the throat. There was a touch of gray in his almost black hair and a suggestion of lines, laugh lines and frown lines, near those peculiar eyes. Calluses had formed on the palms of his hands, so he didn't just play at farming. About thirty-five, she guessed.

Graceful, but strong. With long fingers that touched things so lightly and carefully that her mind inevitably wandered... It couldn't be helped. Those were facts, too.

When the tea and dishes were arranged to Eleanor's satisfaction, she and Jack joined Liz by the stove. "Are you warm yet, Elizabeth?"

"Toasty. Thanks, Grandma."

Jack looked at her over his teacup. "Eleanor tells me you've come to help her organize her things before the move."

Liz nodded. "I'm still having trouble picturing you in an apartment, Grandma."

"You won't once you see it. It's really very nice. All the suites are on the ground floor, with doors lead-ing to tiny private yards. Tenants can plant flowers and vegetables, if they want. Isn't that a thoughtful touch? It's almost like a house, except there's help if you need it. I'll be very comfortable."

"But it's in town. And it'll be so small."

Eleanor smiled. "Exactly. With no stairs to negotiate." She topped up their cups even though they were nearly full. "We have to decide what I'll take with me, what I'll give to relatives, what I'll sell or donate...we have quite a job ahead of us, I'm afraid."

"If you need help with the heavy things, give me a call," Jack said. The silvery eyes turned back to Liz. "Was it a rough trip?"

"Just long." His steady gaze made her self-conscious. She tucked some frizzy strands of hair behind her ear, but they jumped right back. "With an aggressive breeze coming through the window half the time. And I nearly hit a deer, avoiding the car that came out of your driveway."

Eleanor's cup clattered onto its saucer. "I'll shoot those useless creatures myself one of these days, I really will!"

"The alfalfa field across from my house attracts them," Jack said. "I counted more than thirty out there last night."

"And each one doing its best to get hit by a car. You have to keep your eyes open out here, Elizabeth. Deer, porcupine, skunks...your brother nearly went off the road avoiding a chipmunk the other day. A chipmunk." Eleanor's worried irritation faded. "No sense getting our blood pressure up. You must be hungry, after all you've had to contend with. Will you have some pie? It's your favorite."

Eleanor removed the cover from the serving dish,

revealing a ten-inch pie, an appealing shade of burnt orange with visible specks of spice. She lifted a wedge onto a dessert plate, balanced a fork on the side and handed it to her granddaughter. "Jack baked it himself, from his own pumpkins. He has a lighter hand with pastry than I do."

The violin-playing neurosurgeon could bake? "It looks delicious." Liz lifted a small forkful of pie to her mouth. Two pairs of eyes watched her chew. She realized some kind of review was expected. "It's wonderful. So spicy and creamy."

"And he's going into blueberries. Soon there'll be blueberry pie, too. Next year, Jack, or will it take longer?"

"There might be a small crop the first year."

Liz wondered at her grandmother's proprietary tone. She sounded as if she had some stake in this stranger's plans, as if a member of her own family were trying something new and needed encouragement. "Blueberries can be difficult to grow, can't they?"

"I guess I'll find out." He didn't seem worried about dealing with complications. "I've planted a hundred of a lowbush variety that's supposed to be hardy. If they do well, I'll put in more."

"You found a good location," Eleanor said. She leaned toward Liz with a pleased expression. "He's going to plant Christmas trees, as well."

Liz looked curiously at the man next to her. Although he gave no sign of it, he must be a bit of a romantic to choose those crops. "Sort of a holiday express."

"That's right." He emptied his teacup with two big gulps and pushed back his chair. "Your granddaughter looks exhausted, Eleanor, and she's still shivering off and on. I'll be on my way, so she can get settled in." He took his coat from one of the hooks by the door. After all that arranging of tables and dishes, it was a sudden departure.

Eleanor pushed herself out of her chair. "You'll have to come to dinner soon, Jack. Maybe Elizabeth will prepare something for us both."

"I'm not much of a cook, Grandma."

"A little practice will fix that."

"Mr. McKinnon won't want to be my guinea pig."

"Just let me know what evening is good for you, Jack."

"I'll do that. Thanks for the tea, Eleanor. Good to meet you at last, Ms. Robb." He strode through the door, the dogs on his heels.

Liz watched them go, three silhouettes and a small, bobbing light. He'd stayed as long as courtesy demanded and left as soon as he could. Had he emphasized the words *at last?* He wouldn't suggest, half an hour after meeting her, that she ought to visit her grandmother more often...if he had, though, she couldn't disagree. Letters and phone calls, and even invitations to Vancouver, weren't adequate replacements for time at home. She wasn't going to make dinner for him, that was certain. She had a way with scrambled eggs and toast, but her grandmother would expect something more impressive. A lot of pots would be involved, and some of them were bound to burn.

Eleanor turned from the window. "I don't like it when Bella and Dora go out at night, but they always want to follow him. He sends them back when he's nearly home."

Liz began clearing dishes to the sink. "He visits often?"

"Oh, yes, he always has, right from the start. I invite him for dinner, or he brings something he's baked. He's lonely, I think, working and living on his own in a strange place. I enjoy hearing about his plans. Of course, he hasn't yet convinced people around here he knows what he's doing."

The grain farmers and ranchers around Three Creeks couldn't be blamed for a little skepticism. The growing season was hardly long enough for pumpkins to ripen, and no one in the area had ever tried to grow blueberries or evergreens commercially, not that Liz had heard, anyway. She remembered city people showing up in the area occasionally, pipe dreams in tow. They settled down or sold as impulsively as they'd bought and disappeared. "What do you know about Mr. McKinnon, Grandma?"

"You sound suspicious. It's not like living in Vancouver, we don't have to be careful of our neighbors here."

"I'm just curious."

"I can't say I know very much about him. He told me he had his own business in Winnipeg. Something with computers, but he decided he didn't want to do it anymore."

"You mean he sold computers? Or was he one of those people you call to solve all your problems, like when you pour coffee on your laptop?"

"I have no idea. He doesn't seem interested in talking about it. He's looking ahead." Eleanor picked up a tea towel and began to dry the dishes Liz put in the drainer. "Two weeks will go so quickly. Can you stay longer? Everyone wants to see you."

Liz's stomach gave a flip. "Everyone?"

"Well, all the Robbs and all their off-shoots, of course. Jean Bowen and Marge Sinclair both told me they want to have you over for coffee, and Daniel, you know, Daniel Rutherford—"

Liz's 4-H leader, her grade nine English teacher and the ex-Mountie who had helped them solve all their horse problems. "I doubt there'll be time."

"If you can't visit everyone individually, they'll understand. You'll be able to see most of them tomorrow, in one fell swoop."

Liz stared at her grandmother. She had been sure she could slip into town, lend a hand for a while and go. "What's happening tomorrow?"

"Your Aunt Edith has arranged a barbecue. You and I are to take a salad. Any salad we choose, she said. I always wonder what's to stop everyone from bringing the same kind. It never happens, though. Now up you go, Elizabeth. Jack's right, you need to take care of yourself, or you'll catch something. You've got the back bedroom—there's a hot water bottle tucked at the bottom of the bed. I hope you'll be warm enough." The upstairs rooms were heated by small, square metal grills that let air rise from the first floor.

"I'll be fine." Liz kissed her grandmother's flannel-soft cheek. "Good night. Sleep tight."

The back bedroom was her favorite, the room where she and her cousins had played house and dress-up when the weather kept them indoors. Flower-sprigged wallpaper covered the sloping ceiling and short walls, the same wallpaper she had watched her grandfather apply twenty years before. The bed was soft with a thick feather quilt. The Robb women used to make them, visiting around a table and ignoring sore fingers while they pulled the quills from bags and bags of goose feathers.

Liz unpacked her pencil case and sketchbook. Sitting on the side of the bed, she flipped to a new page and began to draw. She needed to get the deer out of her mind and safely onto paper before she slept.

Quick lines caught the animal's terrified immobility. Panicked eyes bright in the headlights, body tensed to spring away, muscles bunched and twitching. Long thin legs bent as if it wanted to run in three or four directions at once. Hooves polished, tiny, sharp. Coat heavy for winter, velvet under coarse surface hairs. Eyes huge and liquid brown, ears surprisingly large and held to the side.

After she had filled several pages with full and partial sketches of the deer, her hand began to draw a face. Jack McKinnon's face, but longer and thinner than it really was, with silver eyes full of secrets. Leaning away from her sketchbook, she studied the drawing and felt a familiar stirring of anticipation. This would be her next hero. He didn't belong in the real world. The story would have to be a fantasy. Whether he belonged to the hills of Tara or the rings of Saturn, she didn't yet know.

THE DOGS FOLLOWED JACK through the woods, moving silently along the path narrowly lit by his flashlight. They were alert, aware of sounds and smells that passed him by entirely. At the edge of the clearing, he stopped. He'd like to keep Bella and Dora with him—they were large enough to give intruders second thoughts—but he'd made a promise to Eleanor.

"Go home, girls." They stood at his feet and waited expectantly, eyes glowing, tails wagging slowly. He would have to say it as if he meant it. He pointed to the northwest. ‘‘Home.’’ Their heads sagged, then they turned and disappeared into the night.

Unable to shake the feeling that caution was needed, Jack kept to the edge of the woods, studying the house and its surroundings as thoroughly as the yard light allowed. The car that had nearly hit Elizabeth Robb was long gone. There was no sign anyone had stayed behind, no sign of trouble.

Except the light. When he'd left for Eleanor's, he'd switched on the light over the back door. Now, it was off. He crossed the yard to the back stoop and reached up to check the uncovered bulb. Not burned out. Twisted loose.

He tried the door. It was still locked. People tended to be casual about security around here—the Ramseys' locks would have sprung open if you'd frowned at them, so he'd installed deadbolts as soon as he moved in. Edging his way around the house, he checked each ground-floor window. All shut and intact. The front door was locked.

Someone had come into his yard, loosened the light over the back door, then left in a hurry, headlights off to avoid being seen. Someone expecting easy access to a TV and VCR in the trusting countryside? It didn't look as if they'd found a way in, so why was the back of his neck still so tight it burned?

He let himself into the house and stood quietly, listening. The lights he'd left on still glowed. He moved from room to room, upstairs and down. The few things of value—his espresso and cappuccino maker, his laptop, the CD player, his guitar—all sat where he'd left them.

Could have been kids, just as Eleanor said. Halloween was only a couple of weeks away. He'd likely be spending Saturday washing spattered egg off the outside walls.

What was bugging him? Jack began another circuit of the house. Was something out of place, something that had only registered at the back of his mind? Faint scratches beside the lock on the door? Dirt tracked in on someone else's shoes?

Finally he found what had been nagging at him. A small thing…smudges in the dust on the coffee table. The books, magazines and sheet music he'd piled there had been moved, then returned to their places.

So, someone had come into his yard, loosened the light over the back door, searched for something, *then* left in a hurry, headlights off to avoid being seen. It didn't make sense. Nothing was stolen, nothing was vandalized.

The tension in his neck eased. Reid. They hadn't talked for a couple of years. It would be his style to get back in touch in some convoluted way. Leaving a few hardly noticeable clues was how they used to signal the start of a new round of their favorite game, a sort of puzzle-solving treasure hunt they'd played all through high school and university. The guy must be bored out of his mind to have gone to all this trouble, driving an hour and a half from Winnipeg…

Moving quickly, Jack lifted the trapdoor near the kitchen table. He bent his head to avoid bumping into rafters and creaked down the stairs into the dirt cellar. Deep shelves where the Ramseys had kept canned goods over the winter lined one wall. Along another were bins for root vegetables. He'd filled most of them with pumpkins waiting for their Halloween trip to the city. Stepping over more pumpkins lined up on the ground, he dug one hand to the bottom of the potato bin and brought out a resealable sandwich bag. Inside the bag was a plain black diskette.

He returned to the kitchen and switched on his laptop. When the menu appeared, he checked the security logs. Sure enough, an attempt had been made to get into his files, today at 2018 hours. Not unexpected under the circumstances, but it still made his heart beat a little faster. He slipped the diskette into its slot, then rebooted the computer and waited for the prompt. As soon as it flashed onto the screen, he relaxed. Reid hadn't tried to open the hidden Linux partition. He had no reason to suspect it was there, no reason to look for it.

Jack popped the small black square out of the machine and into his hand, curling his fingers around it. He could throw it into the Franklin stove right now. Probably should. He could delete the partition and its contents. Absolutely should.

He slipped the diskette back into the sandwich bag, and started down the cellar stairs.

CHAPTER TWO

LIZ BUMPED HER HEAD on the sloping ceiling over the bed when she sat up. It made her think of her grandfather, solemnly checking every door frame, table and chair she'd bumped into as a child and assuring her it was undamaged. Even if her eyes were full of tears from the collision, she couldn't help laughing at his concern for those sharp edges. Couldn't help being just a little bit mad, either.

At night, when she'd made a quick trip down the hall to the bathroom, the bare floor had been icy cold. Now there was a warm path where pale sunlight streamed in. Liz followed it to the window, then stood back from the draft of cool air seeping through the glass.

The yard was huge, reaching to the poplar woods at the back, and to the garden and hip roof barn at one side. Her grandfather's small orchard, hardy crab apple, plum and cherry trees, grew at one end of the garden, and her grandmother's raspberry patch at the other. Her arms stung just looking at it. She and Susannah used to wade right in to find the ripest berries. They didn't notice all the long red scratches on their skin until they were done. Tiny green worms wriggling inside the berries didn't bother them, either.

Maybe in a day or two the *Twilight Zone* feeling would wear off, and she could look outside without seeing twenty different scenes at once, her life passing before her eyes. In little pantomimes all over the yard she saw herself playing with her cousins and her brother. Had they spent any time at their own houses, or were they always here, rolling in this grass, climbing these trees, raiding this garden?

Their swing still hung from the oak tree. Strange to see it empty. Someone had always been on it, leaning way back with arms stretched and legs pumping, trying to go high enough to look at the world through the tree's lower branches. Once, they'd all tried to fit on at the same time—they'd made it to seven, with Liz and Susannah and Tom dangling from the ropes, before someone's mother had called that they'd break the tree if they didn't watch out. They were always tanned and laughing…at least it seemed that way. Untouchable.

It was going to be a ghost-filled visit. Maybe that wasn't such a bad thing. She might manage to scare a few of them away. How, she had no idea. Threaten to draw them? Or ignore them, like bullies? That would be best. Ignore them, and keep her mind on why she was here—to help her grandmother and to say her goodbyes to the old house. Then she'd go back to Vancouver and stay there. Back home.

She hurried into a pair of jeans and a sand-colored sweatshirt, then made her way downstairs, holding the banister as she went. Very little light turned the corner from the living room windows. She could hardly see where to put her feet. It was a dangerous staircase for her grandmother, narrow and steep, and a dark house for her to live in alone all these years. Liz had to think and count…nine years.

Eleanor was in the kitchen, leaning over a steaming waffle iron. "Good morning, Elizabeth! I put the kettle on when I heard the floor squeak. It won't be a minute.''

''Great, I could do with a cup. Don't tell me you're making waffles.''

''How could your first morning home go by without them?''

Liz hovered, wondering if she should offer to help. She had tried to make waffles once and had ended up yelling at the supposedly nonstick pan and going out for breakfast. When the kettle whistled, she hurried to the stove and poured the boiling water over tea bags waiting in a warmed Brown Betty, glad of something useful to do. The dogs looked at her with mild interest, but didn't move out of her way or wag their tails.

She pulled a tea cosy over the pot. ''This is pretty. Is it new?'' It was leaf green, with a pattern of pink geraniums. There wasn't a single tea stain on it.

''Isn't it nice? Jack saw it at a craft sale and thought of me.''

''He goes to craft sales?''

''It was in Pine Point. He wants to experience every aspect of country life.''

''I hope you told him farmers don't go to craft sales unless women drag them.''

Eleanor looked amused. ''I doubt I could influence him. Besides, he likes to support work that's done locally.''

Liz felt an uncomfortable twist of distrust. Jack McKinnon seemed to be going out of his way to please her grandmother. ''He's awfully friendly.''

''For a stranger, you mean?'' Eleanor poured more batter on the grill and closed the lid.

''I suppose that's what I mean.''

''He's not a stranger to me, Elizabeth.''

Liz wandered back to her grandmother's side. She

hoped she hadn't sounded too small-minded. "It's no wonder he thought of you when he saw the cosy. You've always got geranium cuttings on the windowsills." She leaned closer and breathed in the aroma of toasted vanilla. "What's the plan for today, Grandma?"

"We'll start with the furniture, I think. It's a three-room apartment, so I can't take much with me. The dining room suite is my main concern." Since her marriage just before the Second World War, Eleanor had been caretaker of a black walnut table that came with sixteen chairs and a matching sideboard. Liz's great-great-grandparents had brought it with them from Ontario in 1883. "Your brother is willing to take it, but Pamela is reluctant. She prefers a modern style. Smaller scale, lighter wood. She asked Thomas if they could strip and bleach it..."

"Oh, no."

"I'm not sure what to do. There's general agreement that it would be a pity to sell it, but that it's too big and too dark for anyone to take."

"We can't sell it." Every family occasion had involved gathering around that table. "Remember how we used to go from house to house at Christmas? Aunt Edith's for Christmas Eve, here for dinner on Christmas Day, our house for games and turkey sandwiches on Boxing Day. This was the only place big enough for everyone."

Eleanor lifted the lid of the waffle-maker. Two fragrant circles fell away from the grill. "The children never need to sit at a card table in another room. I like that. I like babies at the table."

"I don't remember babies—"

"You were one of them. And you missed the next batch."

"I just remember Emily being smaller than the rest of us. Not quite a baby, though. A toddler." Emily was born a few years after Liz and Susannah, the only child of Eleanor's only daughter, Julia. She had shadowed her older cousins as soon as she could move fast enough to keep up. Now, she was a teaching assistant at the elementary school, dividing her day between the kindergarten room and the library. She still lived with her mother, about a mile down the road from Eleanor's house. "This barbecue tonight, Grandma. Do we have to go?"

"What a question." Eleanor looked startled and not at all pleased. "It's in your honor. Your aunt has gone to a lot of trouble." Using a tea towel, she pulled a plate of waffles from the warming oven and added the two she'd just made to the pile. The stack had fallen over, forming a large, rounded mound, enough to feed them all week. "Would you get the syrup? There's raspberry preserves, too."

Liz rummaged in the fridge. Of course she couldn't avoid the barbecue. It was a few hours with family and friends. She'd be glad to see everyone. She'd fill a plate and mingle and then, if necessary, plead jet lag, or burn herself on the grill, and they'd understand why she had to leave early.

"The syrup's right there, Elizabeth, by the milk. Don't let all the cold air out."

The syrup appeared in front of Liz, beside a carton of whole milk she hadn't noticed, either. Wasn't whole milk extinct? Everything inside the fridge had a foreign look to it, now that she thought about it. Three dozen eggs, real butter, whipping cream. Had the news about cholesterol not reached Three Creeks?

As she set the syrup and preserves on the table, heavy footsteps sounded on the veranda. The dogs lifted their heads, but they didn't budge from their spot by the stove. After a token knock, the kitchen door pushed open, and Liz's brother looked into the room. He grinned when he saw her. "Hey, kiddo. How ya doin'?"

Liz wanted to throw her arms around him, but something held her back. She made herself busy carrying the teapot to the table. "I hoped I'd see you today."

"Got you working hard already, has she, Grandma? Waffles—she's got no shame. It's from living in the city. They get used to being pampered."

"Join us, Thomas. We've got plenty." Eleanor was already setting another place.

"I suppose a little more breakfast won't hurt me." If anyone could tolerate two breakfasts, it was Tom. Since their parents had retired and sold him their land a few years before, he'd been farming a thousand acres and raising a hundred head of cattle. Any spare time was spent playing with his three children.

He reached for the serving plate before he was in his chair. He helped himself, then pushed it closer to his sister. "So, Lizzie, what's the penalty for bashing up a rental car?"

She hardly noticed slipping into the bantering tone they used with each other most of the time. "You bashed up my rental car? That'll cost you."

"What'd you do, hit a deer?"

"I hit a rock, avoiding a deer."

"That was careless. I could have fed my family all winter."

From across the room Eleanor said, "Your sister had quite a scare."

Tom's chastened expression gave Liz's heart a

twinge. He looked about eight years old. "You're all right, though?"

"I'm fine. Just a little more aware how nice it is to be breathing." Even now, thinking about her near miss made her queasy. She cut one of the waffles down the middle and put half on her plate. Slowly she poured on syrup, giving as much attention to filling the little squares as she had when she was a child. "How are my nieces and my nephew?"

"Let's see." Tom's face brightened just thinking about his children, but he spoke in an offhand tone. "Jennifer's had her ears pierced, Will says it's not fair. Anne has joined Brownies, Will says it's not fair. Will's going to play hockey this season, Jennifer says it's not fair. We've made a rule they all have to do an hour of chores on Saturdays before they play and they all agree it's not fair—"

"Pretty much business as usual, then."

"But more so. Pam's bursting to see you. She says she'll be around to help with the sorting and packing when work allows." Tom's wife taught grade five at the local school. Half the teachers there were at least distantly related to the Robbs. "I suppose you'll still be in the house for part of the winter, Grandma? Need some firewood?"

"Thank you, but I'm all set. Jack brought me a good load last week. It should be enough with what I have left from last year."

Tom's cheerful mood was gone, just like that. "What's Jack McKinnon doing bringing you wood? I've always brought you wood."

"You've been so good about it, but look at all you have to do."

"Bringing you firewood has never been a problem—"

Bella and Dora stopped scrutinizing each forkful traveling from Liz's plate to her mouth and ambled to the door, nails clicking on the hardwood floor. More company? Liz hadn't even washed before coming downstairs. There was a light tapping on the door, and then Emily stepped into the kitchen, beaming. Liz's chair scraped back, and she hurried to her cousin, reaching for a hug.

"You finally, finally came home!" Emily said. "How long can you stay?"

"A week. Maybe two."

"Not longer?"

Eleanor brought another plate from the cupboard. "I'm sure it will be two. We need at least that much time to get the work done. We're starting with the furniture today, Emily, if you're interested. Thomas, would you pour your cousin some tea?"

"Thanks, Grandma." The dogs followed Emily to her chair. "No, Bella, no matter what you might think, and no matter what happened last time, I'm not going to give you my breakfast. Is that your car in the driveway, Liz, with the big dent? Don't tell me you hit a deer."

"She tried her best," Tom said, "but all she got was a rock. There's not much point hitting a rock."

"I swerved to avoid a car and the deer came out of nowhere. You'd think it had transported in—"

"Transported?" Eleanor didn't watch much television.

"Like in a sci-fi program," Liz explained. "Beamed from one spot to another...the idea is, they break you down into atoms and reassemble you at your destination."

Eleanor grimaced. "I don't think I'd like that. Although I wouldn't mind a shorter trip to Winnipeg, especially in the winter—and I suppose you could drop in and out of here more often, Elizabeth.''

''And we all could have made it to Susannah's wedding,'' Tom added.

''Oh, could you believe she did that?'' Emily asked. ''Marry a guy like Alexander Blake in the middle of the badlands when we'd stopped thinking she'd ever get married at all, and not wait for me? I'm afraid my telegram turned into a bit of a lecture—''

This time there was no knock, and no warning from the dogs. Susannah's father stepped into the house as if he owned it. He was tall and tanned, with graying hair cut very short. A pale band of skin just below his hairline showed where his cap usually sat, pulled down low to shade his eyes.

''There she is!'' He took Liz's face between two large hands and kissed the top of her head loudly. ''Looking like a million bucks, as usual. Got all your dad's beauty and your mother's brains.''

Liz smiled. It was a long-time claim. ''Hi, Uncle Will.''

''And Emily. Look at the two of you. All we're missing is Susannah. Shove over, Tom.'' Will squeezed into a chair next to his nephew. ''Got some coffee, Mom?''

Eleanor set a jar of instant on the table. ''I bought a special kind for Elizabeth.''

''Hazelnut Heaven? Sounds like a lady's drink to me...I suppose I'll still get my caffeine, though, won't I?'' Will smiled at Liz. ''Quite a dent on that little Cavalier out there. Brand-new car, too. Reminds me of when you were learning to drive. I kept telling you to aim for the road— Oh, well, why change now?'' He stirred a heaping spoon of coffee crystals into a mug of hot water his mother placed in front of him, then flinched when the smell of hazelnuts hit his nostrils. "Did you get the extra insurance?"

Liz nodded. She'd checked the rental agreement before bed.

"Always get the insurance. Otherwise, something goes wrong, you're on the hook for the whole thing. I'll take the car back for you—" He raised one hand to stop Liz's protest. "I'm going into the city on Saturday anyway. I'll settle everything, take the bus back. They won't give me any trouble."

"Uncle Will—"

Tom spoke under cover of their uncle's confident voice. "Give up, Liz."

"I'll need a car—"

"You can use Grandma's. It's old, but it's in good shape."

"We're all set then," Will said with satisfaction. "So, angel, here's the thing. Your aunt wants you to stay with us for a while. How about it? You can use Sue's old room and keep us company."

"I've come to help Grandma, Uncle Will."

"How about over Christmas? I'm sure Sue'll be finished at her quarry by then. Of course, it won't be quite the same, will it? She'll have Alex with her." He frowned into his cup. "The way they got married, in such a hurry, with no family— It's been tough on your aunt. She saved a picture of the perfect wedding cake from some magazine twenty-odd years ago and she was heartbroken not to have the chance to make it."

Tom spooned a big dollop of raspberry preserves on a second waffle. "If they'd waited one measly day we could have got to Alberta in time. Would one day have made such a difference?"

"That's what I said," Will agreed.

Liz tried to defend her cousin, although she'd been disappointed to miss the wedding, too. "There aren't all that many flights to the Gobi Desert."

"Trust you to be in favor of a rushed marriage, Liz. What is it with you and eloping, anyway—" Tom broke off when Eleanor made a warning sound. With a guilty glance at his grandmother, he apologized.

Liz forced a smile. "That's okay. I did elope. It's no secret."

"And everybody was very happy for you," Will declared, "no matter what they said at the time."

Emily jumped up. "Let's get the dishes cleared away, Liz. Then we'll take a look at the furniture. My mother's hoping for that cabinet radio, Grandma."

Eleanor tapped the table. "Settle down and enjoy your breakfast, Emily. Your cousin isn't a child with a short attention span. You can't distract her that easily. And you, Elizabeth, I'm sorry to say it, but you bring it on yourself. If you'd transport in here more often, people would be done commenting on that episode of your life."

Episode. Liz smiled weakly. It was beginning to look as if two weeks would be more than she could handle. At this point, two days was in question.

JACK SCOOPED SOIL INTO a specimen jar and twisted the lid tight. Eleanor's field looked promising. Coming through the woods he'd noticed a few small conifers growing in the shade of the poplars…if nature was already beginning to diversify the deciduous forest, it just might be willing to accept a push from him. He should know for sure in a week or two. So far it had never taken longer than that for the provincial lab to fax the test results.

He yawned and stretched. He'd been awake most of

the night, his mind ricocheting between Reid, who had somehow found a way into his house, and the granddaughter with the spicy hair. Cinnamon, with darker strands, like cloves. She smelled like Christmas. She shouldn't. People who refused to visit their grandmothers for as long as she had should smell like Scrooge—all dust and cigars.

In the middle of the field he used a trowel to dig a small hole so he could get another sample from deeper down, where the trees' roots would be looking for nourishment. He was hoping for a slightly acidic soil, the kind white spruce and balsam firs preferred. Balsams were a safe bet to grow. They were always popular because of their thick growth and festive smell and because they hung on to their needles longer than some trees. The more sparsely branched spruce he liked for old times' sake. It was the kind he and his uncle had always decorated.

When he straightened from collecting the second sample he noticed a figure coming across the field. A female figure. Tall and slender, with light curly hair tousled by the breeze. Elizabeth Robb. She was heading right for him. Striding toward him, in fact. Barely arrived after an absence of fifteen years, Eleanor's granddaughter had spotted a trespasser, and she wanted to do something about it. Jack waited, surprised how glad he was to see her.

She stopped a couple of yards away. Even at that distance he was sure he caught a whiff of cinnamon. Maybe she wore cinnamon perfume. Was there such a thing? If there wasn't, his nose was hallucinating.

After a guarded greeting, she said, "I didn't expect to see anyone way out here."

"There never is anybody." Usually he could walk

for half the day without seeing a single person. It was one of the things he liked about country living.

She had noticed the specimen jars nearly hidden in his hand. "I was thinking about you this morning, wondering if everything was all right when you got home last night."

"Because of the car? Everything was fine. It must have been someone turning around in my driveway. I wondered about you, too. The accident didn't leave you with any aches or pains?"

"It wasn't much of an accident." She was still eyeing the specimen jars. "The car seemed a bit sinister without headlights and disappearing the way it did, but I guess the simplest explanation is usually the right one."

"I hope you warmed up eventually."

A brief smile relaxed her features. "I don't think I'll warm up until I get back to Vancouver."

"Overheating isn't a problem in these old houses," Jack agreed.

"They *do* provide some protection from snow during the winter."

"And they keep the coyotes out."

"But not the mice." She squelched the growing feeling of friendliness by adding, finally, "I'm not sure if you realize you're on my grandmother's property."

He nodded. "I'm collecting soil samples."

His calm admission stalled her for a moment. "I suppose you're looking for somewhere to grow evergreens."

"That's right." He started walking, and Liz fell into step beside him. He shortened his stride to match hers.

"My grandmother won't sell this field. It's part of the original homestead."

"Nobody else is using it."

"I'm sure my brother would like it for pasture. He's expanding his herd."

"It borders my land. It's miles from his."

They walked in silence, dry grass brushing their legs. He saw that her shoes were splotched with paint, nearly every color ever invented as far as he could tell. For the first time it occurred to him that illustrating children's books meant she actually painted pictures.

They had reached the edge of the field. A well-marked path led to Eleanor's; Jack would have to cut through the woods to reach his house. He found he didn't want their conversation to end. He tucked the offending specimen jars into his pockets. "Have you and Eleanor been working this morning?"

"We've being going through the furniture, making lists of everything. She has to get rid of most of it."

"That must be hard for both of you."

"The time had to come eventually. It's just stuff."

He scuffed the toe of his hiking boot into the ground. "And this is just land."

As soon as he said it, he wished he hadn't. She looked at him indignantly, all her suspicions in place. He understood. He had never belonged anywhere in particular, she had always belonged here. They both knew what roots were.

DESPITE THE DULL BROWNS AND GRAYS of late fall, Will and Edith's place looked beautiful. Evening sunlight sparkled through the leafless oaks and elms, and small fires flickered here and there in the yard so guests could warm themselves. Coal oil lamps stood on picnic tables, ready to light at dusk. People had come prepared for the temperature to dip when the sun went down—coats were open over sweaters, hats and gloves stuck out of pockets. Children ran through groups of chatting grown-ups, playing Statues, or jumping in fallen leaves.

Liz pulled over, as far off the road as she could get without driving into the ditch. If she parked in the field that was already bumper to bumper with cars her escape route might be cut off by people arriving later. She pulled down the sun visor for one last check of her appearance. The view in the small rectangular mirror wasn't reassuring. She looked pale and pinched, like someone in the dentist's waiting room anticipating a root canal.

"You look lovely, dear."

"Thanks, Grandma."

Pretending not to notice the curious faces that had turned their way, Liz offered Eleanor an arm out of the car, then lifted a monster salad bowl from the back seat. When she turned around, she found herself inches from a small woman with short, graying hair and bangs, and a girl who looked about ten.

"Aunt Edith—" Liz was swept into an embrace that nearly cut off her air supply. With one hand, she held the heavy bowl away from her body, tilting precariously.

"I'll take that, Auntie Liz." Jennifer, Tom's oldest child, rescued the bowl before it fell.

Edith's grip loosened. "I always said you'd come home eventually. Now, if only Susannah were here. My nest is empty, I'm afraid."

"Empty, but visited often," Eleanor said dryly. Susannah's brothers, Martin and Brian, lived just down the road with their families.

"Of course, it's a long time since Sue lived at home, but it always seemed that she was still *ours*."

Liz nodded. She felt as if she'd lost a bit of Susannah, too.

"This Alex, I don't know, he obviously considers her *his.* I suppose I'll have to adjust. Seeing the wedding for myself would have helped that process, I'm sure. Jennifer, dear, will you put that bowl with the other salads?"

Edith led them along the driveway, edged by curving perennial beds. Most of the flowers had died down and looked like tufts of straw, but a few rust-colored mums still bloomed. "Eleanor, let's find you a comfortable spot and a hot drink. Jennifer, there you are. Salad safely stowed? Good. Will you look after your aunt? Just take her around the yard and help her mingle until she gets her bearings."

Liz could sense anxiety in the air, and restrained excitement, as if people were waiting to see the Queen, or Santa Claus at the end of a long parade, and thought someone might get in their line of vision. Was she the source of all that feeling, or had it just been too long between parties? She watched her aunt and grandmother walk away so she could avoid looking at anyone else. There was a barrier between herself and the people who'd come to welcome her, and she didn't know how to cross it. She didn't want to cross it.

"Who do you want to meet first?" Jennifer asked.

"How about your dad?"

"You had breakfast with my dad. Anyway, he's barbecuing."

Liz could see Tom across the yard, lifting the lid of one of four gas barbecues, tongs in hand. A spicy, smoky smell she'd noticed earlier intensified. Teriyaki something.

Jennifer lowered her voice. "Everybody's looking at you, like they're waiting."

Her niece's discomfort made Liz ashamed of her hesitation. "Let's just go into the fray and talk to everyone at once."

Pleasant faces and friendly voices greeted her. Liz found it easy to respond the same way. Part of her even began to enjoy the evening. She spoke to the couple who'd sold her mother eggs and cream, and to the repairman who'd nursed her family's appliances through mishaps years after their warranties had expired. There was her Sunday School teacher, completely unchanged, and her grade-one teacher, unrecognizable, and in a wheelchair. Second and third cousins who'd never made the trip to Vancouver dived right into the middle of family stories, as if she'd only been away for a few weeks. Parents of young children told her which of her books they'd borrowed from the library and which they'd bought. Someone brought her a cup of cocoa, a few people mentioned her dented car and everyone agreed she'd done well for herself. Through it all, Jennifer followed along, saying hello to each person by name, in case Liz had forgotten.

As she moved away from signing a book one father had thought to bring with him, a pair of arms came around Liz from behind and a chin rested on her shoulder. "Gotcha!"

Liz recognized the voice and the freckled arms. She turned to smile at her sister-in-law. "Pam. I wondered where you were."

"In the kitchen, of course. Why is it that as soon as I manage to get out of mine I find myself in someone else's? Emily and Aunt Julia are still there, keeping the cocoa going."

Interpreting her mother's arrival as permission to abandon her aunt, Jennifer ran off to join the other children at the far end of the yard. They were holding out brown grass to three sorrel mares, and even though the horses could graze the same grass themselves, they reached eagerly over the fence to take it.

Pam pulled Liz's elbow. "Look. There's the new cutie."

Jack McKinnon stood a few yards away, holding a pie in each hand. His deep voice reached them. "Sorry I'm late, Edith. Pumpkin pies, just as you asked." A picture formed in Liz's mind, a silver-eyed fairy king going to market, a string of pies floating behind him...

Definitely Tara, rather than Saturn. Not the pretty, child-friendly kind of fairy, though. The primitive kind, with nature's beauty and force and heartlessness. Dressed in dry fall leaves. No, not dressed...part of the leaves, nature personified. Liz's hand ached for a pencil.

"I just love him," Pam said, in a near whisper. "He's your grandma's new neighbor."

"I met him last night."

"Imagine, he grows pumpkins. He wants to grow Christmas trees."

"Appealing, isn't it? There's something about him, though—"

"I'll say."

Liz looked at her sister-in-law doubtfully. "Does Tom mind all this appreciation?"

"He values an innovative farmer as much as I do." Pam caught the eye of a white-haired man standing nearby. "Isn't that right, Daniel?"

"Isn't what right?" Daniel came closer, his step slow and stiff, so different from the energetic stride Liz remembered. He might not be able to outmuscle a misbehaving horse anymore, but he hadn't lost the ramrod bearing he'd picked up as a Mountie, or his air of authority. "Good to see you, Liz. Thought you'd never come back."

"I wasn't sure I would, either." She smiled. "Now that I'm here, I'm glad I did."

Daniel nodded. "So, we had some excitement last month." He waited until Liz started to prompt him, then continued, "Your cousin came through town with her new husband." He paused again, and Liz remembered that he'd always talked that way, stopping as if to wait for a response, but then going on if you tried to make one. "I saw him through the car window when they were driving back to Winnipeg to catch their plane. Your poor aunt planned a whole get-together for them. Thought she could have a sort of reception, at least, if not the wedding. Managed to get the family together, I hear, but they only stayed for an hour, just long enough to introduce the husband, and then they were gone. Wouldn't you think a daughter would make time?" He stopped to take a breath.

Quickly, Liz said, "I'm sure Susannah would have, if she could."

"She would have," Daniel said, nodding pointedly, "if it had been up to her. I guess there's not much chance she'll ever move back home now, not with a husband like that, always gallivanting around the globe digging up dinosaurs."

"Sue's always digging up dinosaurs, too."

"Doesn't seem like real work, does it?" Daniel's gaze wandered past her, and with a nod he moved on, joining some friends beside one of the small fires.

Jack had deposited his pies on a picnic table. Liz watched him wander through the yard, speaking to a few people, politely accepted, but not really welcomed. It would be years before anyone believed he belonged in the community. Years, or never. He might always be the guy who'd bought the Ramsey place.

Pam dropped her voice suggestively. "Got your eye on Jack?"

"Of course not. I'm just sorry for him. This isn't an easy place to fit in."

"Half the people around town say he's growing marijuana." In response to Liz's surprised glance, Pam explained, "City guy, failed business, money to spend. Talks about organic farming. Case closed."

"I don't think his business failed. Grandma told me he wanted a change."

"My dad says a businessman from the city wouldn't choose to farm unless he was crazy or desperate. That's the way most people see it."

Jack had come to a stop under a maple that looked soft with age. He was alone, and suddenly Liz felt the need to protect him. Murmuring to Pam that she'd talk to her later, she hurried over, intending to offer a real welcome. Instead, she found herself saying accusingly, "Why didn't you tell me my grandmother gave you permission to take soil samples from that field?"

He took a careful sip from a disposable cup full of steaming cocoa before answering. "She did more than give permission. She suggested I test it."

"You let me think you were trespassing."

"I didn't want to take the wind out of your sails." Jack gently swirled the cocoa around his cup, catching bits of froth clinging to the sides.

Liz's cheeks warmed at his description of her behavior. "She told me if the field's right for evergreens, she'll rent it to you, not sell it."

"I wouldn't think of trying to take it away from your family after all these years."

"I thought—" Liz stopped. It was an awkward thing to come right out and say.

"You thought I was an evil rancher out to steal an old lady's land?"

She smiled. "An evil Christmas tree farmer."

At last some warmth crept into his eyes. Liz wasn't sure if she'd really moved closer to him, or if it just felt as if she had. She took a step back just in case. This was her grandmother's neighbor. It was almost wrong to think of him any other way. He was the pie maker, the pumpkin farmer who'd been taken under Eleanor's wing. She shuffled through her mind for a safe conversational topic, something far removed from cocoa-touched lips. "You've chosen some unusual crops," she said finally. "This has always been a wheat and oats kind of place."

"That's what everybody says. Newcomers growing new crops? Whatever is the world coming to?"

She decided not to tell him about the marijuana theory. "It's not that people are unfriendly. The same families have been here for more than a hundred years, though, and they're slow to accept new faces. In twenty years you'll still be a newcomer growing new crops."

"And you, even if you don't set foot in the place again in all that time, will still be the town's favorite daughter."

There was some truth to what he said, but something else came through, a bitterness or disapproval he'd almost managed to hide. "Maybe not the favorite daughter," she said lightly. "Second, even third or fourth favorite, I'm not sure."

From the center of a group of men standing near one of the picnic tables, a familiar voice rose. Liz stiffened.

"Elizabeth? Is something wrong?"

She hardly heard Jack's question. What was Wayne Cooper doing here? She hadn't seen him when Jennifer had led her around the yard. He must have come late. He was standing comfortably, hands in his pockets, shooting the breeze. Anyone would think he had nothing in the world to regret.

He turned, and saw her. "Liz!" He sounded happy, as if they were old friends. Before she had time to react, he'd reached her side. He glanced at Jack, then ignored him. "Hey, Liz. You look great."

"You, too," she said automatically. "Almost grown up."

Another quick grin. "Almost, almost. Gotta avoid that last step, where you turn into your old man. Anyway, the wife likes my boyish charm." His wiggled his eyebrows, his signature comedic move ever since grade two.

"You're married?" Liz looked around for her grandmother. Would she mind leaving early?

"Yeah, someone took me on. Hard to believe, I know. You remember Sally, she always had that long ponytail—"

"I remember you pulling someone's ponytail."

Wayne smiled at the memory. "That's her. How about you, Lizzie? Got a man tucked away somewhere?"

Liz felt a burst of anger. He was smiling, waiting for an answer, as if he had every right to ask her about her personal life, about who she loved. The world could fall apart around him and he would still smile, as pleased with himself as ever. She was aware of wanting him gone, and then suddenly he was. Jack had moved between them, and without taking any steps at all that she was aware of, they were halfway across the yard. They kept moving, Jack's hand on her arm, until they reached the fence that separated the yard from the pasture. Three grazing heads came up, ears flicked forward, and the horses sauntered over to meet them.

"I hope that wasn't high-handed," Jack said. "You seemed to want to get away."

"I can't believe he's here. Aunt Edith wouldn't have invited him."

"There were notices about the barbecue on the community bulletin boards."

She had forgotten about the boards. The town was too small for a newspaper, but you could find out nearly everything that was going on if you kept an eye on the messages people tacked up in the stores and the post office.

The horses had crowded close to the fence, competing for position. One touched its nose to Liz's shoulder, pushing gently. "Hey, sweetheart," she said softly. "It's not fair, is it? The people have all the treats. Where's the alfalfa? Where's the bran mash?" All three horses listened, but the first mare kept the other two away. "So you're top dog, are you?" Liz pulled her hand over the heads of wild oats growing near the fence, collecting seeds, and held it out flat. The horse ate, tough lips nuzzling her palm, delicately picking up each kernel.

"How can you be afraid of Wayne Cooper, and not of these two-ton beasts?"

"I'm not afraid of him. I just don't like him." She wasn't sure how to explain without telling the whole story. "Wayne...likes to find your soft spot and give it a squeeze."

She brushed the last few oats from her hand. "I need to get out of here. Do you think you could find my grandmother for me, so I won't risk bumping into him again?''

''Sure.'' Jack didn't move. ''It's none of my business, but do you mind if I give an opinion?''

For some reason, she didn't mind. She wanted to hear what he thought.

''I don't know what's going on, so I could be wrong—leaving might be the best thing for you to do. Cooper would be chasing you away, though. If you let people scare you off, you never stop being scared. That's basic, Elizabeth.''

''Liz.'' She took a deep breath and felt her muscles relax a notch. ''I don't know how to deal with him.'' She knew Jack didn't understand. Wayne must seem inconsequential to him, a little obnoxious, but harmless.

''Want a suggestion?''

''If you've got one.''

''Let's help ourselves to whatever your brother's been cooking, and then you can introduce me to your friends. Cooper won't get near you again if you don't want him to, I can promise you that. But he'll see you ignoring him, having a good time in spite of him. If he's hoping to intimidate you, it'll be hard for him to take.''

It was, as Jack said, basic. Her instinct to put herself in a whole different time zone than Wayne Cooper had been stronger than her good sense.

Liz had been looking at Jack's chest throughout the conversation. Finally, she looked up. Right away she could see that the image of the heartless primitive fairy was all wrong. His face was warm, concerned. ''I really appreciate this. I didn't have you pegged as a white knight.''

''That's good. I'm no kind of knight.''

There was a touch of sadness in his smile. Launcelot exiled from Camelot, she thought, Arthur from Avalon. Instead of a violin, a lute for those long fingers to strum. Instead of a pie in hand, a shield. Could she do a story about knights, or had children already seen all they wanted of swords and dragons and wizards?

CHAPTER THREE

THE BLADE SANK ALMOST A QUARTER of an inch into the glued pages. Jack sliced in between the lines of text, removed the point of the knife and sliced again. When he'd cut three sides of a four inch square, he bent back the paper like a door. He placed an unlabelled diskette inside, smoothed a little glue on the cut edges, then pressed the pages down. He had opened the book at random, but King Lear's line, just above the cut, would amuse Reid if he noticed. *Who loses, and who wins; who's in, who's out…* Not that the game ever really had a winner or a loser. It was the challenge they enjoyed.

The shelves of the built-in china cabinet in the dining room were full of books: paperback thrillers, textbooks of computer and mathematics theory, gold-lettered classics. Jack slipped *The Complete Works of Shakespeare* back in its place.

He'd spent a lot of time he didn't really have preparing the clues contained on the disk. Reid might not even find it. He would try, though. Housebreaking was a new twist to the game, and Jack didn't like it. He lifted the box he'd got from Daniel Rutherford onto the kitchen table. A surprising man, Daniel.

The bulletin boards were one of the things Jack liked about Three Creeks. Birthday announcements, cards of thanks, lost dogs, free-range hens, help wanted, jobs wanted. One of the ads had always made him smile. *Punks a Problem? Poachers Got Your Goat? Call Daniel Rutherford...Taking Care of All Your Security Needs Since 1975.* Not expecting much, Jack had decided to see what Daniel had to offer.

The older man lived alone on the edge of town, in a story-and-a-half house with crocheted doilies protecting his sofa and chair from the touch of his head and hands. Down in his basement, it was another world. Metal shelves were filled with precisely organized equipment—cameras, tape recorders and other machines Jack couldn't identify. It turned out Daniel wasn't a retired farmer, as he had supposed. He was a retired cop. RCMP Special Branch, long disbanded and replaced by CSIS, the Canadian Security Intelligence Service. A retired spy? He couldn't be.

Once Daniel knew Jack was there on business his tendency to gossip had stopped, just like that, like turning off a tap. Still, Jack was cautious. Taking his cue from Daniel's ad, he'd said kids were poking around his place, not causing any real trouble, but he wanted to find out who they were. He had come away with two small cameras that could be hidden under the eaves near his front and back doors, and an electric eye to place at the end of the driveway. Anyone driving or walking in would trigger the cameras, so intruders would film themselves. Daniel liked the irony. And Jack liked knowing Reid wouldn't surprise him again.

ELEANOR HAD SETTLED INTO THE CHAIR by the woodstove, her feet up on a three-legged stool one of her great-grandchildren had made in shop class. "Do you mind if we don't work today, Elizabeth?"

"Of course not," Liz said quickly. Over the past few days, they had decided the fate of nearly every stick of furniture in the house. Eleanor had struggled to be objective, but each piece held a bit of personal history, and some choices had been hard to make. ‘‘Are you all right, Grandma?’’

‘‘It’s nothing a quiet day won’t fix. You’ll find you slow down a little in your ninth decade, too.’’

Liz reached for a banana muffin. Eleanor would hate it if she fussed. ‘‘I can use the day to finish getting ready for my visit to the school tomorrow.’’ She had agreed to show Pam’s students how a book was made and to help them make books of their own.

‘‘That will be such a treat for the children.’’ Eleanor closed her eyes.

Liz felt a jolt of concern. How could her grandmother be tired in the morning, after a good night’s sleep? She’d been old for as long as Liz had known her, but she’d always been strong and full of energy.

For every bit of work Liz had saved her grandmother since she’d arrived, she’d probably caused just as much. Tonight she’d take care of dinner, something simple, soup and sandwiches. Tomorrow, she’d get up in time to make breakfast. When Eleanor came down to the kitchen she’d find tea and eggs ready and waiting.

‘‘Are you enjoying your visit, Elizabeth?’’ Eleanor’s eyes were open again, and they looked clear and alert. ‘‘I hoped it would be more than work for you.’’

‘‘It is, much more.’’ Liz wasn’t exactly enjoying it, but she was glad to be here. She was getting used to finding ghosts around every corner. Relatives, too. People were always dropping by for a hot cup, keeping a finger on the pulse of each other’s lives. ‘‘I’m not sure how well I handled things at the barbecue, though.’’ Other than agreeing how attractive the yard had looked and how good the food had tasted, they had avoided discussing Saturday's party.

"Very well, I thought."

"Except when I saw Wayne Cooper."

"It would have been more thoughtful for him to stay away."

"Jack...sort of rode shotgun for me."

"That sounds like Jack."

There was the proprietary tone again, as if Eleanor had raised him herself and was proud of how he was doing. She acted almost as if he were her grandson or nephew. Maybe that was it. Maybe he was the unacknowledged offspring of a wandering great-uncle and he'd come to Three Creeks to claim what he thought was rightfully his.

"Nobody minded giving an opinion about Susannah's wedding."

"Uninformed opinions and plenty of head-shaking. Interest in Susannah's marriage will die down soon."

Liz hesitated. "Was there as much gossip about me?"

"When you left? No. People were very quiet about that." Eleanor sighed. "It was all a long time ago, Elizabeth. You were angry and you wanted nothing more than to put this place behind you. But fifteen years...wouldn't it be best for you to make peace with what happened once and for all?"

Liz looked away from her grandmother. How could she make peace with it, even if she wanted to? That was like saying it didn't matter, all was well that ended well, water under the bridge.

"Ah, my dear. But you came to help me anyway, feeling as you do about the place. Sweet child."

"I'm thirty-three, Grandma."

"A baby. But you'll grow up one day, I suppose."

It almost hurt to see the affection on her grandmother's face. For the first time Liz got an inkling of what tending her anger at the people of Three Creeks had cost her. "I'm sorry I didn't come to see you before." Uncertainly, she added, "I think you've been disappointed in me."

Eleanor didn't deny it. "It's always a pity to waste time. Now, you need to get out and get some fresh air. Who knows how long these lovely fall days will last? Why not return that pie plate to Jack for me? I meant to do it days ago. Take the girls with you—they'll enjoy seeing him, too."

THE DOGS HURRIED AHEAD when they realized they were going to Jack's. By the time Liz got to the house, all three of them were waiting for her on the back stoop. Jack looked distracted, as if he had been deep in thought or in the middle of some engrossing project, and was having trouble adjusting to the interruption.

"I should have called—"

"No need for that." He leaned down, rubbing the dogs' ears. "Good girls," he said soothingly. "Fine, beautiful girls." They rested their heads against his legs.

"You're so good with them. I'm surprised you don't have a dog of your own."

"I've thought about getting one. Some big, friendly mutt who'd follow me from my truck to the field to the foot of my bed…I don't know. Pumpkins are needy enough." He gave a quick grin. It didn't erase the impression that he'd meant what he'd said.

She held up a neatly creased paper bag. "Grandma asked me to return your pie plate."

He gave each dog one last pat, then took the bag

and moved aside so Liz could get through the door. "I was just going to make a hot drink. Join me?"

"That would be great. It was a chilly walk. Is it cold for October, or have I forgotten what it's like here?"

"Snow by Halloween, people are saying."

Liz followed Jack into the kitchen. It was a large room, the most important room in the house at one time, with space for cooking and canning, separating cream from milk, churning butter, eating and visiting. It didn't feel welcoming, though, not like Eleanor's kitchen. Wires and pieces of something mechanical were spread out on a Formica-topped table, competing for space with a fax machine and laptop computer. "I'm interrupting you."

He hooked a finger through the handles of two mugs and grasped a bag of coffee beans with his other hand, closing the cupboard door with his elbow. "I was ready for a break…and I'm glad to have company."

The coffee grinder whirred into action. Jack packed the grounds into the filter of a stainless steel espresso and cappuccino maker. "Should I froth some milk?"

"I'll take it straight. It's days since I've had a proper cup of coffee."

Steaming liquid, dark and pungent, flowed into one mug, then the other. Jack led the way into the living room. "Make yourself comfortable. I'm afraid it's a bit of a mess." He sounded surprised.

Liz looked around for a place to sit. Jack and the dogs had congregated near the sofa, and an acoustic guitar occupied one of the chairs. Another chair doubled as a shelf for newspapers, books and videos. "Isn't this the Ramsey's furniture?"

"It came with the house. They just took personal things, pictures and so on."

Nails still protruded from the walls here and there, surrounded by discolored squares and rectangles where pictures had hung. How long had Jack been here? A year? It looked as if he were camping in someone else's house, with or without their permission.

He handed her one of the mugs, then moved the guitar, leaning it against the wall.

"Thanks." When Liz sat down, dust drifted up from the upholstery and tickled her nose. "You play guitar?"

"A little. Just to relax." He moved some newspapers to make room for himself on the sofa. "Sorry about all this. There hasn't been much time to think about the house. Every now and then I run a cloth over the tables, but I haven't got around to buying a vacuum."

"You've been busy establishing your farm."

Books were piled on every surface. Liz turned her head sideways to read the titles on the table beside her. *Blueberries for the Prairies. Growing Heritage Pumpkins. So You Want to Grow Christmas Trees.* "Do you really think you can learn to farm from books?"

"That's a funny question for a writer to ask."

"It's like cooking. You taste something delicious at a party and you get the recipe, but when you try to make the dish, it doesn't turn out the same. People leave out subtle details."

"I guess I'll learn as I go. I'm doing all right so far."

"Christmas trees, blueberries and pumpkins." Liz smiled. It sounded like the beginning of a song. "You must have a bit of the child in you."

For some reason, it was the wrong thing to say. Jack

seemed to withdraw. "To choose those crops? It's just good business sense."

"If you had good business sense you wouldn't be farming."

She'd meant it as a joke, but he responded seriously. "Everyone wants blueberries in summer, pumpkins in October and evergreens in December. An abundant local supply, organically grown, can't fail."

Barring drought, pests, early frost or a downturn in the economy. At least he had the optimism a farmer needed.

Peeking out from under a Three Stooges video and a seed catalog, Liz noticed the corner of a familiar book cover. *The Intergalactic Pirate* by Elizabeth Robb. She moved the video and catalog and lifted the book to show Jack. "Researching me?"

"I was curious," he admitted. "I read it with you in mind, trying to decide what it told me about you."

"Absolutely nothing."

He smiled as he zeroed in on his point. "And my choice of crops tells you absolutely nothing about me."

Liz laughed. Bella and Dora looked toward her with interest, their tails thumping on the floor. She smiled at them instead of at Jack. "Did you enjoy the story?"

"It's fun. Brave, resourceful kids right at the center of the action. Grown-ups on the sidelines if they're there at all."

"Children like that…a chance to feel like the powerful ones." The more they talked, the less Liz could concentrate on what they were saying. Jack wore a dark gray sweater that drew her attention to his eyes and his fair skin. He must have just shaved—his face looked smooth. She found that she wanted to touch it, to let her fingertips drift along his cheek.

His hand came up to his chin. ''Have I left some breakfast on my face?''

Liz flushed. She had always been a tactile person. It was all right most of the time—shopping for bedding or towels, admiring the grain of an oak door, trailing her hand in the water—but definitely not a tendency to indulge when returning pie plates to her grandmother's neighbor. ''Was I staring? Sorry. It's a bad habit. After all that effort as a child learning not to do it, they encourage it in art school.'' She went on, blurting out the truth. ''I was just thinking you must have been a beautiful little boy.''

His quick, assessing expression had nothing to do with fairies or knights of the Round Table. ''I don't know about that. I heard a lot of complaints about my unwashed neck.''

''Mothers are like that.''

''My uncle, actually.'' Abruptly, he stood. ''More coffee?''

''I still have lots.'' She'd been savoring it, letting the caffeine drip slowly down her throat and directly into her bloodstream. She followed him as far as the doorway and watched while he prepared another cup for himself. He'd been relaxed and friendly, with an enjoyable trace of something more. Now his back was one big Do Not Disturb sign. ''I was so grateful for your help at the barbecue. You didn't wait for an explanation. You just...stepped in.''

Jack leaned against the counter, refilled mug in hand. ''No problem.'' His stiffness was already disappearing. ''We had fun when things settled down. I got the feeling I was missing something, though. Everyone was smiling and visiting and saying how wonderful it was that you were home, but there was an undercurrent I didn't understand.''

Newcomer or not, Liz was surprised no one had filled him in. "A bit of tension is to be expected after all this time. I could have used a couple of quiet days between the trip and the barbecue. You know how it is before a holiday."

"The last minute stuff?"

"No matter how organized you try to be, something always crops up."

"What happened this time?"

She wasn't sure if he was really interested or just relieved that they weren't talking about him anymore. "Breakfast was the first problem. I had to get rid of all the perishable stuff in the fridge, so I ate a half carton of beef in black bean sauce, a slice of mushroom pizza and a scoop of potato salad."

"That's what the garbage can's for, Liz."

"I'll try to remember that. Then I made a quick trip to the pharmacy for antacids and before they'd even had a chance to work I cornered my landlord and risked his disfavor by reminding him about the window in my kitchen that doesn't close all the way. A lot of rain, gray squirrels and burglars can get into an empty apartment in two weeks. I left him muttering about rent increases and headed to the airport, but on the way I stopped at my publisher's to hand-deliver the manuscript and illustrations for my new book."

"It doesn't sound as if life's all that much better in Vancouver. Chaos with a view."

"And then there was the drive—"

"And the car—"

"And the deer at the side of the road."

"Anyone would think you didn't want to get here."

Liz stared at him. Of course she'd wanted to get here.

"You must have a really good reason for staying away."

The comment would have surprised her, coming from a man who didn't like to talk about his own private life, but he didn't seem to be asking for information. He was just noticing. He almost sounded protective. Something warm and pleasant stirred inside her. "Going to put me in a pumpkin shell?"

He looked baffled. She'd meant him to laugh.

"Mother Goose. Remember? *Peter, Peter, pumpkin eater…*"

"I don't know much about children's literature. That's your department."

"I thought everyone had those rhymes embedded in their brains. Peter puts his wife in a pumpkin shell and keeps her very well…" No expression of sudden recognition came over his face. "Your concern made me think of that. It was just a joke." He was looking at her as if she was the silliest person he'd ever met. "Some people think political messages were hidden in the rhymes. In those days you couldn't just write an editorial."

"Sort of a code. That's interesting."

"Does it have to be useful to be worth talking about? Can't it just be fun?"

"Codes are fun."

"Right. They're math, Jack."

"Not always. Sometimes they're a silly rhyme."

"You're hard to peg."

"Are you trying to peg me?"

"Don't look so pleased. It's nothing personal. It's what writers do."

"All in a day's work?"

"That's right. In fact, I'm thinking of doing something with a pumpkin grower next, maybe a variation on the Cinderella theme. The hero could be a fairy king, incognito, or the modern version of a fairy, an alien. Instead of a carriage, the pumpkin could become a spaceship…no, I guess that's too corny." He looked horrified at the thought of having a character based on him. Most people liked it. "Don't worry. You're safe for a while. I can't work here."

"Why's that?"

Because it's a narrow-minded, destructive place. "Oh, I don't know. Too many distractions. I'll be gone soon, though. Grandma and I should be able to organize things in another week. If not, Emily could help."

"You're eager to get back to Vancouver?"

"The sooner, the better." Trying to sound less vehement, she added, "A couple of weeks away from my own life is enough. Oh! I almost forgot. My grandmother's hoping you can come for dinner tomorrow."

"I'm afraid not. I'll be in Brandon until late."

"Saturday, then? Be warned—I'm cooking."

"Sounds good. What can I bring?"

"Besides dinner?" She smiled. "Just yourself." She put her mug down on the kitchen table. "I've kept you from your wires long enough. Thanks for the coffee."

Halfway to the trees, she turned to look at the house. Jack was still at the kitchen window watching them go. In spite of his tendency to raise the drawbridge without a moment's notice, she felt good when she was with him. Was she doing what she always did? She tended to see more than was really there when she first met men. It was nice at first, but it led to disappointment down the road.

JACK WATCHED LIZ DISAPPEAR into the woods. Even wearing jeans and running shoes, and with the dogs for company, she looked as if she belonged in the city. Her walk gave her away. You could see she was used to well-tended parks, not overgrown, twisting paths.

He'd almost invited her to go to Brandon with him. A novel date, shopping for farm machinery. It was just that every time they talked, he didn't want the conversation to end. Not because of her looks. Green eyes, fair skin, spicy hair, willowy body, that dreamy, off in the distance expression that made him want to go after her or pull her back…nope. He could resist all that without any trouble. Well, without much trouble. What got to him was how easily she trusted him, even though she hardly knew him. That, and the tenderness he'd seen between her and Eleanor.

Peter, Peter, pumpkin eater. Now that the words had percolated for a few minutes, they sounded familiar. His grade one teacher was always making them play with their fingers, spiders going up spouts and dickie birds flying here and there. Maybe she had recited Liz's rhyme. Miss…he couldn't remember. She'd loved that stuff. Plums, candlesticks, clocks. No wonder Liz unsettled him. You shouldn't be attracted to someone who reminded you of your grade one teacher.

He picked up a Phillips screwdriver and tried to remember how far he'd got with the project on his table. Hardware wasn't his specialty. Daniel's penciled instructions looked more like directions to Pine Point than a system of electrical wires. "It's as easy as pie," Daniel had said—absolutely deadpan and professional, but Jack knew it was a crack about his baking.

LIZ AND EMILY SPRAWLED on the living room floor surrounded by albums and boxes of photographs.

"I won't have room for all of these," Eleanor said. "I suppose the rest of you would take some? I'd hate to throw them away."

"Of course we'll all take some!" Liz exclaimed. "We'd never throw away photos."

"It's the saddest thing—I don't know if you've ever seen this—someone's family pictures in a secondhand store. A young man you don't know in a fine mustache and straw boater, fishing. A row of children in their Sunday best, solemn before the camera. And people buy them for some reason." Eleanor touched a picture of her brother in his RCAF uniform. "I'd hate it if that happened to these."

"No one will ever take your photos to a secondhand store," Emily said. "We won't throw them away, either, not even the blurry ones or the ones of strangers. And especially not ones like this." She held up a picture of a young woman in an evening dress, satiny material clinging to her curves. "Don't tell me that's you."

"That's me."

"You didn't wear that, Grandma!"

"I did! I saw a dress just like it in a magazine and set my heart on it. I knew I wouldn't be allowed to have something so…well, sophisticated, shall we say? So I made it myself. From the lining of my bedroom curtains."

Liz and Emily laughed, trying to imagine their practical grandmother ruining curtains in an effort to look glamorous.

Eleanor's face was warm with the memory. "I went out the back door, wearing my everyday dress in case my parents saw me, and changed in the storehouse, if you can imagine that. Me, in my underclothes, in the storehouse! I was sure every sound I heard was my father coming to catch me. My friend waited in his car, just out of sight of the house and we went to a dance in Pine Point. The dress was completely wrong for the occasion. It would have been more suited to sprawling on a chaise lounge with a cigarette holder in hand, but I didn't care."

"My grandmother, a wild, disobedient girl?" Liz shook her head.

Eleanor looked pleased. "I wasn't wild. I was an absolutely normal girl. It was the rules that were unreasonable."

"Who was the friend?" Emily asked. "Was it Grandpa?"

"It was a while yet before I starting seeing your grandfather." Eleanor's face softened. "This was someone else entirely."

"Was he your true love?" Liz asked. Unthinkable if Grandpa wasn't.

"I don't know about that. Certainly my first love."

"You're being mysterious," Emily said. "Who was it? Spill, Grandma."

Eleanor just raised her eyebrows and went back to sorting photos, smiling faintly.

Who could it have been? Liz wondered. Some rakish stranger, chugging down the road in a shiny two-seater roadster? A movie star, or some English aristocrat, or even the Prince of Wales, on his way to his ranch in Alberta?

It was clear Eleanor didn't plan to tell them more, so Liz went back to leafing through the photo album on her lap. The Robbs took the same pictures every year. Children on ponies. Children leaning over cakes, blowing out three, then six, then eleven candles. The family sitting around the table at Christmas, everyone wearing new blouses or new sweaters, everyone with forks near their mouths.

Her hand stopped. There, at the bottom of the page, next to pictures of herself and Tom, was a small shot of Andy. "Grandma?"

"Hmm?"

"You have a picture of Andy."

"Of course. He was a member of the family."

Liz took a deep breath to ease the sudden tightness in her chest. "No one else thought so. Mom and Dad thought he was a mistake."

"I'm sure they didn't," Emily protested. "They were just surprised."

"He was a sweet boy," Eleanor said. "I liked Andrew."

Liz blinked a few times. They would be so embarrassed if she started to cry.

Eleanor set aside the photographs on her lap. "I think we've had enough sorting for this evening. Tea?"

Emily jumped up. "I'll make it. I'll even make toast."

Stepping over boxes, Liz carried the album she'd been holding to the hutch cupboard. "Leave the boxes, Grandma. I'll get them."

"In that case, I'll help your cousin."

When she heard her grandmother's footsteps in the kitchen, Liz reopened the album, easily finding the page with Andy's photograph. He looked younger than she remembered. They had been sure they were all grown up, eager to jump into their lives, impatient with the restrictions put in their way. But his cheeks were smooth, still slightly rounded. It wasn't a man's face.

She hadn't packed any pictures of him when she'd

left Three Creeks. She'd gone quickly, hardly thinking, leaving most of her things behind. Andy was so much with her then, real and vivid, she never would have believed she'd need a picture to remember him. Somehow, unbelievably, the details of his face had slipped her mind. Whenever she'd tried to draw him after the first year, he'd looked like a stranger, someone observed in a crowd.

"Liz? Tea's ready."

"Coming!" She slipped the photo into the pocket of her jeans before putting the boxes and albums away.

CHAPTER FOUR

PAM AND EMILY HAD TOLD LIZ all about the new school, but she still went into town expecting to see the old one. It was a bit of a surprise to find a new cement-brick building stretching across the spot where the four-room schoolhouse, baseball diamond and maple grove had been. Inside, walking past the gym and the band room, standing at the front of Pam's large, bright classroom, she didn't even feel as if she was in Three Creeks. She could be in any town or city. Except that her niece was sitting a couple of arm-lengths away, looking at her with pride and embarrassment.

Liz held up a single piece of paper covered with tiny, hand-drawn squares. Inside each square was a simple pencil sketch. "This is the first draft of my new book, *There's a Dinosaur on Your Right.*"

Jennifer and fourteen other children sitting at three round tables leaned closer. Kids loved the idea of a book in miniature, no matter how little detail was in each drawing.

"It looks like a comic strip," one boy said, tilting his chair so it balanced on its back legs. He wore an Edmonton Oilers' hockey jersey that reached halfway to his knees. Only the tips of his fingers showed at the end of the sleeves.

"Stephen," Pam said.

He rocked the chair forward so all four legs touched the ground.

"It's called a thumbnail layout. You can see why." Liz held up one thumb so the children could compare her nail to the squares she'd drawn. "It's a quick and easy way to find out if there's enough going on in the story you're planning."

"You should call it a two-thumbnail layout," Stephen said.

Liz smiled. She moved closer to the blackboard, where she'd lined up a series of larger drawings, the ones she'd brought to show her grandmother. The final paintings were with her publisher, but she thought the sketches of a ten-year-old heroine trapped in a subterranean world of dinosaurs would appeal to the children.

"After the *two*-thumbnail layout gives me an idea what will happen, I make a mock-up, also called a dummy." She heard the expected giggles. "I draw bigger, more detailed versions of the sketches I've decided will do the best job of telling the story, with a few words added, so I can keep track of what I want to say on each page. Then I spread it all out like this to see how the story flows."

Liz pointed to the first two sketches. "The story opens with a girl, ten years old, falling into a dark hole in the ground, so deep there's no way out. She sees footprints. Huge, three-toed footprints."

"Dinosaur tracks!" A dark-haired boy leaned forward, his elbows on the table, one foot on the floor, the other knee on his chair. He pointed at the third drawing. "And that's a shadow of a Tyrannosaurus Rex."

Pam spoke firmly from her corner of the room. "Sit down, Dave."

He sat, without taking his eyes off the line of pictures.

"Why did I draw the T-Rex's shadow, rather than the T-Rex itself?"

"It's scarier," Dave said.

"That's right. Not knowing is always scary, isn't it? We start with a dark hole in the ground, then the footprint. Both of those things are scary, but our heroine is sure there must be a reasonable explanation."

"Until she sees the shadow," Jennifer said.

"With that huge head and those little arms and those long sharp teeth and claws...we know what's coming, don't we?" Liz had placed the next drawing with its back to her audience. Now she turned it, so the kids could see the T-Rex close up and suddenly, the way her heroine did in the story.

"Whoa," said Dave.

"These first three pictures build suspense and the fourth one delivers. Now our heroine has some problems to solve. Any ideas what those might be?"

"Not getting eaten," Stephen said.

"Getting out of the hole."

"Finding out what happened! How come there's a live dinosaur down there?"

"Yeah, and how does it fit? T-Rexs are huge."

Liz caught Pam's eye. Now that their interest had been tweaked, it seemed like a good idea to let the children start their own projects. "Answering those questions gives us the plot," Liz concluded, "and as the girl in the pictures solves those problems, we'll find out what kind of person she is."

Pam began distributing paper and pencils. Liz leaned against the desk at the front of the room, keeping out of the way while the children got settled. She couldn't imagine starting a first draft with someone peering over her shoulder.

Stephen looked as if he could use some help,

though. He slouched in his seat, twitching his pencil back and forth, knocking an eraser across his empty paper. After a few minutes, Liz joined him. "Having trouble getting started?"

He shrugged. "I don't like make-believe stuff."

She decided not to mention comics or movies or video games. "Your story doesn't have to be fiction." She held her pencil over his paper. "Okay if I show you something?"

Stephen nodded grudgingly.

She started by drawing a series of small squares. Inside one, using the first idea that came to mind, she sketched a man wearing jeans and a button-up shirt. She rolled up his sleeves to show he was hard at work. Inside the next square, the man crouched down, putting something small and oval into a concave spot in the ground.

"A guy planting seeds," Stephen said.

The boy next to Stephen was watching, too. Liz had to think for a moment to remember his name. Jeremy. He was smaller than the other children, enough that he looked two or three years younger. "Hey, that's Mr. McKinnon, isn't it? My dad worked with him in the summer. Planting and stuff."

"Your dad works all over the place," Stephen said. "Odd jobs."

Liz noticed a slight, protective recoil from Jeremy. "Good for him. That means he knows how to do all kinds of things." The boy's small body relaxed.

Tiny leaves unfurled in a third square, grew bigger in a fourth and snaked all across a fifth. Small fruit with vertical ridges appeared on the vines.

"Pumpkins," Stephen said.

Finally Liz drew long-fingered hands carrying a

large pumpkin, and the same hands pushing a knife through its shell.

Stephen leaned in. "Can I do that?" Pressing heavily on his pencil, he drew a pair of triangular eyes, a matching nose, and a crooked sharp-toothed grin. He smiled at the result, but Liz could see his interest was fading fast.

"I've never been a pumpkin farmer," she said, "but I know what pumpkins look like and I know how to plant a garden—"

She could see when his idea hit. Stephen reached eagerly for a fresh piece of paper. "I'll make a book about winning the Stanley Cup! I know what the rink looks like and the goalie and the uniforms—"

Jennifer muttered, "The refs, the penalty box—"

"I know what the Cup looks like, and I know what it feels like when you win." He sat forward, feet tucked around the front legs of his chair. At the top of the paper, he wrote *Chapter One* and underlined it three times. He thought for a few moments, then added, *by Stephen Cook, Three Creeks Elementary, Grade Five.* This was underlined twice. Liz waited, but no thumbnail-size squares followed. Not even two thumbnail-size squares. He indented and began to write. *My team made it to the play-offs…*

He was out of his seat, she was sure, a fraction of a second before the lunch-hour bell rang. Faster than they would have for a fire drill, the children emptied the classroom.

JACK PULLED THE BOOK he'd just bought out of its bag. It was tall and wide, so he rested it against his truck's steering wheel and slowly turned the pages, sometimes smiling at the illustrations, until he found the verse he wanted.

Peter, Peter, pumpkin eater…

Strange to hear a grown woman quoting a nursery rhyme as seriously as if it were Shakespeare.

Had a wife and couldn't keep her, put her in a pumpkin shell, and there he kept her very well…

Nonsense, he would have thought, the kind of rhythmic nonsense children enjoyed. Could it mean something, as Liz had suggested? What was a pumpkin eater, anyway? He'd heard of potato eaters. It was a derisive term for the poor during the 1800s, for anyone who couldn't afford better food. Were pumpkins common when the rhyme came to be, or a rare luxury?

Peter put his wife in a pumpkin shell—in fact, he couldn't keep her until he put her there. Did the shell represent a nice house, and was the wife unwilling to stay with him until then? She cared more for possessions than for love? Maybe he should pay more attention to the phrase *couldn't keep her.* The pumpkin might be the back alley cardboard box of its day. It was the best Peter could do, but they were happy.

Or did it suggest a prison, maybe the Tower of London? Was Peter a well-known person, the Lord Mayor, or a king, with a wife who tended to stray? And why was any of that appropriate reading for children?

Jack slipped the book back into its bag and tucked it under the seat. Plenty of time to think about it during the drive home. He couldn't tell Ned he was late for lunch because he was reading nursery rhymes. Ned already thought he was crazy.

He locked the doors of his truck and walked out of the shopping center parkade onto Princess Avenue. Lunch-hour traffic crowded the usually quiet street. As much as he loved walking through the countryside, the only human in sight or hearing, it was a nice change to see hurrying men with briefcases, mothers pushing strollers, teenagers laughing and jostling each other, certain all eyes were on them.

Brandon University was only eight blocks away, welcome exercise after the drive from Three Creeks. It stretched along 18th Street like the city's centerpiece. Two beige brick buildings from the late nineteenth century were flanked by newer ones, including the Brodie Building, a glass and cement structure that housed the science faculty. The math and computer science department was on the first floor. Jack strode along, checking nameplates on doors until he finally saw Dr. Edward Hardy. Voices came through the open door.

"...and it runs in linear time," a young-sounding voice finished. "So you can't say all sorts run in *Omega-n-log-n* time."

"All *comparison* sorts run in *Omega-n-log-n* time," Ned replied.

"But this is *linear.* Why use QuickSort at all?"

Ned and his student both turned when Jack stepped into the room.

"There you are, Jack, right when I need you most!" Ned said. "Ray, this is Jack McKinnon, an old school friend of mine. He's a lowly technician compared to me, but even I have to admit he's an artist with a computer program. Sort of an idiot savant—"

"That's very generous, Ned. Good to meet you, Ray."

Ned tossed Jack a piece of chalk. "We've been going over this for a while. Want to have a go?"

Jack looked at the chalk as if it were an unfamiliar instrument. He felt a little sorry for Ray, standing there both hopeful and embarrassed. He went to the board, covered with formulae and diagrams, and found a bare section big enough for his needs. "We sort things every day,'' he began. ''You sort your socks, you sort your change, you sort your Halloween candy.''

Ray allowed himself a small smile.

''For our purposes, we're trying to help the computer store and retrieve numbers. When I came in you were arguing the benefits of the Counting Sort, and you've got a point. When the conditions seem right for it, why use a more complicated method, like QuickSort? You're glossing over some important details, though. Say you're sorting *n* things—integers, whatever. Okay?''

Ray nodded. ''Yeah, sure.''

Jack wrote a list of nine numbers on the board—5,7,1,1,3,2,7,5,7—and underneath them, $n = 9$. ''You want to sort these numbers. You've figured out how to do it by using the Counting Sort, so you count how many 1's you have, then how many 2's, all the way up to the sevens.''

''That's right.''

''Okay. That's good as far as it goes. If I add, say, another 5 and a 7 to this list, it's clear that we'll see a linear increase in how long it takes to do the sorting.''

''Right,'' said Ray, ''so it runs in linear time with respect to *n*.''

''What if I make this list?'' Jack jotted another series of numbers on the board—5,7,1,1,3,2,7,5,7, 300 000. ''It'll take a heck of a lot longer to sort, won't it? The time it takes depends on the range of possible numbers in your list, not just how many you need to sort.''

Understanding dawned and with it, greater embarrassment. Ray swore under his breath, then apologized before swearing again. There was nothing like that moment when you saw something you should have seen half an hour before.

Jack set the chalk on the ledge under the board. "Don't worry about it. Maybe one day I'll tell you about your prof's first year in comp sci."

"That's something I'd like to hear." Ray hitched his backpack higher on his shoulder and, with a few words of thanks, was gone.

Ned came forward with his hand outstretched. "It's good to see you in a classroom, Jack. You're a better teacher than I am. I gotta ask, what in the world are you doing growing pumpkins?"

Jack had known that was coming, but as a greeting? "Avoiding eyestrain."

"I'm serious, Jack."

"So am I."

Ned stared at him. "You give up years of study because you don't want to look at a monitor? Come on. You can hire someone to do that for you. If you didn't like running a business you could have detoured into research any time. Any university would take you, starting with this one. We went into the semester short two people."

"I'm not looking for work."

Ned eyed the wall and the floor before saying quietly, "Some of the guys are wondering if you're having a meltdown. I told them of course not. People make career changes all the time."

"Thank you."

His friend nodded and stared at the floor some more. Finally, sounding both apologetic and encouraging, he said, "But this is a dramatic change. And an impulsive one, from what I could see. So if there *is* something…I mean, it's nothing to be ashamed of. One of the guys on the psych faculty here has a private practice and I'm told he's good. Discreet."

"I thought we were going to have lunch."

"We are." Ned checked his watch. "There's a great Chinese food buffet just around the corner on Victoria. We'll load up there and I'll harangue you about getting back to work at something that matters."

"Pumpkins don't matter?"

A new expression crossed Ned's face. "Lots of farmers' daughters out there?"

Jack couldn't help laughing. That would be an explanation Ned could understand.

"A farmer needs a wife, Jack."

"Heigh ho the derry-o."

"Jack?"

"Just some reading I was doing. Nothing to worry about."

THE THREE WOMEN SAT elbow-to-elbow in a study room off the library, their feet up on chairs on the other side of the table, a plate of tomato and cheese sandwiches in front of them.

"Liz is a natural," Pam told Emily. "Too bad she can't come by the classroom every term."

"A natural?" Liz asked. "Those kids couldn't wait to get out when the bell rang."

"But they didn't groan. Not once."

Emily handed Liz a mug of clear tea. "Careful, it's hot."

"The hotter the better. I've been cold ever since I got here. Jack says it's going to snow by Halloween."

Pam looked meaningfully at Emily. "*Jack* says."

"Don't start, you two. Small talk about the weather doesn't mean anything."

"Bothering to deny a harmless observation might

mean something.'' Emily pushed the plate of sandwiches closer to Liz. ''I was prepared to believe Jack glued himself to your side at the barbecue because he was shy, or because you'd asked him to make sure no mosquitoes landed on your neck—''

''Or because he had a microphone and she was dictating a new story,'' Pam said. ''There are lots of reasons for a man to hover protectively beside a woman he's just met—because I thought his posture was protective, didn't you?''

''Like a shield,'' Emily agreed.

''Did you do anything at the barbecue besides watch me?''

''We watched Jack, too.''

''I'm not denying he's attractive—''

Pam whispered to Emily. ''She thinks he's attractive.''

''But Jack has his mind on pumpkins and Christmas trees, and I'm going back to Vancouver in a week. There'll be narrow mountain passes and glaciers and grizzlies between us.''

''Us,'' Emily repeated.

Liz stared into her teacup, hoping they would soon be done with this line of questioning. They couldn't really think she and Jack were about to embark on a relationship, could they? Just because he was one gender and she was the other and they had enjoyed a couple of conversations?

''Come on, Liz,'' Pam said. ''How long is it since you've gone out with someone you really like? Jack is so nice and so good-looking and he seems interested, who knows why—''

''I'm enjoying the single life. The unattached, uninvolved, uncomplicated life.''

''Voluntarily, you mean?'' Emily asked. ''I'm enjoying the single life because I haven't met anyone I'm willing to complicate it for.''

''You will, hon,'' Pam said.

''Not if I stay in Three Creeks.''

Liz looked at her cousin in surprise. As far as she knew Emily had never considered leaving. ''Are you thinking of moving?'' She could come to Vancouver. There'd be four at Sunday dinner.

''Of course not. This is my home.''

Liz knew Emily meant she couldn't leave. That was what she believed, anyway. When she was still in junior high she'd told Liz and Susannah that she would always stay with her mother. Julia lived in a world of her own, that was the phrase everyone used, and it was a world where stove burners were left on high while she lost herself in her book collection. People said she'd always been like that, but the tendency had got worse after her husband died when Emily was eight.

Emily re-focused the conversation on Liz. ''I don't believe you want to be single. You love falling for guys. You call me every time it happens, chirping like a songbird.''

Liz laughed at the description, and hoped it wasn't true. She did like the feeling of being smitten, but it rarely developed beyond that. ''I'll admit I like men—taken as a group, a subspecies. Taken individually, though, they're never as wonderful once I get to know them as they are at first sight.''

''Poor guys, give them a break!'' Emily said. ''They're not knights in shining armor. And you, much as I love you, cuz, are not Guinevere.''

''That two-timing bit of fluff? I should hope not.'' Liz jumped when the bell on the wall near her ear rang. ''Already?''

Pam put down her half-empty cup. ‘‘That’s only the first bell. We have five minutes till class starts, but I like to get into the room before the kids do. Otherwise I have to sort out whose fault something is.’’

Liz and Pam were almost out of the library, when Liz stopped as if she’d banged into an unexpected wall. Over the door was a oil pastel she hadn’t seen in fifteen years. It showed a close-up of the smallest of the three creeks, the shallow water still and murky. Through cattails half gone to seed, a wounded mallard floated.

Emily came to stand beside her. ‘‘Your Mom and Dad found it in your room after you left. They didn’t think you wanted it and Andy’s parents didn’t leave a forwarding address. I guess we could have tried harder to find them.’’

‘‘Everyone assumed they didn’t want us to find them,’’ Pam said.

‘‘It was in the hallway of the old school for years, on that wall between the grade five and six and the grade seven and eight rooms. I know he didn’t go to elementary school in Three Creeks—’’

‘‘Over the water fountain?’’

‘‘High up, so it wouldn’t get splashed.’’

Andy had been so angry the day he’d found the duck. He wasn’t against hunting, but he was furious that a hunter would take a shot he wasn’t sure of making. His first impulse had been to wrap the bird in his jacket and rush it to the vet, but he could see how badly it was hurt. It would have died, afraid and captive, before he got to Pine Point. The image of its quiet effort to hold its head up, resisting defeat even near death, had stayed with him for a long time.

‘‘Do you want it back, Liz? That would be fine. I mean, Andy gave it to you.’’

"No," Liz said quickly. "I'm sure he'd..." Her voice trailed off. What was she sure of, where Andy was concerned? She forced herself to look away from the picture. Emily's and Pam's faces were full of concern, so she looked away from them, too. "It was a long time ago. Ancient history."

Hardly aware of Pam at her side, Liz made her way back to the classroom, glad to see the children already in their seats, apparently as eager to get back to their stories as they'd been to go outside. Responding to their questions helped her push Andy's drawing to the back of her mind. It was like stuffing a suitcase too full, though, pushing one last item in only to find it springing back, forcing the lid open.

Jennifer had covered her paper with small irregular shapes resembling squares. They were filled with kittens, stretching and sleeping, batting their paws at nothing.

Stephen's story was well on its way. *Number 10 was coming at me fast. I knew I had to get rid of the puck before he sent me flying into the boards. No one could make that shot, but I had to try.*

Most of the boys had followed the same idea. Dave had drawn a few stick figures with blades on their feet and hockey sticks in their hands. Underneath the sketches he'd written, *Two days before Chrismas the creeks finly froze up and the guys played hockey. There was a blizerd and school was canseled so we played all day. They had to shovel it first.*

"That's all I've got," he said, when he saw Liz reading.

"Could you add some detail?"

He looked at his paper and sighed. "Like which guys?"

"That would help."

"But it's just another line, and I need, like, four more pages. I guess I could say who got checked and who scored." He brightened up as more possibilities occurred to him. "And who was in goal and who got the face-off."

"Now you're talking. You said there was a blizzard...how cold was it?"

"Pretty cold."

"Did your fingers feel like blocks of ice inside your mitts? Were birds falling dead from the branches above you?"

He lifted his hands in front of him, as if showing her how big a fish he'd caught. "The whole thing, you mean." His hands went up and down, tracing brackets in the air.

"The whole thing," Liz agreed. "Not just what happened, but what your five senses noticed about what happened. What you thought and felt. And don't forget dialogue."

Dave looked even happier. "Right! Cause you need a new paragraph for each person who talks...that would take up lots of space. Thanks, Miss Robb!"

She smiled. But as soon as she turned away, the suitcase lid popped open.

CHAPTER FIVE

GOING SO SLOWLY DOWN THE gravel road that a whole herd of deer could have crossed safely in front of her, Liz left the town behind. She felt like the kids in Pam's class—glad to get out of the house that morning; just as glad to leave the school now. The grade fives were going to finish the day with a baseball game, so she'd helped them clean up before the afternoon recess bell, then stopped in at the general store for dinner provisions. A little something for tonight, and salad ingredients for tomorrow.

As she turned into her grandmother's driveway Bella and Dora emerged from the lilac bushes, just as they had the night she arrived. Now their tails wagged, and they looked pleased to see her.

"Hey girls. Have you been good? Did you keep the monsters away?" They wagged their tails harder. "You did? Well done!" She followed the dogs into the kitchen, where she found Eleanor surrounded by dishes, polishing a Spode dinner plate. She carried her brown paper bag to the counter. "I brought you a treat from the grocery store."

"How nice." Eleanor watched as Liz reached into the bag and pulled out a frosty, plastic-wrapped package. "Now what could that be?"

"It's frozen lasagna. It's good, Grandma. Really. I get it all the time." She waved a head of romaine lettuce in the air, followed by a bottle of Caesar dressing. "I'll make salad to go with it."

"Lovely. We can eat in front of the television. Like roommates, with those meals in divided trays." Eleanor looked pleased at the thought. Eating in the living room had always been unheard of in this house, and as far as Liz knew her grandmother never watched anything but the national news and royal weddings and funerals.

Liz tucked the lettuce into the crisper and turned on the electric oven. The lasagna needed to cook for two hours, so she'd have to put it in soon. "I had a good time with Pam's class."

Eleanor began polishing the next plate in the pile. "I thought you would. Ten is a nice age. Did you miss the old school?"

"The new building is beautiful. So bright and roomy." Liz almost mentioned Andy's drawing. Instead, she took a tea towel from the drawer and joined her grandmother at the table. "You've been busy with dishes all day?"

"Dusting and counting. Edith is keen to have the Spode. I wondered if it might be an idea to give each family a share of it. Edith could have the dinner plates, your mother could have the bowls, and Julia the teapot and cups. A few serving dishes for everyone."

"It would be a pity to break up the set." It was actually two sets, with a transferware pattern of soft blue flowers on a white background. It had belonged to the first Julia, who had come to the wilds of Manitoba prepared, believing she would never set foot in a china store again.

Liz picked up a rose colored depression glass platter and held it so light from the window shone through. She ran her hand over the raised pattern of trailing leaves and flowers. There wasn't a chip or a scratch on it. "I always loved this platter."

"Then it's yours. Six small plates go with it."

"I wasn't asking for it, Grandma. You should take it with you."

"I'm content to know it will be with someone who appreciates it."

Liz carefully put the platter down. Maybe it and the six plates could travel safely in her carry-on luggage. She wondered how much of their charm came from their surroundings. Would they look as pretty in a modern apartment? "None of this seems right. I can't picture you living anywhere but here. I'm sorry, I know I keep saying that, and it doesn't help."

Eleanor spoke bracingly. "The house isn't manageable for me anymore, not even with all the help the family gives me. The roof needs to be re-shingled, some of the windows reglazed, the garden dug over, the fruit trees pruned. It's been wonderful living here, but I'll enjoy being in town."

She put down the tea towel, and her voice slowed. "I was going to pack the china away today…but what if I'm still here at Christmas? We'd need it then. And the table." Will had offered to contact an antique dealer about the dining room set, but she hadn't given him the go ahead yet.

"Someone in the family will take it. I'm sure of it."

"And if they don't, that will be fine. I can hardly cling to that piece of wood, can I?" Eleanor pulled the tea towel from Liz's hands. "You're pale after your day at the school. Chalk dust never did agree with you. Why don't you take the dogs for a walk while I finish here?"

"You've been working by yourself all day, Grandma. I'm not here for a holiday."

"Bella and Dora need more exercise than I can give them. Off you go now."

"If you're sure."

"That's more like it! Obedience is a fine thing in a grandchild."

Liz slipped the tray of lasagna into the oven before she left and repeated that she'd make the salad when she returned. As soon as she took her jacket from the hook by the door, the dogs were at her side and the moment the door opened they bolted for the woods. Hands in her pockets, Liz followed more slowly, breathing in the spicy air. The last of the marigolds, she thought, and crumbling leaves.

When she reached the swing, she stopped and tugged on the rope. It seemed secure. One foot on the tire, she pulled herself up, swaying slightly. No ominous sounds came from the rope or the branch, so she pushed with her free foot and the swing went higher. A stronger push, higher still. She'd forgotten the dizzying feeling, part elation, part seasickness.

The last time she'd been here was with Andy. She had climbed up just like this, feeling pretty with the breeze in her hair. He'd taken a running jump onto the swing, sending it flying, and when she'd yelled at the sudden speed and height, he'd wrapped his long, thin arms around her, laughing. That was after the wedding and after the fuss, when her grandparents were the only people who didn't look at them with disapproval.

She jumped off while the swing was still moving and whistled for the dogs. They came bounding out of the bush near the barn, ears pricked forward, then turned and disappeared again. Liz stuffed her hands back into her pockets and started through the garden to the pasture.

The barn's huge double doors were open. From the look of the grass tall and tangled in front of them, they hadn't been shut for years. Although the barn had been empty for just as long, she still noticed an animal smell, soaked into the ground and the weathered boards. No more warm, munching animals with big, brown eyes, glad to be scratched behind the ears. Now it was a place for bats and rats and hornets.

If she took a couple of steps back and stood on her toes, she could see into the hayloft. From the time they were Jennifer's age, it had been one of their favorite places. She and Susannah would stretch out on the bales, chewing long pieces of straw and reading, or talking about all the wonderful things that would happen when they grew up.

How old had they been the summer they'd planned to sleep up there? Grade five, six? The last adventure of their holidays. They'd included their brothers, but Emily couldn't come. Aunt Julia had said she was too young. The five of them blew their combined allowance on soft drinks and chips and packaged cookies and hauled the food and their sleeping bags and some games up the ladder. Most of the mosquitoes were gone by then, but wasps were urgently looking for places to nest, and at night moths fluttered heavily, attracted to the flashlights.

They'd sat in a circle with loose and baled hay all around them and empty swallows' nests overhead. After sunset, they took turns telling ghost stories, voices more and more hushed as they went, bodies more and more crouched, heads closer and closer together, flashlights casting odd shadows on their faces.

And then they'd heard the noises. Crackling sounds

outside, just below the loft. In one motion, they jumped up and leapt from the window, without a thought for broken ankles, and ran as fast as they could for the house. In with a bang, shushing each other loudly as they thumped up the stairs and into the back bedroom. Someone turned on the light and they stood silently, in a circle again, eyes wide.

"Did you hear it?"

"What was it?"

"Whatever it was, it was coming to the barn."

In the morning, brave in the sunlight, they'd gone back to investigate. Three heifers looked at them calmly from the willows near the barn, munching the tall ripe grass between the trees, flattening branches as they went. At first they swore each other to secrecy, but over time they told everyone they knew. It was too good a story to keep to themselves. When they got back to school all their friends agreed they would have run, too.

Bella and Dora darted out of the woods, pulling Liz's attention back to the present. They circled the barn, chasing nothing Liz could see, then looped back into the woods. Hoping they were only imagining whatever had them so excited, she hurried after them. Now and then, they reappeared, eyes bright, tongues hanging out the sides of their mouths. As soon as they saw she was with them, they were off again. She didn't notice they had led her to Jack's until she was about to step out of the trees into the wide yard around his house.

"He's not here, girls. Remember? He's away for the day." It was too bad. She would have liked to see him, too. She tried to whistle, but just blew air. "Bella!" If Bella came, Dora would follow. She was about to call louder when she saw the car. A black car, squarish, parked almost out of sight behind the house.

The dogs had seen it, too. They stood uneasily, ears swiveling like radar. When the kitchen door swung open Bella barked once, in a sharp *Hey, what's going on?* tone. The man who'd come outside froze.

Liz didn't recognize him. She had opened her mouth to call the dogs back, but instead, obeying a feeling she didn't stop to analyze, she moved deeper into the trees. Whether he'd seen or heard something, or just wanted to investigate, the man took a couple of steps in her direction, then froze again when Bella growled.

A second person held the kitchen door open. Liz saw a man's arm and heard a low voice. All she could tell was that it wasn't Jack. Keeping an eye on the dogs, the first man backed up. When he reached the step, he turned and hurried inside.

Liz managed a quiet whistle. One of four ears tilted in response, but the dogs kept watching the house. She started to walk away, hoping they'd sense her withdrawal and follow. She was almost home when she heard them behind her.

She bent to rub their ears. ''Good girls. Why did you take so long? Interrogating them, were you?'' There was an unusual tension in their bodies. She knew just how they felt—her muscles were tight, too. Either they had excited themselves playing in the woods, and she had unsettled herself with too many memories, or the people at Jack's were up to no good and anyone with two instincts to rub together knew it.

Eleanor came into the kitchen to meet them. She looked worried, as if she sensed their unease. ''Elizabeth? Is something wrong?''

"I don't know. There were two men at Jack's. In the house, I mean."

"Isn't he in Brandon today?"

"The dogs were guarding, Grandma. Hackles up, growling."

Eleanor looked at them in surprise. They had stayed close to Liz, pressed against her legs. "These girls?" She put a hand on Bella's head. "Poor things. I send you out for a nice walk and you come back all in a flutter." She smiled at the three of them. "I'm sure it's fine. I'll call Thomas to check into it, though, and then we'll have tea while we wait."

Liz lifted the kettle and gave it a shake. It was nearly full, and almost simmering. She moved it onto the cast-iron burner directly over the fire, and found tea bags in the cupboard. By the time Eleanor came back to the kitchen, the tea was steeping.

"Your brother must be out at the feedlot. I got hold of Martin, though, and he's promised to take a look."

"Maybe I should go with him. There were two of them."

"You'll stay right here with me."

Silently, Liz put two cups of tea on the table.

"That's a welcome sight." Eleanor seemed glad to sit down. "What would you say to a game of cards to pass the time?"

They'd had a few games of double solitaire during the week, and Eleanor had always won. At first Liz thought she was letting it happen, taking her grandmother's poorer vision and slower reflexes into consideration, but increased effort hadn't changed the outcome. She pulled out a chair. "I'll get you this time. I'm alert and razor-sharp, and you're drowsy from resting."

"Resting," Eleanor repeated meaningfully. "I'm ready for you."

Eleanor's hand and eye were consistently faster. After losing a third game Liz said, "You could make your living as a double solitaire shark, going from bar to bar with your deck of cards."

"Maybe that's how I'll pay for the roof."

The teapot was empty and Liz had yet to win a hand, when they heard a truck in the driveway. Liz opened the kitchen door before Martin had time to knock.

"Hello, ladies." While Eleanor moved the kettle back onto the heat, he told them what he'd found. "It was just some friends of McKinnon's. From Winnipeg. They figured he'd be home all the time. Isn't that typical? I don't know how they think a farmer can get his crops to grow from his kitchen, even if it is pumpkins. They were planning to wait for him, so I told them what you told me, that he'd be out of town till late. They said at least they'd had a nice drive in the country." Martin shrugged expressively.

"Everything's all right, then."

"Yup, everything's fine, Grandma." He took a couple of strides to the stove and reached across the dogs to lift the boiling kettle. "Liz was just using her imagination the way a good writer should." He sniffed the air. "Do I smell lasagna?"

HALF AN HOUR LATER, the three of them sat on the scratchy sofa in the living room with trays on their knees, talking over the voice of the CBC news anchor. Martin's wife had surprised him by not minding that he wouldn't be home for dinner. She had the cutout pieces of their two-year-old's Halloween costume all over the kitchen table and nothing on the stove.

"She's going nuts," Martin said. "I bet she'll stuff that costume down the garbage disposal before she's done. Halloween is this big deal now. You wouldn't believe it."

"I do believe it," said Eleanor. Martin's daughter was her youngest great-grandchild.

"I used to find some old coat and hat of Dad's, throw on an eye patch, and I was done. Pat spent forty bucks on this fuzzy cloth to make Nell look like a teddy bear. When I left the house she was tearing out seams and swearing—it's a good thing you called, Grandma. I was glad to get out of there."

"Poor Pat," Liz murmured.

"And where's Nell while all this is going on? Scattering toys from one end of the house to the other and working herself into a mood. When I get home, I'll be the one who has to deal with it. Pat will hide in the bathtub until I get Nell calmed down and ready to sleep."

Eleanor smiled. "What a thoughtful husband you are. Tell Patricia if she's having trouble, I'd be glad to help. Ears and paws are such a nuisance."

"Thanks, Grandma." Martin leaned forward to take a bite of lasagna, so tomato sauce wouldn't drip on his shirt. "Did you know Mom and Dad heard from Sue?"

Liz and Eleanor both stared at him, waiting for him to finish chewing so they could hear more. "How is she?" Liz asked. "She got to the Gobi Desert safely?"

"After a crazy ride through a sandstorm. They're falling over fossils, she says. Every time the wind blows, which is pretty much all the time, something new pops out of the ground." He grinned. "Something old, I should say. Seventh heaven for Sue."

He used his knife and fork to fold a large piece of

lettuce leaf into a small square and popped it into his mouth. "Mom keeps complaining about the wedding. The main thing is, Sue found a guy she likes and she married him the way she wanted to. Good for her." He glanced at Liz. "Now you and Em are the only holdouts."

"Really, Martin," said Eleanor.

"Uh-oh. Sorry, Grandma. It's just—" He hesitated, glancing at Eleanor. "I suppose I assume everybody else would like being married as much as I do."

"There's a lot to be said for the single life," Liz said. "Don't you remember?"

"No, I don't! And I'm sticking to that story."

Martin didn't stay long after dinner. Liz sent the rest of the lasagna home with him, in case Pat hadn't eaten. After washing the few dishes, she started getting ready for the next evening's meal.

She was setting the table with Eleanor's china when Will arrived to pick up the rental car. He leaned into the dining room to take a look at her preparations. "Fancy. Having company?"

"Not until tomorrow. Jack McKinnon's coming over."

Will made no effort to hide his interest. "Is that so?"

"Grandma invited him." Liz handed her uncle the rental agreement and keys. "Thanks for doing this, Uncle Will."

He tucked the folded papers into a pocket. Jingling the keys in one hand, he said, "Hope Mom's not working you too hard."

"We're having a good time. It's kind of sad, though, going through her things." She caught Eleanor's eye and smiled. "And Grandpa's things."

"Your aunt and I threw around the idea of buying the place. Keep it in the family. All your stuff could stay then, Mom. The table."

There was an uneasy silence.

"Problem is, we're attached to our own house. Kids grew up there." He looked uncomfortable, as if he was afraid he and Edith were being unreasonably selfish. "You ever think of coming back, Liz?"

Coming back? "To live?"

"Why not? You can write and draw anywhere, can't you? The Internet connects everybody, coast to coast. You could e-mail your books to your publisher."

"I can't e-mail paintings."

"Courier. Next day delivery. The world's getting smaller, hon. Think it over."

Eleanor put a hand on Will's arm. Liz wasn't sure if she was restraining or comforting him. "Elizabeth, he just likes to say these things. It's a form of entertainment. Ignore him."

Liz started to laugh, but her uncle went on, apparently serious. "It'd be like old times. Imagine, going into the woods to get a Christmas tree, fishing the big creek in the spring, when the water's high." He had that look on his face, the one that had always convinced them how much fun it would be to take a polar bear swim or camp out in the north field all night to watch a meteor shower.

"You make it sound tempting."

He smiled. "Think how happy it would make your Grandma."

"For heaven's sake, it wouldn't make me happy at all. She has her own life. And so she should."

"Just a thought." With a farewell jingle of the keys, Will was out the door.

JACK YAWNED AS HE HUNG HIS COAT on the hat stand beside the back door. He'd had a good day, but it had started at five a.m. He was ready to fall asleep on his feet. That changed when he stepped into the kitchen and saw a sheet of paper waiting in the fax's document tray. In two long steps, he reached the machine. The logo at the top of the page, the provincial government's stylized bison, was instantly recognizable, so he skimmed the text, looking only for numbers. Anything from 6 to 6.5 was the ph range he needed for white spruce and balsam firs.

There it was: 6.2. Perfect! He was in business. Jack checked his watch, even though he already knew the time. It was too late to call Eleanor. She'd be pleased. She was almost as eager as he was to see a crop of Christmas trees growing in that field.

A pang of longing for his uncle came out of nowhere. This was news Jerry would have liked to hear. The academic stuff, things like scholarships or being accepted into Waterloo's graduate program, hadn't excited him all that much. Not that he didn't care. He just couldn't see why anyone wanted to sit at a desk or do calculations all day long. Jerry liked working outside, with his hands, so as far as he was concerned his job in a lumberyard couldn't have been better. He loved the grain and the smell of wood. He would have got a kick out of being on the other side of the equation.

Jack nudged up the needle on the thermostat. Maybe he'd plant a tree for Jerry. Right in the middle of the field, a place where he could get some shade when he took a break from pruning or cultivating. The idea might be a little on the sentimental side, but he liked it.

He left the lab results on the kitchen table and went

to the living room. As he had each night since hiding the diskette, he reached for *The Complete Works of William Shakespeare.* Every time he checked the book it fell open to page 1005. The difference this time was that the paper door he'd glued shut was torn open and the disk was gone.

That was fast. He really hadn't expected Reid to come back so soon. How had he happened to pick a day when Jack would be gone for hours? It was enough to make a guy feel like he was being watched.

Jack checked the tape in the VCR. It was full. Good to know the surveillance system had worked. He rewound the tape, turned on the TV and pressed the VCR's play button. At the bottom left-hand corner of the screen was the time recording had begun—10:35 a.m.

At first there was nothing to see except the outside of his house. That made sense. Whoever had activated the camera had to get up the driveway.

Then, as casually as if he belonged there, Reid appeared. He wasn't alone. Two other men had come along for the ride. One other man, anyway, and a pair of legs…the third man didn't get close enough for the camera to catch more than that.

"All right," Jack muttered. "Show me how you got in."

The legs disappeared around the side of the house. Reid and his friend stood by the back door, as if they had rung the bell and were waiting for someone to answer. The friend had his back to the camera. Jack could only see dark hair and a black leather coat.

He fast-forwarded until there was movement. Ten minutes into the tape, the door opened from the inside. The two men wiped their shoes on the mat before going into the house. "Thanks, guys. Nice of you to think about the floor."

He pressed the fast-forward button again, whizzing past five and a half hours of back door scenery. Then Reid appeared on the stoop. He seemed to be looking out at the yard, or toward the woods. He went down the steps and out of camera range. After a few minutes the door opened, and Jack saw an arm in a black leather sleeve. Reid came into view again, walking backward. Why would he walk backward? Away from something, watching something?

There was nearly a half hour more of nothing to see, and then the recording was finished. Six hours at least, these guys had been in his house. Jack wished he'd installed cameras inside. He stopped the tape. It hadn't told him much. Just that Reid had gone way over the line, and that he was angrier about it than he'd realized.

He took a flashlight from the glory hole under the stairs, pulled his coat and gloves back on, and went outside. Going in the same direction as the third man, he shone the light on the downstairs windows. They were all shut tight. He didn't see any broken glass. The cellar windows were locked from the inside. The air vents that prevented moisture build-up under the house were too small to provide a way in. He shone the light upward, to the second floor. Each pane of glass reflected the light. He'd made sure after Reid's first visit that the upstairs windows were locked. They were heavy, with secure metal catches. He was confident they couldn't be forced open.

How had that little creep got in? Not through a door, not through a window, not through an air vent. That left the roof, and the ground. The house didn't have a fireplace anymore, so there was no old brick chimney big enough to let sweeps and raccoons inside. The chimney for the Franklin stove was too small to climb down. The furnace chimney might let sparrows in, but that was all. When he'd climbed up to check for loose shingles and rot before he bought the place he hadn't found any surprises. No hidden sunroof, no gaping hole into the attic.

Jack began a slow walk around the house, flashlight aimed at the foundation. There wasn't a coal chute, or a miniature two-way door system for milk delivery. Could there be an old well that led to the house?

Finally he noticed a few branches broken from a foundation shrub. He held the bush away from the wall. Behind it was a simple, plywood door. A hook and eye held it shut. The hook lifted easily. That couldn't be it, there had to a be a lock.

The door swung open partway, stopped by the shrub. Jack got down on his knees and peered inside. It was a crawl space, under a newer part of the house, an extra bedroom the Ramseys had added.

He lay on the ground and turned his body until it fit through the opening, digging his toes into the ground and pushing. At first glance, the space seemed empty. There was nothing but spiderwebs, and from a faint, unpleasant smell—mice.

Wriggling on his stomach, Jack worked his way further in, shining the flashlight along the wall that met the original building. There. A window, one that would have let light and air into the cellar before the addition was built. It was wide open, accommodating a heating duct to the added bedroom. The window was small as it was, but the heating duct made it virtually impassable.

Impassable for most people. The third man on the tape, as far as Jack had been able to see from the short, narrow legs, had a slight build. Slight enough? If he could squeeze through into the cellar, it would be a simple matter to open the trapdoor into the kitchen. But how had they found the plywood door? Jack hadn't noticed it in the year since he'd bought the place. That would teach him not to weed the shrub bed.

He crawled back outside. The hook and eye seemed a bit pointless, but he fastened it anyway. He brushed dirt from his coat and pants, thinking of Reid bringing strangers to break into his house while the other disk, the one that mattered, sat at the bottom of the potato bin.

Reid didn't know about it. Ergo, he couldn't be looking for it.

What if he did know about it, though? Would he look for it? Maybe. To try to persuade Jack to use it, yes. To suggest a business partnership, yes. To break in and steal it? Probably not.

Still, a little more protection might be a good idea.

CHAPTER SIX

IT WAS A JUVENILE TRICK.

When he'd double-clicked on the A drive, an empty screen had come up, as if Jack's diskette was blank. Did Jack think for a minute anyone would be fooled by that? Revealing the hidden menu was child's play. With a couple of clicks of the mouse, Reid told the computer to show the menu, and the diskette's files appeared.

Okay. Reid smiled. That was more like it. Two hundred files crowded the screen, give or take a dozen. Still, the strategy would only slow him down, not stop him. Give the man a B for effort.

A few minutes later Reid began to have a better idea just how much it would slow him down. A password had been applied to each of the files. He sat back in his chair and stretched, hands clasped behind his neck. An unintentional sigh caught his partner's attention.

"Problem?" Croker came to stand beside Reid. "What's McKinnon doing?"

"Hiding a needle in a haystack."

"You can still find the needle, though." It wasn't so much a vote of confidence as an order.

"Of course. It might take a while, though."

"A while?"

Croker hadn't let up since they'd found the diskette. He was like a kid constantly asking his dad if they were there yet. "It depends how careful Jack was. He might have followed all the rules for creating virtually unbreakable passwords, or he might have used his mother's middle name for each file. I don't know how hard it'll be to get in. I'll run a password cracker program. It might open all the doors in seconds. Or days. Or weeks. There's a small possibility of never."

"But you'll be using more than one computer. You've got a network here, right?"

Reid nodded. His head had started to ache, and the movement made it worse. He got up from the desk, making sure his body language conveyed his determination that his schedule was his business. He would take a walk to the corner, get some fresh air and some pizza, despite the early hour, and, more importantly, a break from this insistent man. Without Croker's humorless impatience, the project could be fun. Like the games he and Jack used to play.

The invisible band around his head tightened.

JACK ANSWERED THE DOOR in his pyjamas. A heavy robe, its collar half twisted under, hung open over dark gray bottoms and a navy sweatshirt that was worn to soft comfort. With one hand he kept feeling for the other end of the robe's tie. He smiled groggily when he saw Liz. "Is it morning?"

"Officially." She had been up since six, sketching, making a fruit salad for her grandmother's breakfast, thinking about the black car and the two men and the gentle dogs growling, forcing herself to wait before coming to Jack's. Wishing she could backtrack a few minutes, to just before she'd clanged the cowbell hanging beside the door, she reached behind him and found the trailing tie. "Here you go."

''Thanks.'' Jack squinted at the sun. ''Eight-seventeen?''

''Not bad.'' She showed him her watch. ''Eight-twenty.''

He didn't ask what had brought her to his door at that hour. He stepped back, and the dogs rushed into the house. When Liz followed, they acted as if they hadn't seen her for days. Being around Jack turned them into puppies.

He headed straight for the coffeemaker. ''Espresso, I think. Doubles.''

Liz took a quick look around the kitchen. At first glance, at least, nothing seemed to be disturbed. If she'd been a burglar, she wouldn't have left the stainless steel coffeemaker on the counter, or the laptop and fax machine on the table. Jack's guitar would be worth taking, too.

The last time she was here, it was in the living room and now it leaned against the kitchen wall. She imagined Jack sitting beside the table, the guitar balanced on his knee, fingertips strumming. Did he sing, too? She'd like to hear that, his mellow voice lilting with music. Bittersweet tunes about lost love, and love to come, hiding his feelings behind the lyrics. Could a knight be a balladeer? Why not? A warrior-poet, equally adept with sword or song.

The sound of the coffee grinder dispelled the pleasant picture. ''I guess I woke you.''

''Good thing, too. I meant to get up at seven.''

''Even at Grandma's, people don't drop over this early. Unless they want breakfast.''

''Do you want breakfast?''

''No! I came to make sure everything was all right.''

He looked at her curiously. ''Everything's fine.''

"Good." He seemed to be waiting for an explanation. "The dogs and I were out walking yesterday, and before we knew it we found ourselves at the edge of your woods." She pointed backward over her shoulder, then swiveled her finger a hundred and eighty degrees. "Those woods—"

Strong coffee, almost syrupy, hissed into the first mug. Jack handed it to Liz, then began filling one for himself.

"We saw a car parked behind your house, completely off the driveway, almost as if it was being hidden from the road intentionally. Then two men came out the back door. Well, one came out and the other one sort of lurked out of sight." Jack didn't look the least bit startled, so she added, for emphasis, "They'd been inside."

"I'm sorry they worried you. A friend of mine dropped in." Jack held his drink near his mouth, breathing in the steam. He blew gently over the surface of the coffee.

"Oh." He knew, and he didn't mind. She could have slept in. "They told Martin they were friends of yours, but I wasn't sure. It would have been easier to believe them if they hadn't been in the house, and if the dogs hadn't been growling."

"Your cousin was here?"

That, at least, had surprised him.

"We had a whole little flap about your visitors. The dogs quivered angrily, I rushed home to tell Grandma, she called Martin, he stomped over demanding an explanation...this is what happens when there's no movie theater for miles. We've got to entertain ourselves somehow."

Jack was laughing, the caution she usually saw in

his face gone. ''I'm lucky to have such thoughtful neighbors.''

''There's a fine line between neighborly concern, and nosiness, though.''

''Maybe there's not a line at all.''

''Hey—''

He left his mug on the table, and took a carton of eggs out of the fridge. ''Breakfast?''

''No, really.'' She had satisfied herself that he and his house were all right, so she should leave, not hang around enjoying the coffee and the opportunity to stare at Jack in this appealing morning mode.

''I'd like the company,'' he said. ''I'll have everything ready in a few minutes.''

''Can I help?''

''Just relax. I have a routine.''

He poured olive oil into a cast-iron skillet, followed by a clump of butter—that had to be the day's recommended fat intake right there. While the butter melted, he took two plate-covered bowls from the fridge, and after sprinkling paprika and garlic into the fat, emptied first one bowl, then the other, into the pan. Precooked potatoes and sausages began sizzling on contact, the potatoes turning a glistening golden red.

''I never thought of precooking things for breakfast.''

''My uncle and I always did it. Otherwise we wouldn't have time for something hot.''

The uncle, again, the one who complained about his unwashed neck and never read him nursery rhymes. Liz wanted to ask why Jack had lived with his uncle. What had happened to his parents? He tended to retreat when the conversation became even slightly personal, though. Besides, whatever evidence she'd provided to the contrary, she wasn't nosy. It was just that his house was between town and her grandmother's place. She couldn't help going past it. She couldn't stop the dogs from running to it.

Jack flipped the potatoes and pushed the sausages back and forth, then broke four eggs into the pan. "It won't be long now. Couple of minutes." He took cutlery from a drawer, plates and glasses from a cupboard and ketchup and a pitcher of orange juice from the fridge, swinging doors open with his foot and shutting them with his elbow or his hip. Liz leaned against the table, wondering why it was so relaxing to watch a man who was self-sufficient in the kitchen.

Bella and Dora had chosen places beside the table and were watching every move Jack made. Their eyes moved up when he lifted the spatula to turn the eggs and down when the eggs returned to the pan. After a few seconds, Jack divided the breakfast in half and slid equal portions onto two plates. He made room for them on the table, pushing his laptop to the far end and piling seed catalogs and assorted papers beside it. "I guess I should work at my desk."

"Then you wouldn't be beside the coffeepot." Warmed by a friendly glance from Jack, Liz began to lower herself onto the nearest chair. His hand shot out, holding her steady, then pulling her upright.

"Better take the other one. It's rickety, but this one's losing its leg. Fixing it is on my to-do list."

Still aware of Jack's touch, Liz sank onto the chair that was less likely to dump her on the floor. He was stronger than he looked. His hand had cupped her elbow gently, but she was sure he could have lifted her with one arm. She said the next thing that popped into her head, and then wished she could take it back. "I've based a character on you after all. A fairy."

Uncertainty, consternation and amusement scrolled

over his face. "You found you're able to work here, then. That's good."

"You don't mind?"

He sat with one leg out at an angle to help balance the damaged chair. "Do I have green leggings and those gauzy wings?"

Smiling, she shook her head.

"That's a step in the right direction. Magic?"

"I don't know yet."

"Am I a king?"

"More of a knight."

That idea seemed to agree with him. Dotting ketchup on his potatoes, he said, "So there must be battles."

"I haven't worked out the plot yet. Would you like to be in a battle?"

"Of course. With swords and trumpets and tiny horses to ride. Otherwise there's not much point being a fairy."

Liz smiled at the image. He must have read some children's fiction as a boy. Maybe he'd borrowed books from the library when he was past nursery rhyme age, using a friend's card because his uncle wouldn't let him have one, and riding his bicycle because his uncle wouldn't drive him, and reading under the covers at night so his uncle wouldn't stop him. "Do you prefer a personal conflict, or a showdown between good and evil?"

"A showdown, I think. A big, important victory."

"Followed by an epic poem from the court bard and gold from your king?"

He looked amused, but she saw that trace of sadness or longing again, as well. How had she ever thought his eyes were silver? They weren't cold and metallic. They were more like a cloud...no, like water, cool water on a cloudy day. Deep enough to lose yourself in. Reflective. And hiding something.

"More juice?"

Liz blinked, bringing Jack's face back into focus. "No, thanks. It was good, though. Almost like fresh-squeezed."

"It is fresh-squeezed."

"That explains it." She'd squeezed an orange once and got all of two gulps for her efforts. "How was your trip to Brandon? Did you get what you needed?"

"I had a great day. Found a cultivator right off the bat, then had lunch with a friend who told me nineteen different ways what a fool I was to get into farming. In the afternoon I tracked down a secondhand tree baler from a grower just outside the Brandon Hills. Beautiful place. You wouldn't know there was a city just down the road."

"What does your friend think you should be doing?"

After a pause long enough that Liz began to wonder if he would answer, he said, "Ned thinks computers are my vocation, not just a job I tried for a while."

"Were they just a job you tried for a while?"

He smiled, then gave a little shrug. "They were a vocation."

That didn't sound as if he sold or repaired them. "But not anymore?"

"Not anymore." His tone said there shouldn't be any more questions, either.

Bella and Dora had positioned themselves in the promising zone between Jack and Liz, but so far they'd been ignored. Liz gave each of them half of her last sausage, then placed her knife and fork across her empty plate. "That was delicious. I suppose now I can't make eggs for dinner."

"Were you going to?"

"Scrambled eggs and stir-fry are my two specialties."

"I love stir-fry. Want me to come early and chop?"

"I want you to come early and cook the whole dinner, but that's not what we're going to do. You and Grandma can't lift a finger tonight." She carried her plate to the sink. Before she could touch the tap, Jack was at her side, taking the dish away.

"I don't ask women who drop in for breakfast to wash dishes."

"I didn't—"

"I'll clean up later. Why don't you come outside with me? I'd like to show you something." He took a jacket from the hat stand and held it out to her. "That sweater won't be warm enough."

He wrapped his robe tighter, stepped into a pair of green-soled rubber boots and headed down the back steps with the dogs right behind him. Liz followed, pulling on the coat he'd given her. The sleeves dangled past her hands.

"I look like Stephen."

"Then Stephen must be awfully pretty." Jack reached out to fiddle with her collar. She heard a zipping sound. He unrolled a shiny, nylon hood, and tied it under her chin. "Did you know you lose ninety per cent of your—"

"—body heat through your head," she finished, more pleased than she had been in years to learn that a man thought she was pretty. "And you without a hat."

In answer, he turned up the collar of his robe. Liz fell into step beside him, wishing she could tuck her arm through his. Was it because he was friends with her grandmother that she kept getting the feeling she already knew him? She had to remind herself not to behave too intimately, given the five minutes or so they'd spent together. How much time had it been? Two hours in all? Three?

"Where are we going, Jack?"

"Not far."

"Give me a hint."

"About three hundred feet east, and fifty feet north."

Liz looked around, getting her bearings. She preferred to have distance described in terms of left or right, in front or behind. What three hundred or fifty feet looked like, she had no idea. "We seem to be walking in your front yard. Would your lack of decent clothing be a clue we won't be leaving it?"

"Maybe."

"There'll be a notice about you on the bulletin board if you're not careful. *Newcomer Jack McKinnon was seen flaunting his pyjamas Saturday morning while decent people were hard at work.*"

His laughter felt so companionable, she nearly did put her arm through his. They walked side by side, close enough that she sometimes bumped against him. He didn't try to widen the distance between them. Bella and Dora trotted in circles, nosing the dry grass. Every now and then they found something promising, a branch, a stone, or paper waiting for the next breeze, and picked it up eagerly before racing to Jack. He accepted each offering, throwing it for them to find again.

He stopped when they reached the oak grove.

"Is this our destination?" It didn't seem likely, since she could see it from the road.

"Not quite."

"Susannah and I used to play out here."

"In the Ramseys' yard? Why, with all those acres of your own?"

"This place was on our rounds. Mrs. Ramsey made great oatmeal cookies."

"The crunchy kind, or chewy?"

"Crunchy. Raisins, no nuts."

"Mrs. Duncan, three doors down from us, made the chewy kind. She'd meet me at the door sometimes when I brought her newspaper, and give me a cookie in exchange. She made 'em big." Jack held his hands six inches apart, thumbs and forefingers curved in a circle.

"You had a paper route?"

"Oh, yeah. For years. They nearly gave me a gold watch when I retired."

Liz smiled, trying to picture him as a boy, but all she could do was make him shorter. His face, guarded and kind, stayed the same, and his eyes were still that soft, warm silver.

"Now for the fifty feet north." He led the way beyond the oaks to a cultivated bed about as wide as he was tall, but much longer. Tiny evergreens grew close together in rows six inches apart. "This is it. My transplant bed. A thousand seedlings."

"They're just twigs. It's hard to believe you could ever make a living from them."

"I could have started trees from seed, but I bought these when they were a couple of years old, to save time. They've been in the ground for a year, developing good root systems."

"You're giving them a head start?"

"That's right. I'll plant them out in the field the spring after next. By then they'll be strong enough to do well without coddling." He paused. "I hope this won't be a problem for you, Liz…I've heard from the provincial lab. Your grandmother's field is perfect."

She felt one little pang of something unpleasant. Not jealousy exactly. Traces of territorial imperative? But that was all, and it was gone in a second. "I'm glad, Jack. How long will you have to wait for the first harvest?"

"Eight, ten years."

"You're a patient man."

"I'm learning. Farming fosters a Zen state of mind."

"I don't know if I could take the frustration. When you grow wheat you've got a loaf of bread in your hands by the end of the season."

Jack smiled. "But children don't look at a loaf of bread in awe." His face sobered. "At least most of them don't, thank goodness. Not in this neck of the woods, anyway."

"Is that why you're doing this? To make things magical for kids?"

He didn't answer right away. After a moment he gave an embarrassed shrug. "That sounds so plaintive. I've got a detailed spreadsheet on my laptop. I've got a business plan. I've projected when I should break even, and how many blueberries, pumpkins and trees I'll have to sell to make the profit I'm looking for—"

"In fact, you're a coldhearted businessman."

He looked more comfortable at that. "Now you understand."

She wanted to ask him to hold her. His arms would feel warm and strong and she could burrow in…ridiculous. She would have to remember what she'd insisted to Pam and Emily yesterday. As nice as Jack was, their lives were moving in different directions. Whatever they were starting to feel, the only sensible thing was to ignore it.

AFTER HIS PATHETIC DISPLAY of independence, sulking off for breakfast pizza, Reid returned to his office, ready to work no matter how annoying Croker was. He began running the password cracking program, and in less than an hour the first password fell. *Program1.exe,* the file was called, a promising sounding name if he'd ever heard one, although he couldn't believe Jack would give an important file a promising sounding name. More likely, *Family Pics*, or *One Dish Meals for the Single Male.*

He double-clicked to open the file. Up popped a box with a title bar that said, "WinZIP Self-Extractor." That meant Jack had compressed many files into one, and had thoughtfully provided a program to decompress them.

A second box materialized underneath the first. It showed files being extracted from Jack's diskette and downloaded onto Reid's hard drive, one after another, the progress bar zipping along like crazy. Without him even asking, it went on downloading the other files on Jack's disk. Reid sat patiently, thinking about what he might see when the download stopped and he could look at *Program1.exe.* It didn't seem likely that he'd luck onto the code while opening the first of two hundred files. It couldn't be that easy.

It couldn't be that easy. That was exactly what he was thinking when another box jumped into the picture. An attention-getting warning box. An unknown virus had found its way onto his system.

Reid's hand, already on its way to the reboot button, dropped onto his lap. The bug was on his *system.* Not on Jack's disk and not in the computer's RAM, where it could easily be zapped by rebooting. He'd run a virus check! That sneaky...

There was nothing he, or his soon to be replaced antivirus program, could do. He sat watching Jack's bug do its stuff. Very pretty stuff, he had to admit. Protective, not destructive. It put some kind of shell around all the downloaded files. Interesting. He'd like to know how Jack had programmed that.

The problem was Reid's cutting-edge cracker program was now useless.

Or maybe not. He popped the diskette out of the first computer and into a second one. He would find a way to isolate and destroy the virus, then he'd attempt another download.

Not so fast, he could picture Jack saying. The virus had done one more job. It had written over everything on the disk. Near the end of Reid's minute or so of swearing, Croker came into the office.

"Something wrong?"

"You could say that." Briefly, Reid explained the events of the past few minutes. Of course, Croker didn't understand.

"What can you do about it?"

"Not a thing."

Croker blinked at the unwelcome reply. "Not a thing? This is what you're here for."

Reid stared at the monitor until he was sure his response wouldn't sound angry. How could he best explain what Jack's virus had accomplished? "If you wrote on the sand and someone came along dragging a fistful of sticks through the letters, could you put all the grains of sand back the way they'd been, leaving the original letters intact?"

Croker looked at him as if to say, "Yeah, sure you can, if you know what you're doing." The guy didn't know the first thing about computers. He seemed to think they were magic, and that Reid was one lousy magician.

Reid tried to sound patient. "It'll take time to figure this out. It's a difficult problem." Actually, it was an impossible one, but the more he got to know Croker, the less willing he was to tell him things like that.

"I don't want to hear how difficult it is. I want it fixed."

Good for you. Being really firm when you're absolutely ignorant always makes problems go away.

With a frown on his face and a cell phone to his ear, Croker left the room. Reid pulled a paper lunch bag out of a desk drawer, took one look at it and swallowed two Tylenol and a couple of antacid tablets instead.

LIZ AND JACK SAT SIDE BY SIDE in two Muskoka chairs that had been on the veranda for as long as Liz could remember. Their coats were fastened, their hoods pulled up, and their gloved hands wrapped around mugs of cocoa to keep either from getting cold. Liz could feel Jack in the dark, even more aware of his body and its energy than she was in daylight. His voice sounded deeper, too. More personal.

"That wasn't so bad." No one had collapsed halfway through dinner, pointing a blaming finger in her direction as they breathed their last, so she was happy.

"Dinner? It was great."

"I cheated. The vegetables were from Grandma's garden. They were frozen, but they still tasted fresh-picked. It made all the difference."

"You mean you should have grown them yourself?"

"And the rice came from a package, brown and

wild mixed together, with the simplest, no-fail instructions you ever saw."

"Good choice. Knowing what to shop for is half the battle."

"You're not going to agree that I'm a bad cook, are you?"

"Not to your face."

Liz stretched out her foot to give Jack's leg a little push.

"Are you sure Eleanor is all right?"

"She's been turning in early most nights. Going through sixty years' worth of stuff is tiring. It's hard for her to think of strangers living here."

"For you, as well?"

Liz wasn't sure what to say. She hadn't been prepared for the depth of loss she sometimes felt packing away her grandmother's things. It had hit her tonight, too. In the middle of dinner her pleasure in the evening had faded briefly, and she'd wished that the table the three of them were sitting at and the dishes they ate from and the candles they saw by didn't all squeeze her heart. But then she had looked at Jack, on the other side of the wide table, and she'd thought that she could look at him for months, trying to understand all the angles and shadows and fleeting expressions of his face. Across a picnic table, across a carton of takeout food, it wouldn't matter. The trouble was, they didn't have months.

"It's just a house," she said finally.

Jack's silence was comforting. He seemed to know she didn't mean it, that a house was never just a house, but always full or empty of something that mattered. If she asked him what he was thinking, would he say that? Or would he say he was thinking of getting a refill of cocoa, or a new car, or tickets to the Bomber game?

"Eleanor often talks about you, you and Tom and your cousins. It sounds as if you spent a lot of time over here when you were growing up."

"All the time we could. It was a wonderful place to be a child. Not just here, though. The woods, the creeks, even the town—we managed to have fun everywhere. Property lines didn't mean much to us. It all felt like ours. It seemed…set in stone. Perfect and unchanging."

"That's how it seems to me now." She heard a note of humor in his voice. "Nearly perfect, anyway."

"It isn't unchanging, though. It's changed a lot."

"For example?"

"Oh…the store, for one thing. Where that miniature supermarket stands, there used to be a little general store. Fishing bait in the freezer beside the meat, blocks of livestock salt beside the dish detergent. We went there at lunchtime, for jawbreakers and chips. And we used to gallop our horses on a strip of railway allowance on the edge of town. Now the track's gone and it's all houses, all in a city row. There was an alfalfa pasture where they've built the seniors' home. When the flowers were open, the whole field buzzed. The new school's an improvement. Pam and Emily love working there."

"But you preferred the old school?"

"It was more homey. Four rooms for eight grades, creaking floorboards, a hand-rung bell. When it was too cold or wet to go out at lunch, we played in the basement."

"You liked it here. Why did it stop being a place you wanted to live?"

The question seemed abrupt, a sudden wall in their conversation.

"Maybe you changed," he added quickly. "Needed something else."

"Art school." She was grateful for the detour. "Galleries. Book launches."

"I bought a few of your books while I was in Brandon."

Her voice lightened. "A few?"

"Read them this afternoon. Got comfy in that big dusty chair in my living room, with Lenny Breau in the background and a glass of Tullamore Dew in hand—"

Laughing, Liz said, "I wonder how often my books are accompanied by mournful guitar and Irish whiskey?"

"It was a bit of a contrast," Jack admitted. "One of the books was nonfiction, about all the life on and around and under a huge oak tree. It was fun when I recognized the tree. It's the big one in the grove in my yard."

Liz nodded, smiling.

"I enjoyed it. Enjoyed all of them. That was you in some of the illustrations, wasn't it? Always with another little girl."

"Susannah."

"The cousin who was supposed to come with you, the thoughtless one who got married in Alberta without her family."

"That's the one. My uncle Will always said we were more sisters than sisters would have been. Except we look nothing alike. Sue has long dark straight hair, and mine's all short and wavy, with no particular color. Brownish-blondish."

"Cinnamon," Jack said. "Cinnamon and cloves."

He touched a curl that framed her chin. "It's not all that short."

In the silence that followed she thought she could hear his breathing. She could see it, puffs of white fog each time he exhaled, mingling with the puffs that came from her. "It's cold. We should go in."

They got up quickly, and took turns standing aside at the door, then went into the living room looking at everything but each other. The table lamp was on its lowest setting, giving the room a candlelit glow. Jack went straight to the stack of records Liz and Eleanor had dragged out of a closet the day before. He picked up as many as he could hold, fanning them like a hand of cards. "Wow. Original Chet Baker, Billie Holiday, Ella Fitzgerald."

"My grandfather was a jazz fan." Liz shut the living room door so they wouldn't disturb Eleanor. "There's another box full of big band 78's."

"Duke Ellington?"

"And Fletcher Henderson, Count Basie…just about everyone."

"I wonder if Eleanor would be willing to sell some of them to me. Or does your family want to keep them?"

"We're not finding many takers for Grandma's stuff. I'm sure she'd give you all you want."

"No one else wants these?" Jack's voice was disbelieving. He looked at her grandfather's record player the same way she'd seen him look at the dogs, his face soft and affectionate. "What a wonderful machine. No bells and whistles at all." He slid an LP from its cover. Holding the edges between his fingertips, he placed it on the turntable and carefully set the needle in place. When the first notes came from the speakers, he smiled. "Hear the static? I love that sound."

Liz had moved closer to listen. When Jack straightened, they were only inches apart. She didn't have any inclination to move back. She had to consciously keep her foot on the floor so she wouldn't step forward, right into his arms. "Want to dance?"

"Want to, sure, but it's a skill I never mastered."

"It's easy. We stand close and move our feet back and forth."

"Like advanced walking?"

"There's a complication. We're supposed to hold each other, too."

"Oh, right. And there are all sorts of different ways to do that."

"I think, since we're listening to Ella, we should do it the old-fashioned way." Liz took hold of Jack's left hand with her right and rested her left on his shoulder.

"And I put my arm around you." His hand came to rest on her lower back.

"Higher, I think. Halfway up, in the middle, and then you press gently, to let me know where we're going."

His hand traveled higher. "Here?" Light pressure brought her closer to him.

"Just right." She could feel his chest rise and fall with each breath he took, then the tightening of his thigh muscles as they began to dance.

"You smell like gingersnaps."

Liz leaned away so she could see Jack's face. "There's no way I could smell like gingersnaps."

"You always do. Is it your soap? Your perfume?"

"You're imagining things. In spite of all your spreadsheets and good sense."

His arms tightened around her. ''It's a nice thing to imagine.''

When the song ended, they danced for a moment to the sound of the needle on vinyl. Liz eased her hand out of Jack's, feeling the roughness of his palm. ''Did your skin get like this from one year of farming?''

''Mostly.''

The second song began, slow and bittersweet, but they had stopped dancing. ''You have a scar.'' It was an old one, slightly jagged, deep where it started under his forefinger and shallow by the time it stopped under his ring finger.

''A saw went its own way.''

''What happened?''

''Sometimes I worked construction in the summer.''

It wasn't much of an explanation. He was so reluctant to talk about himself. ''After retiring from the newspaper business?'' She touched the hardened tips of his fingers. ''And this is from playing guitar?''

''Um-hum.''

She held his hand to her cheek. It felt like warm sandpaper against her skin. When the impulse occurred to her, she moved without thinking, slipping his hand inside her blouse. His fingers fanned out, rising with the rise of her breast, stopping when they met a closed button.

''Liz?''

''Yes, Jack?''

''Is this the cocoa talking?''

She laughed, and firmly shut the door on the part of her mind that was trying to remind her why she had come home and how soon she was going back to Vancouver. She wanted to undo the button that had got in his way. She wanted to feel that warm roughness against her softest skin. The thought made her body hum.

"Liz. Are you going to step away and turn on some more lights, or am I?"

"Not me."

"Then I should."

"No." She needed him, that was all there was to it. She said so, her lips against his neck, and felt an answering need in the tightness of his muscles, in the way his hands moved over her. She leaned closer, as close as she could, so his leg fit between hers and she could feel his heart beating against her chest. She would erase the sadness around his eyes, be as tightly with him as another person could be, rub out the solitary air that surrounded him. They were on the floor, his hands protecting her head and her back as they went down. She didn't care how itchy the carpet was. They pulled at buttons and zippers, pushed cloth out of the way, and she made room for him, pulling his hips toward her. Then he made a sound that startled her, worried her, and the heat of his body was gone.

"Jack?"

He took a deep breath, almost laughing as he let it out. "Sorry. Dinner with you and Eleanor. I brought wine and pumpkin loaf. That's all."

She needed him back, she needed to feel his weight. "I don't know what's wrong with me, but I completely forgot to bring prophylactics on my visit to my grandmother's. Had a last-minute list and everything. You always forget something." She was angry with him for thinking of it.

He pulled the sides of her blouse together, trying to locate the right buttonhole for each button. "I don't even have anything at home...it's been a while."

"Me, too." Liz sat up, gently pushing his hands

away. "I'll do it." They were nearly naked, on her grandmother's rug, with the light on. What had they been thinking? "I hope Grandma's sleeping."

"The door's shut. It's a long hallway."

"It's a good thing you remembered, Jack. I would have eventually, during the night or in the morning, and then I would have been so worried. I should have paid attention when you suggested turning on more lights. We could have listened to music, that would have been nice—"

"The evening was perfect." Jack helped Liz up, then got his shirt buttoned and tucked in. "I'll get out of here while we still have any resolve. Next time, dinner at my place? I'll go into Pine Point first."

She followed him to the kitchen door. She wanted to follow him all the way home, to make do with privacy and cross her fingers about the rest. "Or Winnipeg. If anyone we know saw you in Pine Point, there'd be a whole round of phone calls."

Jack pulled on his coat. "You're kidding."

"I'm not."

"Almost makes you long for the big city, where nobody knows you and nobody cares." He smiled. Liz couldn't tell if he meant it.

The dogs, who'd been sleeping by the stove, now waited expectantly beside Jack. "I'll send them back to you once I'm home."

"I'll be here." Wide awake, and delivering a no-nonsense lecture to herself, whether she wanted to hear it or not.

CHAPTER SEVEN

JACK MOVED RESTLESSLY AROUND the kitchen. He'd been awake half the night thinking about Liz. Not just thinking, but almost feeling her. After dinner, when they'd sat on the porch together, and when they'd danced, he'd wanted two things. To go to bed with her, right then, and to stay with her forever. *To make her his.* It was an old-fashioned phrase. Too possessive for anyone's good. This morning, he felt more civilized. His brain was working, telling him to slow down, to approach any potential relationship cautiously, the way he always did.

He waited until nine o'clock to call. After the fourth ring he began to consider hanging up, but then he pictured Liz picking up on her end, breathless from hurrying, only to hear the click. There was one telephone, in the dark hall between the kitchen and the living room. She could be outside, or in the bathtub…just when his mind was about to go down that path, he heard Liz's voice giving a company-polite greeting. Her tone didn't change all that much when she realized she was talking to him.

Jack walked as far as the telephone cord would let him. He looked out the kitchen window, to the woods Liz had disappeared into after her last visit. "I had a little trouble settling in last night." He tried to keep his tone light, but he heard a certain intensity creep in. "Did you sleep?"

"Not that well."

"How about some breakfast over here...apple pancakes?"

"I can't, Jack. I'm taking Grandma to church. The minister's in town this morning. It's his one Sunday a month in Three Creeks."

"That leaves lunch or dinner. Or both."

"I can't," she repeated. "There's a family get-together."

He hadn't thought of that. Sundays in Three Creeks were for big, hot midday meals followed by dozy conversations. When Eleanor had the Robbs over to her house, she usually invited him, too, and her relatives treated him with an elaborate courtesy that made it clear they'd be happier if he hadn't come. "Who's having it this time?"

"Tom and Pam. So I have to go."

She didn't sound very disappointed. "What's the matter, Liz?"

"Nothing's the matter." She took a deep breath, then let it out. "We got carried away last night, Jack. Don't you think?"

"I thought we showed a lot of self-control."

"It was an awful way to behave, with Grandma down the hall."

"It was a little embarrassing. I guess a lack of self-control came first, then the abundance of it. Isn't that more commendable, though? Putting the brakes on rather than never needing them in the first place?"

He'd hoped he could make her laugh a little, or at least relax, but it didn't happen. Her voice became even more reserved. "I'm leaving soon, so that sort of involvement really doesn't make sense. I'm not looking for a holiday fling.''

''Wait a minute—'' He stopped, unsure of what he wanted to say. He wasn't going to beg her to see him.

''Grandma's ready to go.''

''At this hour?''

''We're decorating—fall leaves and vegetables. And Grandma has a carafe of tea for the minister.'' Liz lowered her voice, speaking so quietly he could hardly hear. ''I'm sorry if I sent the wrong signals, Jack.'' Gently, she replaced the receiver.

He stared at the silent telephone. Sent the wrong signals? They'd all but made love on Eleanor's living room floor. What kind of signal had she meant to send?

Holiday fling. Thanks, Liz.

She had a point. Fifteen hundred miles separated her home from his, her work from his. They had connected, though. He'd never felt such a sudden, strong connection with anyone. He really didn't like the idea of her going back to Vancouver just as he was getting to know her. He almost smiled. Maybe he could put her in a pumpkin shell. Keep her safe, keep her here, keep her his. It was tempting, but a wee bit dysfunctional.

Jack grabbed his coat, made sure his gloves were in his pocket, and slipped on his hiking boots. As soon as he felt the morning air on his ears he pulled up his hood. Snow by Halloween? He wouldn't be surprised if it came before. That might keep Reid and his friends from dropping in whenever they liked. Yesterday he'd bought a padlock for the plywood door. It wouldn't stop them if they were determined to get in—they could force the hinges off—but at least it told them he'd found their entry point.

He looked up to locate a honking sound overhead. Geese, just a few stragglers, but still holding to a small V-formation. He'd heard them in the city occasionally, but here they were part of the swing of things, telling you that spring had come, telling you to dig out your winter clothes. Too bad they didn't travel stealthily, and at night. They mated for life, raised a family all summer, then had to fly past a gauntlet of hunters every fall. Try as he might, he couldn't think of them as dinner. He wasn't a vegetarian, so it was illogical and sentimental. If he didn't watch out, he'd be writing a children's book full of talking geese smoking pipes or some ridiculous thing.

Breakfast in Pine Point sounded good, and then maybe he'd take another look at Eleanor's field. When he'd arrived for dinner last night she'd had a rental agreement all ready for him to sign. It was the first time he'd ever had to negotiate to get someone to raise their price.

Maybe Liz was backing away in general, not specifically from him. The noise and inquisitiveness of a big family might be overwhelming if you found yourself in the middle of it. At the barbecue last Saturday she'd hardly been able to eat her dinner. Every time she took a bite of food, someone had asked about her life in Vancouver, or how long she planned to stay, or whether she was involved with someone. Privacy was an unknown concept.

Except for that one area of restraint, the question he'd most like answered. What was behind the tension between Liz and the people in town? He'd sensed that Eleanor felt guilty about something relating to her granddaughter, but she had never revealed what. Everyone in town, usually so quick to tell him what and when and who, as well as what they thought about it, were silent when it came to Liz.

TWO KITTENS HUDDLED ON THE STEP, just out of the way of any foot traffic. One was gray; the other was half marmalade and half tabby, clearly divided down the middle. They crouched low, fur bristling, lifting first one paw, then another, mewing forlornly. Liz stood beside Jennifer on the landing. The storm door was open, and they watched the kittens through the glass window of the screen door. Liz wanted to bundle them under her sweater, away from cold cement and unseasonably wintery breezes.

"What unusual markings the little one has, half and half."

"That's Charlotte."

"After the spider?"

Jennifer nodded. "The gray one's Smoke. Dad named him." She looked at her mother, mashing potatoes with enough energy to make it clear she wished they'd stop chatting and give her some help. "Can't they come in, Mom? Just for a while?"

"You know they can't."

"They're cold."

"Then they can go back to the barn, where it's warm."

"They don't like it in the barn. There are mice in the barn. And it smells."

Liz moved to the stove and gave the gravy an unneeded stir. Pam had everything under control and a particular way she wanted things done. When Liz had started to put out pickles, Pam had swooped in with a different dish; when she'd tried to drain the vegetables Pam had exclaimed that she wanted to save the water for soup. Stirring gravy seemed to be a safe gesture of good will, but suddenly Pam was at the oven wanting room to check the cabbage rolls and perogies. The rice-filled cabbage leaves and soft potato and cheese filled turnovers weren't part of the Robb menu until Pam had joined the family. Now she was asked to make them all the time.

"There's so much food, Pam. It's like a holiday dinner. I can hardly wait to eat."

"You'll hardly have to." Pam lifted two round roasting pans out of the oven. "You can put the cabbage rolls and perogies into the serving bowls, Liz." She glanced at her daughter. "Shut the door, Jennifer."

"In a minute, Mom."

"They're no happier with you watching them. It's kinder to ignore them, so they'll go back to the barn." One corner of Jennifer's mouth trembled. Pam's voice softened. "You're always scolding me about the environment. Think of all the extra oil the furnace will burn while you let cold air into the house."

There was a soft but definite click as Jennifer closed the door. Pam handed her the salad tongs. "Toss the lettuce with a little of that dressing I made and put it on the table. Not too much. It's supposed to be salad with dressing, not the other way around. Liz, would you tell everyone to sit down?"

Liz's hand, holding a slotted spoon, hovered over the perogies.

"Never mind. I'll tell them." Pam hurried from the room. Liz could hear her voice rising above a political discussion and opinions about the new television season, telling everyone to come to the table. Then she was back in the kitchen, taking the spoon from Liz. "Go sit down, Liz, across from Aunt Julia. She was saying she's hardly talked to you yet." Emily's mother hardly ever talked to anyone, but Liz was willing to try.

With its extra leaf in for company, the dining table filled most of the available space, leaving little room for people and chairs. Even if Pam had wanted it, Eleanor's black walnut set wouldn't have fit. Besides, it would look out of place in this modern room. Eleanor's house was always dark, no matter how many lights were turned on, and it always seemed dusty, no matter how recently it had been cleaned. Here, light streamed into every room, and there wasn't the smallest suggestion of family or local history to be seen. Pam said there were enough disadvantages to living on a farm without being surrounded by other people's old stuff.

Liz squeezed past Tom at one end of the table and into an empty chair between Emily and Martin, across from Aunt Julia. Julia was busy trying to read the identifying mark on the bottom of her plate and didn't say hello when Liz greeted her. Beside Martin was his wife Pat, with a flushed and sleeping toddler on her lap—Nell, looking exactly like early photos of Susannah. Liz smiled. Nell would be a very sweet teddy bear.

Then Uncle Will at the head of the table, and around the corner, Aunt Edith, still in her church clothes. Eleanor was next, looking especially pretty—happy, maybe, that she'd heard the St. George's organ that morning and listened to the minister's measured voice sorting its way through an illogical but well-meant sermon. The seat closest to the kitchen had been left for Pam, so she could refill serving dishes and keep an eye on the children's table. It wasn't the whole family—Brian's bunch was spending the day with his wife's parents—but it was more than Liz had seen at once for a long time. She blinked quickly, hoping no one would notice the sudden moisture in her eyes.

Emily touched her hand. "Okay?"

Liz blotted a drip that had grown big enough to fall. Almost under her breath, she said, "You know how it is when something makes you so happy you feel sad?"

Emily smiled in understanding, but on Liz's other side Martin said, "Good grief. Not mixed feelings again."

"Martin, don't be hard on your cousin."

"Thank you, Aunt Edith."

"That's just the way she is," Edith went on, "the way she's always been. An absolute compote of feelings. Bits of everything. What is it you're feeling mixed about, dear?"

Martin answered for Liz. "She's so happy, she's sad."

Pam set the biggest standing rib roast Liz had ever seen in front of Tom. "Don't tell me you've never heard the word 'bittersweet,' Martin."

"It's a kind of chocolate, isn't it?"

Tom waved the carving knife in the air until everyone paid attention. "I'll serve Grandma first. Then Liz—" he smiled at his sister "—because I'm so glad she's come home." Ignoring good-natured rumbles of disagreement about his second choice, he offered Eleanor a well-browned and seasoned outside piece, then cut three medium-rare slices so thinly they crumpled as they fell onto Liz's plate. "That still how you like it?"

"Perfect. Thank you, Tom." She sat back, listening as her family continued to debate the hierarchy of service. After everyone had been given roast—now cold—the rest of the food was passed around the table: potatoes and gravy and horseradish, cabbage rolls in tomato sauce, perogies and sour cream, carrots and peas and green beans dotted with butter, home-pickled beets and cucumbers, dressing-laden salad. Liz had a sudden picture of Jack, alone in the Ramsey kitchen. She turned to her brother. "I thought Jack might be here today."

"Jack McKinnon?"

There wasn't any other Jack. "He doesn't have family in the area. I thought you might ask him to Sunday dinner."

"Great-grandma always does," Jennifer called from the kitchen.

"Because he's her neighbor," Tom said.

"And because he's good company." Eleanor's quiet voice dared anyone to say otherwise. "Besides, he does thoughtful little things for me, and I appreciate that."

"Like bringing you firewood." From Tom's tone, anyone would think Eleanor had given Jack the biggest piece of cake.

"Jack is just being neighborly," Emily said.

"There's neighborly and then there's odd." Tom looked at Martin, who nodded in agreement. "He's a young guy from the city, no wife, no kids, a business he doesn't talk about, and suddenly he's calling himself a farmer and spending half his time visiting an old lady—no offense, Grandma—who happens to be selling her place, ingratiating himself by doing odd jobs and taking her baking like he's some old woman himself—''

''Tom!'' Liz, Pam and Emily all spoke at once.

''—and the next thing I hear he's all set to rent a field I've had my eye on for quite some time.''

''Ingratiating?'' Eleanor said. Although she spoke quietly, everyone stopped eating and stared.

Tom's knife and fork froze above his plate. ''I'm sorry, Grandma.'' The two looked at each other across the table.

''It's true that Jack is a young man from the city who lives alone. And it's true that he has embarked on a new way of life. He's also a very good neighbor.''

''And a very good cook,'' Edith said. ''I really do enjoy his pie. Although, it will be nice when it's blueberry.''

There were small movements as knives and forks began working again. Will looked around the table and zeroed in on Liz's plate. ''Is that all you're eating, sweetheart? Somebody send the cabbage rolls back this way for Liz.'' He motioned for the bowl, ignoring her protest.

''She's dieting,'' Martin said. ''She hardly touched her lasagna when I was there the other night.''

''Oh, but you shouldn't diet, Liz.'' Edith sounded concerned. ''That's what they say now. It does something…what does it do to you, Pam?''

''It slows your metabolism, because your body thinks it's starving.''

''Maybe she's still full from last night's dinner,'' Will suggested. He raised an eyebrow at the rest of the group. ''I was at Mother's Friday picking up the car Liz dented, to take it back to the city. The place was quite the hive of female activity. Liz was getting ready to cook for McKinnon.''

Pam said, ''I knew it.''

''Everyone knew it,'' said Martin. ''If you were at the barbecue you couldn't miss it.''

''Miss what?'' Tom asked. ''Liz and McKinnon? You're kidding, right?''

Aunt Julia spoke for the first time. ''Leave the girl alone.''

''That's right,'' Will agreed quickly. ''If you aren't careful she won't come home again. I talked to her the other day about coming back permanently. She's thinking about it, aren't you, Liz?''

''To live?'' Emily asked.

Edith blinked happily. ''Oh, wouldn't that be nice!''

Liz focused on her meal, letting her family's noise wash over her. If she stayed longer, for a month or two, would it be as if she'd never gone? Maybe Uncle Will's idea wasn't as far-fetched as it sounded. She could move back and keep house for her grandmother and work in the bedroom under the eaves. The light was good, there was plenty of floor space to spread out pictures and visualize a story. Her neck got tight just thinking about it. It wouldn't be easy, but she could do it. And Jack would be there.

Edith was talking about Susannah's wedding again. ''I know I need to let it go. But I had dreams, what mother doesn't? I always saw Susannah in my wedding dress.''

Patiently, Martin said, ''It wouldn't have fit her, Mom. Sue's a foot taller than you.''

''But not even to attend my own daughter's wedding.''

There were murmurs of agreement around the table. It had always been like this. Every member of the family had at least one opinion about whatever the others did. What would they do if she got up and left, a silent protest, just walked out of the dining room and out of the house? Most likely, they wouldn't bat an eye. Someone would ask, "What got into Liz?" and then they'd turn back to their meal, with cheesecake for dessert, no doubt, just to be sure no one's body was fooled into thinking it was starving.

WHEN HER MOTHER left the kitchen to get another stack of dishes from the dining room, Jennifer hurried outside, a slice of roast beef dangling from her fingers. Liz followed her to the back step, and found her ripping the meat into small pieces for the kittens.

"Maybe we should take these poor things to the barn."

Jennifer picked up Charlotte. She touched the kitten's nose, then her paws. "See how little she is? She wouldn't be in the way. She could stay in my room the whole time."

Liz crouched down to get Smoke and received a scratch in thanks.

"It's just that he doesn't know you," Jennifer said quickly.

"If you encourage them to stay by the house, what will they do when it's dark? Shiver on the step all night?"

Reluctantly, Jennifer agreed the barn would be warmer. They each took a dish, one with the scraps and another with water, and crossed the long yard.

The barn was older than the house, a practical, easy-to-build peaked roof design, white with green trim. It was rarely used for animals anymore. Most of the cattle spent the winter in the feedlot, with shelter from the woods and warmth from each other's bodies.

"Are there other cats out here?" Liz asked.

"Charlotte and Smoke's mother disappeared a while ago. There's another cat around somewhere. She goes to the granaries and the other outbuildings."

They heaved open the sliding door. At first they couldn't see anything but hazy streams of light coming from small windows high on the walls. As their eyes adjusted, empty shadowed stalls came into focus. A group of calves milled around a large, straw-bedded enclosure.

"Somebody had their bull out in the field too late," Liz said.

"I guess. Dad told Mom they were such a good price he couldn't say no. They're too young to winter outside. There's a light. Just a sec." Jennifer found the switch and warm light from a row of three dangling bulbs filled the barn, making it suddenly cosy. The calves pressed closer, wide noses lifted over the partition. "They don't need anything. They've been fed and watered." She went past without looking at them. Liz understood. No sense developing feelings for somebody else's dinner. Still, she lingered, rubbing faces, scratching behind ears, looking into dim, gentle eyes.

"Auntie Liz?"

"Coming, hon." Liz joined her niece near a stack of straw bales. A dusty blanket had been used to make a warm cave between two of them, but the kittens refused to go inside. Their hopes were still pinned on Jennifer. "It's not such a bad life for a cat out here, you know."

"These aren't the kind of cats that like to live in a barn."

"You've made up your mind about that."

"I know them better than anybody else does."

Liz nodded. Maybe she did.

"Are you mad at everybody, Auntie Liz?"

Even without the sudden change of subject the question would have startled Liz. "Mad? No, of course not."

Jennifer looked at her doubtfully. "Mom thinks you're mad. I heard her tell Dad."

"Your mom and I have been friends forever, since kindergarten. So we've been mad at each other lots of times. We've always got over it, though."

"And what are you mad about this time?"

"I'm not, sweetheart. Really. I love your mom. Now, I should go do my share of dishes. Coming?"

Jennifer shook her head and transferred her attention to the kittens again. Liz kissed the top of her head, wishing she could do something that would actually help, and went back to the house alone. Emily and Pam had started washing and drying anything that hadn't fit into the dishwasher.

"How's my daughter?" Pam asked.

"Worried. Feeling misunderstood."

"Well, that's just normal, if I remember my growth and development classes." She rinsed a glass and placed it upside down in the drainer. "Those kittens come from a long line of barn cats. They'd never adjust to life in the house."

Liz picked up a tea towel and beat Emily to the glass. Out the window, she could see Tom and Martin and Uncle Will playing road hockey on the driveway with young Will and Anne, using a tennis ball since there was no snow for a puck to slide over. Edith's and Pat's voices came from the living room, discussing Nell's sleeping habits. "Where's Grandma?"

"Lying down in the girls' room. I guess things got a little boisterous for her at the table." Pam gave Liz a reassuring smile. "It's nothing to worry about. It'll be good for her to get into the seniors' home, though. She'll have less work to do, less to worry about, less time alone. The doctor visits once a week."

"I hope she'll be all right in that little space. She's always had an unobstructed view, just trees out every window. Her own trees. Miles between her and the next building."

"The home is really nice inside," Pam said. "So many ladies she knows are there, and when she saw she could have a garden—"

"That was the clincher," Emily agreed. "She said if she could have her own salad and roses, what more did she need?"

Well, Liz thought, *her dining room table for a start.*

LATER THAT AFTERNOON, Liz worked at the table by her bedroom window. Every time she picked up her sketchbook, more characters emerged to populate the woodland fairy world she was creating in spite of herself. The fairies were the size of squirrels. She was pleased with the fusion of plant and person. They looked like twigs that had hopped off a tree and walked away, full of their own intentions. If they were lucky, they lived in hollow trees; if not, they dug burrows underground. A female fairy, a sharp, pointy being with hair like dry grasses, had appeared unbidden beside the one she'd based on Jack.

Soon it would be dark enough to go to bed. An

afternoon with her family had worn her out. Maybe if she'd slept last night they wouldn't have seemed so overwhelming. She'd ended the evening with Jack with her nerve endings all aquiver, then laid in bed stiff with need and guilt under a comforter made by who knows how many hardworking Robb women. In the longest, darkest part of the night, Andy had suddenly been everywhere, filling the room, filling her mind, for the first time in years. He wouldn't berate her. If there were such a thing as ghosts, he wouldn't haunt her.

She looked at the small clock beside the bed. There was time before dark. She closed her sketchbook and put away her pencils and gum eraser. The dogs, who had crept up the stairs after her as if no one would notice if they did it slowly and guiltily enough, watched as she took her jacket from the back of a chair.

"That's right," Liz told them. "We're going for a walk."

They wagged their tails in approval. Sometimes she thought they were better companions than a lot of people. They listened as if they understood every word you said, and if you had nothing to say they closed their eyes, content with silence. She couldn't help wondering about Jennifer's kittens, so much smaller and with so much to learn, denied the same warmth and human company. Soon these chilly days would be remembered as pleasant autumn weather. How would the kittens fare then?

Eleanor was resting in her room, so Liz left the house quietly, locking the door behind her. When they got to the woods, the dogs turned toward Jack's house. Liz ignored them, and they soon noticed she hadn't followed. She walked briskly along a path nearly grown over with tall grass and hazelnut shrubs. As she got closer to her destination, she walked more slowly and the dogs lost patience with her. Following trails that stopped at holes in the ground or led out of reach up tree trunks, they trotted here and there, tails high, noses to the ground.

Liz stopped near the edge of the woods, where one of the three creeks, the smallest one, wound damply toward the far away river. It didn't look as if it would ever get there. It looked as if leaf-mold and layers of bent grass would sop it up like sponges. They never did.

The clearing was hardly a clearing anymore. Low-growing shrubs were dotted over the space, and young poplars as tall as Liz but no wider than pencils had sprouted. In the middle of it all, the log cabin stood. It was tiny and roughly made, the first quick shelter her great-great-grandparents had built. The roof was green with moss. When she got closer, she saw that a small tree had started to grow in its softening logs.

The door was gone. Dry brown leaves had blown into the cabin, covering the floor where she and Andy had spent their wedding night. Eloping impulsively was much harder to do than they had thought...there were laws and appointments and frustrating waits for paperwork. But they had kept it all secret, the next best thing to romantic impulse, and when their moment before the marriage commissioner had finally come Andy had given her a grocery store bouquet, a dozen white roses. She'd never had even a single rose of her own before. Her mother grew shrub roses that bloomed all summer, but they were nothing like the long-stemmed flowers she held that day. She was glad she could keep them, that she didn't have to throw them to a waiting bridesmaid. After the short, businesslike ceremony, they'd bought two champagne glasses, a bottle of sparkling wine, and some Belgian chocolates and hurried back to the log cabin for a night that mixed uncertainty and embarrassment with passion. The next afternoon, they had defiantly presented themselves to their parents and held hands tightly during the lectures and tears that followed.

We were children.

Her grandmother thought she should make her peace with the past. Easy to say. She didn't want to sweep what happened under the carpet. That would be turning her back on Andy. He was the sweetest boy in the world, and by now he should have been a man. She couldn't forgive the people who had taken that away from him. Not ever.

CHAPTER EIGHT

THE MAIN THING WAS TO GET BACK to Vancouver as soon as possible. She'd been letting her grandmother and the house and the dogs pull her into family life, Three Creeks life. Belonging was seductive.

Liz pressed a long piece of parcel tape across the flaps of the last cardboard box and set it on top of the others beside the kitchen door. They had packed away ordinary clothes Eleanor was sure some member of the family would need one day, and special things—uniforms, wedding dresses, christening gowns—that had to be kept even if no one would use them again. There were boxes for the church's rummage sale, for the school for dress-up, and for the clothing museum in Pine Point. Brian had agreed to stop by later to take them into town. "That's it, Grandma."

"Excellent. I can't look at another stitch of clothing. Not so much as an apron. Why don't you sit down and visit a bit? You've done nothing but work these last few days."

"We've got to get done. Otherwise you'll have to sell your house with all its belongings, the way the Ramseys did."

Eleanor looked startled at the thought, but then she smiled. "That would save a lot of trouble." She had taken the chair by the woodstove. She put her feet up on the stool and rested her hands on her lap. "I don't know if you heard me on the phone earlier...the real estate agent called. She's wondering when I'm going to list the place.''

Liz looked at her grandmother in surprise. ''I thought you had, in the summer.''

''I couldn't quite bring myself to do it. It seemed better to get things ready first. Mrs. Armstrong says it could take a while to find a buyer, though, especially heading into winter. Months, she said. There's not much of a market for drafty, rambling houses that need a lot of repairs.''

''So you might be spending another winter here.''

''That's all right with me. I don't know that I want to move while there's snow on the ground. Spring would be fine. Then I could plant something in that little bed outside my apartment. Listen to that! My apartment. It'll be like living in the city.''

''Is there more I can do to help get things ready, besides packing?''

''Not a thing.'' Eleanor's smile was probably meant to be reassuring, but she just looked worried. ''It's a matter of deciding how best to do things. I was going to sell the whole package, the house and all the property, but I know everyone in the family wants a share of the land. So it might be better to subdivide, and sell the house and yard site separately. The only thing I know for sure is that I'd like Jack to have the Christmas tree field. Buy it, rather than rent.''

''Uncle Will and Tom might be annoyed about that.''

''There's no might about it.'' Eleanor's voice was almost sharp. ''No one wants the house and no one wants my dark old table, but they sure want my acres.'' She added in a rush, ''You know I didn't mean that, Elizabeth.''

''Why not come back to Vancouver with me?'' It

was an impulsive suggestion and at first Liz wasn't sure if it was a serious one. "You could put your feet up and take it easy—just ring a bell and I'd come running from my easel."

"Wouldn't that be something? I'd get used to all the fuss, though, and then I'd expect it. You'd have to treat me like a queen."

Liz was warming to her idea. "You'd like it in Vancouver, Grandma. It's never cold, there are gardens everywhere and cut flowers for sale on every street corner. You'd be close to my mom and dad. We could transplant the family one by one and start having those traveling Christmases again."

"We do have those traveling Christmases."

Of course they did. Why hadn't she realized the traditions she loved would continue without her? "Are you tempted?"

"I am. But I'd miss the prairie sky. The mountains get in the way in Vancouver."

"That's not the way most people talk about mountains."

"Here the sky is high and wide, it goes on forever. I'd feel closed in with the ocean on one side and the mountains on the other."

That was how Liz had felt at first. It had been a good kind of closed in, though, like being held, as if the ocean had been one arm and the mountains the other.

"It's all for the best, Elizabeth. I do wish I could take the woodstove to town with me, though. That I'll miss. I like heating the kitchen with it, keeping a vat of water hot, the kettle always simmering. And where else would the dogs would make themselves comfortable?" She broke off, overcome by a defeated air that twisted Liz's heart. "Do you think Jack would take them? They'd be happy with him."

Liz bent to scratch behind Bella's ear. "I'm not sure." He'd said pumpkins needed as much as he had to give. He couldn't have meant it. On the other hand, he hardly gave his house enough attention to keep it together. "If not, there's always Tom."

"Tom has dogs. Everyone has everything. New houses, new dining room suites, pets of their own." Eleanor pressed her lips together, as if forcing herself to stop.

Liz had to get up and move around the kitchen. Wasn't anyone listening to how Eleanor felt about this move? Everyone just agreed how good it would be for her. How could it be good for her to divest herself of her entire life?

She reached for the kettle. "Tea?"

"Oh, please. That would be lovely."

Liz made a small pot of regular tea for her grandmother, and a cup of apple cinnamon herbal tea for herself. As soon as she opened the box and smelled the spice, she remembered Jack standing close, his voice deep and soft, making that ridiculous claim about gingersnaps. He saw her in a way no one else did.

He'd come to the door on Monday, bringing another load of wood and some pumpkin muffins. His voice had rumbled upstairs through the grill in the floor and reached her where she sat sorting sheets and pillowcases. The sound had made her happy. Some people might say it wasn't a complicated problem. If the sound of Jack's voice was enough to lift her spirits, why not treat herself to the rest of him? Apologize for being odd, for hurting his feelings, because she knew she had, and find her way back into his arms. That's what she would do, if the distance between his house and her apartment were the only problem.

"Elizabeth? You look so troubled, so tired. It's not that accident, is it? Your neck hasn't been bothering you?"

"Not a bit."

"I thought you seemed a little off on Sunday, and now I'm sure of it. With those circles under your eyes you could be a ghoul for Halloween."

Liz smiled. "Thanks." It wasn't the best time to bring this up, but later wouldn't be any better. "Grandma, I'm sorry to do this when there's still so much work, but I need to get back to Vancouver by the end of the week. Emily can give you a hand with the rest of the packing." She felt she should explain, although she was sure no one expected her to stay any longer. "The thing is, I haven't been sleeping well, and I don't think I will until I get back to my apartment."

Eleanor poured a little milk into her cup, then filled it with tea. "You could run forever, I suppose."

Liz stared at her grandmother. "I said I'd come for a week or two. It's been nearly two."

"I think you know that's not what I mean."

"I didn't *run*—"

"Elizabeth, when you told me you wanted to visit I hoped it meant all the trouble was over. Your first night here, it was clear that it wasn't. For your own peace of mind, you need to do something about this situation."

"Do something, Grandma?" What could she do? Make it all better? Pretend nothing happened?

"Whether you want to gather everyone together and tell them exactly what you think of them, or forgive them and get on with things, I don't care. But, please, think of your health.'' Eleanor's voice was still quiet, but it was unusually firm. ''So much anger…years of it, just moldering away. It's not good for you.''

''I'm not angry.''

''Well, that's good to hear. Because if you had been and continued to leave it that way, you'd have ended up with high blood pressure and who knows what else.''

''Are you worried about me, Grandma?''

''I am indeed.''

''Please don't be. I'm fine. Absolutely fine.''

Eleanor looked her granddaughter in the eye. ''That's more apparent every day.''

LIZ HAD NO INTENTION of taking the kind of action her grandmother recommended, but there were two things she did need to do before she left Three Creeks, and she had decided to do both of them today. When lunch was over and the dishes were done, she pulled on a warm jacket she'd found while sorting through trunks—thankfully, it was in a cedar-lined trunk, not one with mothballs. She gently pushed the door shut against the dogs' noses. This time, she didn't want their eager companionship.

Instead of going through the woods, she walked along the road toward Jack's. A couple of cars passed her, honking hello, and a tractor pulling a swather crawled by taking so much room she had to step into the ditch. When she reached the alfalfa field she saw the rock she'd run into and skid marks cut deep in the road's shoulder. It would take a lot of spring runoff and summer rain to erase those tracks.

Jack was outside, loading pumpkins into the back of his truck. He must have heard her feet crunching on the gravel driveway, but he kept working until she was hardly a yard away. Finally he turned.

"Hello, Liz."

"You're busy. I won't keep you long."

"I have lots of time—there's nothing to do but get tomorrow's delivery ready."

"For the school?" Pam had told her Jack was donating pumpkins for jack-o'-lanterns, but she hadn't realized he was giving so many. "Are you taking enough for everyone?"

"There's one for every three or four kids. Pam says it'll be a valuable exercise in cooperation."

"That's generous of you."

"Eleanor can only eat so much pie." There was a glimmer of amusement on his face.

Encouraged, Liz went to the back step, where pumpkins waited to be transferred to the truck. She picked up a small one, and brushed dry dirt from one side, where it was flattened and wrinkled from sitting on the ground. Just looking at it she could see potential features in a squashed face, scary enough for kids Jennifer's age. "I wanted to talk to you, Jack."

He leaned against the step, waiting. In the bath last night, she'd planned a short, rational speech, but now she found she didn't want to give it. She just wanted to stay with him, to talk all afternoon. "Did you and your friend ever get hold of each other?"

"We've left messages."

"It was a long way to come on the chance of seeing you. He must be a good friend."

"We go back a long way."

"Back to the days of the unwashed neck?"

"Almost. Is that what you came to talk about?"

She took the pumpkin to the truck and brushed off her hands. "I came to apologize."

"There's no need, Liz. We got carried away. You changed your mind."

She wanted him to know it was more than that. "We weren't carried away. Getting as close as we did wasn't just an impulse. It doesn't make sense for us to get involved, though. That's what I'm sorry for. It was careless to start something I couldn't continue."

"Because you're leaving any day now."

"That's right." She tried to smile. "It's one of those might-have-been situations. Kind of romantic, really. Doesn't it make you wonder how often people miss an opportunity for something wonderful to happen? You're walking along a busy sidewalk, you catch someone's eye and you both pause, then turn away and go on."

"And that's romantic?"

Liz nodded.

More emphatically, Jack said, "Squandered chances are romantic."

"Sure. Lost love and all that. It's a popular theme." She wished she hadn't used the word "love."

For a moment she thought he was going to come right over and grab hold of her, but he stayed where he was. "Seeing someone you think you could care about and making room for that person in your life no matter how unlikely it is to turn out well…that's romantic, Liz. A hell of a lot more romantic than a few sad tears as you walk by. People take chances like that every day."

It was true. They did. She and Andy had. "In a way, I'm not free to start a relationship—" She broke off, annoyed with the awkward phrase.

Jack looked as if he'd finally got the point and couldn't believe it had taken him so long. "You're already involved with someone."

Inaccurate, but true. As soon as she began to nod, he turned away, loading up with pumpkins again. The action was as expressive as a closing door. She was glad he'd ended the conversation, because she couldn't look at those cool silver eyes any longer.

LIZ HURRIED THROUGH JACK'S woods. When it was time to turn toward her grandmother's house she headed north instead, going deeper into the trees. She had to force herself to go that way. More than anything, she wanted the comfort of the kitchen.

The weather had changed in the past hour. Before lunch, there'd been some warmth in the sun. Not now. Low clouds and an icy northwest breeze had moved in. Ever since she'd arrived people had been saying it felt or smelled like snow. Today, she believed them.

The ground rose suddenly. Liz hesitated. Maybe this was a bad idea. Morbid.

Maybe she shouldn't think, just walk.

She went on, crossing from her grandmother's property onto Crown land. Gradually the loamy soil became sandy, and the woods thinned, then stopped. Brittle shrubs and patches of brown grass grew where road crews had dug deep into the ground long ago, leaving gravel mounds and a year-round pond. Liz climbed, dislodging stones and grit. When she reached the top of the incline, she forced herself to look at the ice-cold water below. Her eyes closed. *Andy.*

She could feel him. She'd been so aware of him lately, around the house and in the yard and now here. The only place he didn't seem to linger was in the new school, in spite of the picture in the library, and even there she couldn't escape thoughts of him.

Escape. That was the wrong word. She was glad to

think of him. He deserved to be in her thoughts. Where else could he be?

She couldn't see his face without seeing his smile. He was always smiling. His eyes were always full of fun. Even for the math final that June, the last barrier to freedom. Even when her parents opposed the idea of art school in Vancouver. The world was a wonderful place in his book. Everything was manageable.

"Liz?"

She turned toward the quiet voice and saw Jack standing on one of the lower mounds. The breeze had tousled his hair and reddened his nose.

"Careful, there," he said. "Watch your step."

"What are you doing here, Jack?"

"I followed you. To apologize for being holier-than-thou."

"Everything you said was true."

"Come down from there, Liz. It wouldn't be good if you fell from that height."

Liz gave a small, grimacing laugh. No, it wouldn't be good. That was certain; it had been proved. She began to sidestep down the hill. Before she had gone halfway, Jack met her and took her hand.

"This would be a great place to toboggan. I suppose you did that when you were a kid?"

She nodded. "And we swam in the summer."

"Sounds like fun. So why do you look upset?"

He didn't seem to know. Considered too much of an outsider to hear that particular story, maybe. She swallowed, trying to get rid of the tightness in her throat. "Someone died here. Years ago."

His face softened. "I'm sorry, Liz." He took a look around. "Are we closer to my place, or your grandmother's? Your grandmother's, I think. Let's go and get warmed up, then you can tell me what happened."

Liz didn't budge. "We were having a party, an end-of-summer party." Her voice had gone hoarse, as if the cold air had frozen it. "This was a favorite hangout for a lot of people. Not for us, not for Susannah and me, not for Andy. Wayne and his group always got plastered. You know how things get when that happens. It's not fun anymore. But this was the last party. Most of us were going away to school, or to find work. We didn't know when we'd all see each other again."

"I know the kind of party."

Now that she'd got going, she couldn't stop. "We hauled in food and beer. Drinking was the point of the night for some people. Andy seemed to want to keep up. I don't know why. He never paid attention to those guys. *'Have another one,'* Wayne kept saying. Andy took it as a challenge."

"Boys do that sometimes. Proving themselves."

"Then Wayne dared Andy to dive from the highest peak. Andy started to climb, just like there was nothing to think about. Until he got to the top. He stood up there, looking down, and he didn't move." The muscles around Liz's mouth twitched. Her eyes burned. She didn't want to cry. If she started, she wouldn't stop. "Wayne said, *'He's afraid to jump.'* Sue said she didn't see the others jumping. She said, *'Ignore them.'* That would have been best."

"But he didn't ignore them."

"No." She felt Jack rubbing her hands. He unzipped his jacket and tucked them inside, against his sweater. "It turned out he couldn't have done it, not even if he'd been the best athlete in the school. And he wasn't the best athlete in the school. He wasn't an athlete at all."

"No one could have made the jump?"

"The deepest water was yards away from the line

of the dive. Even there, it wasn't deep enough. The point was, Wayne didn't goad anybody else into diving. He chose Andy. The outsider. And everyone said, 'Too bad. Boys will be boys.' People called it an accident. It wasn't. Not really."

"I'm sorry, Liz."

"Pathetic little story, huh? It's not all that uncommon, inebriated boys diving into shallow water. They just prove themselves to death."

Jack's hand was warm against her cheek. "Let's get you home. You're frozen."

"I'm always cold. This place is still in the Ice Age. I should do a book about it, about a little corner of the prairies with glaciers and mammoths—" She could hardly squeeze the words past the tightness in her throat. Her voice dropped, and she said, mostly to herself, "I suppose I already did that with my dinosaur book. Lost worlds are fascinating, though. Children love lost worlds."

THEY HAD TUCKED LIZ INTO BED under the thickest feather quilt Jack had ever seen, with a hot water bottle at her feet and another one, wrapped in a pillowcase, for her to hug to her stomach. In the kitchen, Jack put a cup of tea beside Eleanor. She was too pale for his liking. "I think I should call the doctor for both of you."

"We'll be fine, don't you worry. I suppose this was bound to happen."

"But the accident was years ago. Looking at Liz, you'd think it was today."

"She ran off right afterward. She went to the funeral with Andrew's parents, without even telling us when or where it was, and then she just left. Every few weeks she called her parents, or her grandfather and me, to say she was fine. That was all. She was fine, goodbye. It was a couple of years before she wanted to see any of us. She wouldn't come back here, though. We went to visit her. You'd hardly know anything had happened, except she wouldn't let anyone talk about Andrew."

Jack didn't know what to say, so he just poured more tea.

"We didn't do anything wrong."

"Of course not."

Eleanor's hand trembled when she sipped her tea. "No one was unkind to him, no one in the family at least. Elizabeth told me he had some trouble fitting in at school. It's difficult to move to a small place with a long history. Well, you know that. His family seemed to expect a perfect window box town, a storybook town. Not one full of stubborn people whose forebearers were tough enough to survive here when there was nothing but bush for miles around. People take pride in that. Maybe they show off a little. But Elizabeth blamed everyone for Andrew's death."

"An indictment against the whole community?"

"Yes! That's it exactly. So, off she went to Vancouver. She became an art student, and left the grieving wife here." Eleanor took a second look at Jack's face. "Don't be too concerned. I'm afraid the whole situation was waiting for her. She'll have a difficult time for a while, but she'll be better off in the long run. Things have to be faced. She hasn't ever liked to believe that. How she used to scowl at me—"

"Liz was married?"

"You didn't know? I was sure you did. Strange that none of us told you."

Maybe not so strange. People weren't usually chatty about their flaws and failures. Jack didn't know what he thought about Wayne and the gravel pit and the adults who'd done nothing. Pathetic, as Liz said. Awful. A waste. He'd never believed Three Creeks was a storybook town, so he shouldn't be surprised by the proof. The important thing now was to get some color back in Eleanor's cheeks. Of everyone involved she had the least reason to feel bad. It made him angry to see her hand tremble.

FROM HER BEDROOM WINDOW Liz watched Jack stride across the backyard, his feet lost in shadow. She wouldn't want to walk through the woods at night. There was only a half moon. That wasn't much light to go by.

At least he wouldn't be too cold. There wasn't any wind now, not even a breeze. She could tell by the trees in the yard. Their branches were absolutely still, silvery against the sky. The prairie sky that her grandmother didn't want to leave. There were no mountain ranges to interrupt it, no city lights to make it dim. It was clear and black and endless, crowded with sharp, bright stars.

Some people liked to say stars were souls out of harm's way, twinkling down on the living. Hadn't the ancient Egyptians believed that? Your soul was weighed and if it was light enough, up it went. Of course, stars weren't souls. They were big balls of burning gasses. Sometimes she wished she didn't know anything.

Her eyes closed. This was an old pain. Why was it back? New and fresh.

She had stared at the water that night fifteen years ago, as if her mind could unmake that last moment, that throw-your-heart-and-follow-it leap, and when she saw Andy on the shore it had kept fumbling through the facts, looking for the mistake, the thing it could put in place so he would open his eyes and see her again. She didn't understand how he could disappear like that. How could he be thinking and breathing and feeling at the top of the hill, and then not, a few seconds later, at the bottom? What vapor or essence or electrical impulse had made him Andy, and where had it gone so easily, so fast? Sometimes, even now, she thought she should be able to reach out her hand and find him, that if only she knew how, she could pick him up the way you picked up a child who fell off a swing. Sometimes the thought crept up on her that only geography was between them, only miles of mountains and miles of prairie, that somewhere in those miles Andy was waiting for her to find him.

She was cold, all goose bumps and shivering. She pulled the quilt from the bed and wrapped it around her, right up around her ears and nose, her hands tucked inside.

If only his family hadn't moved to Three Creeks. He would be an artist in Vancouver now, and she would be a gym teacher—right here in town, maybe, having a tea break with Em and Pam every day. Or if only they hadn't met. Or if they'd met, but not married. Married, but stayed home that night. One decision different.

CHAPTER NINE

ON HALLOWEEN MORNING heavy clouds reached down into the tops of the trees around Eleanor's house. By noon a few snowflakes floated in the air. By the time school was out, the roads were a wet, sloppy mess. After the sun set they would be treacherous.

"No one will come around," Liz said. "Not in this."

She carried the third jack-o'-lantern out to the veranda. Eleanor always put one on each step, lighting the way to the door. Jack had brought the pumpkins yesterday, almost tiptoeing, almost whispering, as if he were in a sick room. Liz was sitting beside the stove wrapped in the afghan when he came, still cold a whole day after visiting the gravel pit. She felt numb all over, as if her entire body had been to the dentist. She'd watched Jack and Eleanor spread out newspapers, spoon out seeds and pulp and cut features in the shells, comforted by the remembered actions. When night finally came, she had crawled into bed without washing her face or brushing her teeth and slept deeply.

Today had been a better day. She and her grandmother had worked at a few quiet jobs, not even talking most of the time. She was doing her best to behave like her usual self. After all this time she wasn't really a widow. She'd hardly been a wife. And she wasn't the one who'd died young.

Using herself as an umbrella, Liz leaned over the three pumpkins, one by one, and lit the candles inside. In the middle of a blizzard, the flames looked very small. Wet snow soon put them out. She found flashlights to tuck inside instead, but half an hour later, snow fell so heavily the faint light couldn't be seen from the kitchen window.

Eleanor sat at the table, where she could keep one eye out for children at the door. She looked small and sad. The past couple of days had been difficult for her. "The youngest have usually been and gone by now," she said. "Preschoolers before dinner, grade ones just after dark. Such a disappointment for them."

Liz picked up a box of playing cards. "How about a tournament while we wait?"

"I wouldn't mind a game." There was an ungrandmotherly glint in Eleanor's eye. Liz was glad to see it. Maybe things would soon get back to normal between them. Eleanor had been concerned about Liz, but perplexed by her distress, too. She believed that when something was in front of you, you faced it. End of story. Liz really thought she had faced what happened at the gravel pit. *Take that, Three Creeks. I'm outta here.* In her mind, she hadn't run away, she had run to the life she'd planned with Andy.

They shuffled both decks, and laid their cards across the table. As soon as Liz's last card was in place, Eleanor began moving hers, slapping down red and black cards in sequence and shunting aces to the top. Liz moved to put a Jack of Spades on a Queen, and a nine of Hearts on a ten, but quick and light, Eleanor's hand got there first. Soon Liz was reduced to watching her grandmother play.

An hour later, Eleanor was still unbeaten. A few trick-or-treaters called while they played. The first time Liz went to the door Tom stood just inside the reach of the porch light, hands in his pockets, shoulders hunched up to keep his neck warm, while two small wizards and a princess collected their candy. They were followed almost immediately by Pat, with her hair full of snow and Nell the Teddy Bear in her arms. Nell was terrified of her costume and wouldn't even look at the basket of candy, so Pat took a red lollipop for her and went back into the storm, muttering about a hot bath and a glass of scotch. Last was Stephen, dressed as a hockey player, his oversize Oilers jersey fitting perfectly over his parka. He moved slowly in his knee and elbow pads, a bag for candy looped over a hockey stick. A car waited for him in the driveway, barely visible through falling snow.

"Did you have any trouble on the roads?" Liz asked.

"Nope," Stephen said confidently, but he added, "The Mounties are turning people back on the highway. And we got stuck once, on the little creek road." The hard squared fingers of his hockey glove were as awkward as a robot's hand, so Liz scooped some treats into his bag. "Wow! Thanks."

"Keep safe out there."

"We won't get anyone else," Eleanor said, when he was gone. "Even in a mild year, there's never anyone after eight."

"Good. Then we won't be interrupted." One after another, Liz laid five cards down on the aces in the middle of the table. "You'd better look out. I'm going to get you this time, Grandma."

"Do you think so? A positive attitude can help, I hear."

WET AND HEAVY, THE SNOW WAS nearly over the top of Jack's boots. He'd walked through the woods as usual, sure that he'd be better off on foot than driving. The trees had offered some protection from the wind, but he'd found the swirling snow disorienting. Eleanor's house was invisible until he was only a few yards away.

He climbed the porch steps, using his feet to swipe the accumulated snow to the side as he went. Glad to be under a roof, he stamped his boots and banged at his coat, knocking snow to the porch floor.

Liz opened the door. "Jack!"

He hoped her horrified expression had something to do with the amount of white stuff still heaped all over him. She moved aside to let him in.

"You look frozen! You walked?"

She sounded angry. Jack stepped into the kitchen and found himself the center of attention. Bella and Dora sniffed at his legs and at the bag he carried, tails waving. Eleanor and Liz pulled off his coat and scarf, and pushed him toward the fire, exclaiming over the frost on his eyelashes.

"Don't you know you can die walking in a blizzard?"

She *was* angry.

"You get wet, you get cold, you get tired, you lie down in a ditch and you die!"

It was the way he used to imagine a mother would sound. Not so much angry, as scared and worried. "It's not all that bad out—"

Liz turned to her grandmother, speechless.

Mildly, Eleanor said, "You could get lost in these conditions, Jack. And then the rest of what Elizabeth said is certainly possible."

Liz turned back to Jack with an I-told-you-so expression.

"I'm fine." Like swimming upstream, he made his way past the four females to the table. He set down his bag and loosened the string. Miniature chocolate bars tumbled onto the table. He'd shopped a little too enthusiastically, choosing some of every kind of bar he thought might be someone's favorite. "I was hoping you'd help me. I bought too much candy."

Eleanor and Liz just looked at him.

"You walked through a blizzard to bring us candy?" Liz pointed to their own basket. "We've got candy."

Licorice and lollipops. "Mine's better." He was glad to see a flicker of amusement on her face. She was pale, and there were circles under her eyes. Had she really put off grieving for her husband all this time? A loss could jump up and bite you when you least expected it, long after you thought you'd settled it. That seemed more likely to be what was going on. Some trip home. Too many goodbyes for one person in one short visit.

He looked at the cards spread over the table. "You're both playing solitaire at once?"

"Double solitaire," Liz said. "It's the same as the single person version, only you have eight aces to play on."

"Is there a three person version?"

When she smiled she looked even more vulnerable. "That could get a little wild."

"Yup. Drinking tea and playing solitaire with two country ladies. Could be the wildest thing I've ever done." He moved his bag of chocolate bars to the side and started gathering the cards to reshuffle. Liz found a third deck in the living room. By the time Eleanor had a fresh pot of tea ready, all three decks were dealt and ready to go.

Jack tossed a Mars bar into the middle of the table. "Opening bids, please."

"I'm not sure you can bet on solitaire," Eleanor said.

"Of course you can. I'm betting I'll win."

"Confidence is a great thing." She picked up a handful of candy. "In that case, I'll meet your Mars bar and raise you two Aeros. Oh, why don't I just add them all?" She dropped all the bars she held onto the table. It was Jack's first indication that he might be in trouble.

He soon realized he'd have to play competitively to have any chance of winning, and he couldn't bring himself to do that. He ended up joining Liz on the sidelines, happy to see the light pink that tinged her cheeks when she started to laugh at how hopeless they both were. Her laughter faded quickly, though, and with it the color.

They'd hardly talked since she'd told him about Andy. Going from memories of Saturday night to approaching Liz as a grieving widow wasn't easy. His feelings for her had developed too quickly. They'd got ahead of how well he knew her. He wanted to hear what she was thinking, he wanted to fix things, he wanted to hold her and feel the tension leave her body. Instead he had to act like a neighbor. Not even her neighbor.

Eleanor was scooping her haul of chocolate to her side of the table and suggesting another game when they heard a snowmobile engine above the wind. Snow swirled into the kitchen, followed by Will, covered from top to toe by a one-piece snowmobile suit and a balaclava. He looked approvingly at the table full of cards and treats and teacups.

"Now here's some people who know how to spend

a snowy evening. I don't know what it is with Halloween. Why doesn't everybody just stay home and eat their own candy? You all right for wood and fuel, Mother?''

Eleanor assured her son she was equipped to handle the blizzard even if it lasted all week.

''Good, good. And you have plenty of food, of course, and company.'' He smiled at Liz, then said to Jack, ''The roads are pretty much closed. Need a ride home?''

''Thanks, but I've got to try to win back my losses. Unless I can help?''

Will made it clear that he and his snowmobile worked alone. ''If you're going to stay longer you'd better plan on spending the night. It'd be just plain stupid to go walking out there now.'' He reached toward the pile of chocolate bars, waited for an invitation, then helped himself, stuffing several in his pocket. He smiled at Eleanor. ''I'll check on you again tomorrow.''

''You'll be careful, won't you, William?''

''Always.'' He tapped a finger beside one eye. ''Eyes like a hawk.''

''A hawk with reading glasses.''

''Not to worry. There's no fine print out there tonight.'' He rolled his balaclava down over his face, pushed up his hood and was gone. They heard his snowmobile sputter, roar, then fade away.

Liz and Eleanor couldn't relax after Will left. The cards sat ignored on the table while they paced around the kitchen looking out windows, checking the wood supply and moving the kettle onto the heat in what Jack was beginning to think was a compulsive gesture, like knocking on wood. Bella and Dora had picked up their anxiety and followed them a few steps here, a few steps there.

"Grandma, if Jack's staying I'd better get a room ready for him."

"The one overhead," Eleanor told her. "It'll be the warmest."

The dogs went with Liz as far as the kitchen doorway. Jack gave a low whistle. They came to him and leaned against him while he rubbed behind their ears. They were all upset, all four of them. He'd been naive to think company and chocolate could help. He didn't sense as much distress in the air as he had when he was here carving pumpkins yesterday, but there was enough to make him feel useless.

"Would you take them, Jack?"

He looked up from the dogs' silky heads. "Take them, Eleanor?"

"Bella and Dora."

"Upstairs?"

"Would you take them when I move?"

He'd never thought of the dogs away from this house. "Of course I will. And you'll visit them whenever you want."

"Thank you. I'm so glad. They won't be confused if they're with you."

She looked exhausted. He should have left with Will. "Don't stay up because I'm here, Eleanor. I'll head upstairs—"

Eleanor looked behind Jack, toward the doorway. "Jack's agreed to take the girls, Elizabeth."

Liz's eyes got misty, but she smiled. "That's one problem solved. Maybe he'd like the table, too."

"Maybe I would." He didn't even have a dining room. Well, who said dining room tables had to go in dining rooms?

"Perhaps you should just buy the house then, Jack, and list the Ramsey place with Mrs. Anderson." Eleanor smiled widely enough that Jack thought she was probably joking. Still, it wasn't the worst idea he'd ever heard. She went on, "It'll be fun to think about it while I'm waiting to fall asleep. Good night, you two."

Liz led Jack up the narrow staircase. They passed the room she was using, and the bathroom and stopped at the last door on the left. The window looked out over the front yard, but right now he could only see driving snow. Liz tugged the heavy drapes shut and the room immediately felt warmer. Woodsy, heated air from the kitchen came through the metal grill in the floor. A big old bed was against the inside wall, away from drafts. Even with quilts piled on he could see the mattress sagging in the middle.

"I put a few hot water bottles in," Liz said. "If you give it a little longer they should get the chill out of the sheets. I don't know if you care about pyjamas. We found a whole box of them the other day, different sizes, all in good shape, so I got a pair out for you. They're under the comforter, getting warm."

"Thanks, Liz. I feel pampered." She'd even put a glass of water and some books beside the bed.

"Good. That's what you need."

"You'll never guess what I found myself thinking on my way through the woods tonight."

She gave a faint smile. "Tell me, then."

Now that he'd committed himself to saying it out loud, he was embarrassed. His eyebrow went up, mocking him. "The north wind shalt blow—"

Her smile widened.

"And we shall have snow—" He stopped. What

was sillier than an adult male reciting a nursery rhyme?

"And what will poor Jack do then?"

"Get lectured when he reaches the house. Poor thing."

"Oh, dear. It wasn't a lecture, was it?"

He hadn't minded at all, but he wasn't about to admit it.

Liz leaned against the wall. He wished she'd sit down and get comfortable. "So, you do know some nursery rhymes. This one just popped into your mind?"

"You got my curiosity going, so I bought a book of them when I was in Brandon. Interesting reading, but I've given up looking for secret messages. They can't really be meant for children, Liz. Some of them are nasty, even violent."

"That never bothered me when I was little. They made me laugh."

"The absurdity, I suppose."

She nodded. "And maybe children recognize something in the rhymes—the world as they see it. Simplistic, upside-down, unpredictable. For whatever reason, childhood and nursery rhymes go together."

"They weren't part of my relationship with my uncle." She always looked suspicious when he mentioned Jerry. "He was a good guy. Just not a Mother Goose fan."

"I'll admit if I were reading them to Nell, I'd be selective." She pushed away from the wall. "I'll leave you to get settled in, Jack." Unexpectedly, she came close and reached up to give him a sisterly good-night hug. He could tell she found the contact comforting. It felt wonderful to him. Just not comforting.

"There are extra towels in the bathroom. You have

to run the water a while before it's hot, but then it gets *very* hot, so be sure you don't burn yourself. And be careful if you decide to go downstairs. The steps are odd sizes, so it's easy to lose your footing. You can knock on my door if there's anything else you need." She lingered in the doorway. Her voice more hesitant, she said, "Thanks for listening to that awful story the other day, Jack. I should have told you about Andy right away, instead of cutting you off the way I did."

"You can't tell people your life story as soon as you meet them."

She smiled again, more warmly, then went out, closing the door behind her. It was hard to have her so close, but unaware of her effect on him. He couldn't help wondering how long her resurrected grief would last. When it was over, would she see him as a reminder of all this sadness? He was connected to the place she'd tried to cut out of her life. Picking up where they'd left off might be the last thing she wanted.

Jack felt under the covers. Not bad. A lot warmer than the sheets in his bedroom. He piled the pillows against the headboard and stretched out on top of the comforter. Liz had left him a couple of paperback thrillers, a book about pruning fruit trees and a slightly musty hardcover with fraying edges. He held it closer to the light to read the faded letters. *Roughing it in the Bush* by Susanna Moodie. There was a handwritten name on the flyleaf, faded, too. Julia Robb, 1883.

The first Julia, he'd heard the Robbs call her. That was the year she and the first William had arrived at their new home, nothing more than acres of trees and scrubby meadow. No buildings, no doctor, no roads. He was still adjusting to his move. Sometimes he thought he must have gone thousands of miles from the city, not a hundred, to some far-off place where the cultural rules were anybody's guess. What must it have been like for them?

He had just opened the book to the first chapter when the lights went off.

LIZ FELT FOR THE LAMP SHADE and twisted the still-hot bulb. It didn't come back on, so she crossed the room, feeling for the switch by the door. The ceiling light was out, too. No moonlight reached the hall outside the bedroom, or the stairs.

"Liz?"

"I'm here, Jack. Right by my door." She couldn't see him, not even when he reached her side. "I'm going downstairs. If you're coming, be careful."

One hand on the wall and the other on the banister, Liz eased forward until her foot encountered the first step. She went down slowly, pausing when her hand came to the rounded end of the banister. "Okay, Jack?"

"It's like a fun house at the fair. Pitch-black, and I have no idea what's in front of me."

"I'm in front of you."

A hand touched her shoulder "So you are."

Pleasant waves of feeling rippled through her body. "The front hall is a bit of an obstacle course." She felt her way, careful not to knock pictures to the floor or bang her knees on furniture. She didn't hear any clatter behind her. Jack seemed to be managing, too.

"Grandma?"

"In the kitchen."

"You're all right?"

In answer, a candle flame appeared, with Eleanor's face behind it. She placed the candle on the kitchen table. "We should have expected this. It's the ice and wind," she told Jack. "Even if a line snapped near Churchill, we might feel it here."

"Maybe a polar bear chomped a wire," Liz suggested.

Eleanor smiled. "No doubt that's what happened."

Without power, the oil furnace couldn't heat the house. The water heater couldn't heat water, the well couldn't pump it, the toilet couldn't flush. They began preparing for an uncomfortable night. Jack dragged upholstered armchairs from the living room and added more wood to the fire, Eleanor brought a load of quilts from the downstairs bedroom, and Liz filled the kettle and a couple of stockpots with water that was still in the pipes. Between their chairs and the stove, they made a bed of blankets for the dogs. The rotary phone still worked, so before settling in Eleanor called Will's house to be sure he'd got in safely. She was more relaxed when she came back to the stove.

"Everyone's all set," she said contentedly. "William's enjoying himself enormously."

"He loves storms," Liz said. "I remember my dad going out with him on nights like this, making the rounds. Getting people out of ditches, taking groceries to anybody who was snowed in. They'd come back all red-faced and smiling, and Mom would make a fuss over them." She looked at Jack. "Blizzards must have been different for you, growing up in the city. The ploughs would get out right away."

"We never even got to miss school."

"We did, all the time." She smiled. "Maybe that's why I can't add."

"Your grandfather loved it when the school was closed." Eleanor turned to Jack to explain. "They always found their way over here, on snowshoes if they couldn't beg a snowmobile ride from anyone, and then we had a houseful for a day or two."

"Blankets over the furniture to make forts," Liz said.

"Games of tag all over the house."

"Cookies baked in the woodstove."

"You must have kept your fingers crossed all winter for storms," Jack said to Liz.

"We were lucky to have storybook grandparents." She looked affectionately at Eleanor, then turned to Jack. "And you're a storybook neighbor. A mysterious man from the city. Where he came from, who he is, no one knows."

Jack shifted in his chair. "I don't mean to be secretive. What would you like to know?"

"I've wondered about your vocation."

"His vocation?" Eleanor asked.

"There's not much to tell. I designed computer programs."

Eleanor and Liz nodded, waiting for more detail.

"Individualized programs. The big software companies make standardized packages. We found that hospitals need one kind of database, and grocery stores another. Lawyers need templates for particular forms, schools need others. And so on."

Liz was a little disappointed. It didn't sound very exciting.

"Kind of dry, I know. The process is interesting. The math." He looked from Eleanor to Liz and gave a little shrug. "Eventually it didn't satisfy me anymore. Remember the experiment in school with the bean seed?"

Liz perked up. She understood beans. "You put it in a jar with water and watch it sprout."

"And a green leaf emerges. Then you cut open a

dry bean and there the leaf is, tiny and white, waiting. I decided I'd rather deal with that kind of code."

"Applied mathematics." Liz wasn't sure if she was joking or trying to sound intelligent.

Jack smiled. "You've got it. Outdoor math."

"You'll do well," Eleanor said. "You're very much like my husband. He quietly went about his business doing things the way he thought they should be done, regardless of what those around him said. Now, there were times, I must admit, when listening to others might have done him good, but on the whole I liked his independence." She tried to stifle a yawn.

"Are you warm enough, Grandma?"

"I'm nearly ready to run into the snow, that's how warm I am."

Liz opened the door of the woodstove to check the fire. She would let it burn down a little more before putting in a large log, a piece of the hardened birch they'd been saving. It would take its time to catch, then burn slowly and steadily through the night.

Jack stood beside her. "I'll watch the fire, Liz. Can you sleep sitting up?"

"I haven't really been sleeping anywhere."

He took her hand and pulled her gently back to the chair. "Get as comfortable as you can." He tucked the quilt around her. "Even if you just rest or doze it'll do you good."

"Why did you say you're no kind of knight?"

His face looked blank.

"At the barbecue—"

"I suppose because I don't qualify."

"You're chivalrous."

"Do you think so?"

From behind him, Eleanor murmured, "Definitely."

He seemed uncertain if he was being teased.

"There's no Round Table. I don't fight dragons. And I'm afraid of horses."

Liz smiled. Nothing complimented chivalry better than modesty. He was a knight. He just didn't know it.

CHAPTER TEN

LIZ AWOKE TO THE SOUND of male voices. It was a few minutes before she was alert enough to sort out the pleasantly deep rumble. Jack, sounding calm. Tom, sounding defensive. And Eleanor's soft voice, barely making it through the grill. She hoped her grandmother and Jack hadn't been awake long. The power had come on at about four o'clock, and as soon as they'd felt warm air coming through the registers, they'd gone back to their rooms for some real sleep. Had she slept through breakfast? Tea and miniature chocolate bars, probably.

Liz pulled off the clothes she'd worn to bed and shivered her way into a fresh pair of jeans and a sweater. She smoothed the sheets and the comforter and shook the pillow so it was plump again, then went across the hall to the bathroom.

Above the frost that coated the bottom half of the window, she saw Tom and Jack go outside. Stepping into the holes he'd left on his way to the house, Tom headed to his truck, parked at the end of the driveway, and Jack struggled through unmarked snow to the garage. By the time he got back with a shovel, Tom had unloaded his snowblower. Liz smiled. *Gentlemen, start your engines.*

She sat on the edge of the deep porcelain tub, knees drawn up and arms wrapped around them. Tom's snowblower roared, sending an arching fan of white powder into the air. Sensibly, Jack began with the porch steps and worked his way along the path toward the driveway. His movements were steady and efficient, and despite the snow's depth he made good progress.

She'd liked sitting near him by the fire last night. When they'd come upstairs, she'd liked knowing he was just down the hall. And she liked seeing him when she looked out her window. He had a comforting presence. Sometimes he was funny, sometimes cautious, always kind. It wasn't his kindness that had got to her when they'd made their way downstairs after the lights went out, though. She had been so aware of his body she'd felt it in the banister and in the paneling on the wall. How could her mind have room for Jack?

"Elizabeth?"

Liz started and turned, nearly falling into the tub. Her grandmother stood in the doorway with a tray. "Grandma! You shouldn't have come upstairs."

"I do come up from time to time, you know."

"Let me take that." Liz set the tray, holding coffee and toast, over the sink. "This is so nice of you."

"Is toast enough for now? It's nearly lunchtime."

"It's perfect."

Eleanor looked past Liz, then moved closer to the window. "What a pair. As soon as your brother turned up they started growling at each other about my driveway. I don't understand them. Well, I suppose I do. One wants a grandmother and the other has one. What I don't understand is why it's a problem."

The deep sound of a large diesel engine, in the background for the past few minutes, had become louder. A John Deere tractor with a front-end loader and attached snow-pushing blade came into view. It chugged to a stop at the mouth of the driveway. Idling noisily, it looked ready to push the snow and Tom's blower out of its path. The blade came down and as the tractor moved forward its engine roared. The driver was invisible inside an enclosed cab.

"Uncle Will?"

"Thomas and Jack will have to move quickly. He won't wait all day."

Jack must have come to the same conclusion. He stuck his shovel into a snowbank and hurried to help Tom move his machine out of the tractor's way.

Eleanor began to laugh. "It won't be long now, will it? I'll get lunch ready."

Liz took a bite of toast and a gulp of coffee. "I'm right behind you, Grandma."

"Good." Eleanor gave her an approving smile. "There's nothing like keeping busy."

Liz had just put a plate of sandwiches on the table when the three men came in, stomping snow from their boots, voices booming around the kitchen. Jack and Tom, both with an armload of wood, were teasing Will about the way he'd appeared, engine snarling, a road warrior ready to race. They hung up their parkas, put their gloves on the stove and sat at the table without any "after you, ladies" movements. Will left his snowmobile suit on, unzipped to the waist, the top half hanging down over the bottom.

"This is nothing to talk about, hardly a storm at all," he said. "Not like the whiteout of '77. Remember, Mother? By the time we cleared ourselves out of that one the snowbanks were over our heads."

One by one, Eleanor handed Liz bowls of homemade soup they'd taken from the freezer and heated. "I do remember. The driveway was like a tunnel from the house to the road. It doesn't matter what you're digging, though, does it, William? You used to push your toy grader through the garden dirt just as happily as you cleared snow today."

Will gave a pleased smile. "What was I, six?"

"Younger. It was your favorite thing when you were four. You were particularly happy the day you dug up a whole row of beans."

Tom took a sandwich from the plate, saw that it was tuna salad and put it back. He turned the plate around until he found ham and cheese. "Whose garden did you dig in, Jack?"

Liz looked at her brother gratefully. It was a small step, a simple courtesy, but more than he'd been willing to do for Jack so far. Now, if Jack just wouldn't get touchy…

"I grew up in an apartment," he said, his voice relaxed. "We used to dig in the school yard at recess, but not without paying for it later."

"No garden at all?" Will asked. "I thought people in the city liked balcony gardens."

"Whoever built our apartment didn't think of balconies."

"So you're a true-blue city dweller. High-rise living, cement instead of grass, somebody making the snow disappear before you even get up in the morning. That explains why I was treated to the sight of you tackling a three-foot drift with a shovel. Quite a change for you, coming to Three Creeks."

Jack smiled. "Third floor walk-up, birch trees out the window and snow-packed streets with ruts so deep you could get lost on your way to school. But you're right, things are a lot different in Three Creeks. I don't regret the change of lifestyle at all."

Will and Tom looked speculatively from Jack to Liz. To her relief, they kept whatever thoughts they had to themselves. Tom helped himself to another sandwich and asked, ‘‘What sort of business did you have in Winnipeg, Jack? Something with computers, I heard.’’

‘‘He told us all about that last night,’’ Eleanor said. ‘‘He designed computer programs.’’

Will’s eyebrows went up, and he nodded thoughtfully. ‘‘That’s a good line of business to be in, isn’t it?’’

‘‘It’s a very good line of business,’’ Jack agreed.

‘‘But you left it?’’

‘‘I sold the whole kit and caboodle.’’

‘‘And bought a farm.’’

Liz could see her uncle wondering what to put in the credit and debit columns.

‘‘Quite a step for someone who never had so much as a balcony garden,’’ he said. ‘‘You seemed to find your way around your pumpkin field all right. If you can afford to wait for the trees, maybe it’ll all work out. Next thing you know everybody will want to grow Christmas trees.’’

Jack couldn’t hide his surprise at Will’s interest. ‘‘I hope not. The market’s only so big.’’

‘‘Dad wanted to plant trees, didn’t he, Mother?’’

‘‘Not as a business. He used to talk about having a field of evergreens close to the house. He liked the idea of everyone coming over to choose a tree each year. He never had the leisure to make it happen, though.’’

‘‘Well, since Jack’s renting a Robb field no doubt he’ll let all of us come tree-picking once they’re big enough.’’

Liz looked at her grandmother. They hadn’t talked any more about how she planned to divide her land. She didn’t seem concerned about her son’s assumption.

Will and Tom both got up from the table. Will had Julia's driveway to clear, and Tom needed to get some more feed to his cattle.

"Good lunch, Mother." Will sorted through his gloves as if he had a whole pile of them. "You play any hockey, Jack?"

"Pickup games. Nothing organized."

"There's an old-timers' league starting up at the community center once the ice goes in. We can always use another man."

"Old-timers," Jack repeated.

"That's anybody over twenty-five." Will grinned. "Better get used to it."

"I suppose it wouldn't hurt to have an extra left wing," Tom said, a little stiffly. "Can you manage that, Jack?"

"I'll certainly give it a try."

The kitchen was quiet when Will and Tom left. Eleanor sat down to finish her lunch. "Isn't that encouraging, Jack? My family is beginning to behave itself."

For now. Liz wondered what would happen if Eleanor decided to sell Jack the field.

REID HAD HOPED THE BLIZZARD would paralyze traffic so he couldn't get to the office for a day or two, but the worst of the storm stayed north of the city. There were a few fender benders at intersections along the way, and that slowed him down, but by nine-thirty he was at his desk. Croker didn't seem to believe in weekends. When there was nothing to do, the best minds worked overtime.

Reid's job was to recover the files on Jack's disk. He'd been at it for days. Whenever Croker asked him how things were going he talked about bits and bytes and overwritten fragments. That seemed to satisfy the guy that his expert was well-occupied.

During this exercise in futility he'd had plenty of time to think. A couple of things worried him. You had to wonder how they'd missed the disk the first time they were at the house. The book had pretty much opened to the clump of glued pages, and the cut edges weren't exactly invisible.

Then there was the page Jack had chosen, and the particular area of the page where he'd cut. *Who loses and who wins…* Reid didn't have a copy of King Lear, so he'd found it on the Internet. Not that reading it did him much good. He'd never understood a word Shakespeare said. Certain lines leapt out at him though…talk of enemies and spies, victories and his least favorite, *Come, let's away to prison.*

Coincidence? Or did Jack know about the first break-in, and he was letting them know he did? If that was the case, the disk they'd found was worthless. He hadn't mentioned his doubts to Croker. It was kind of self-defeating not to, but every cell of rebellious fifteen-year-old left inside him wanted to watch the guy flounder a little longer.

He'd honestly thought this whole project would be much easier going. He knew Jack, and Croker knew people interested in making a purchase. Wouldn't you think they could find the product and sell it? And then be very happy, if not forever after, then at least for as long as it took to spend a million bucks? Give or take.

Without knocking first, or saying hello, one of Croker's chums came into the office and whispered something Reid couldn't hear. A second later Croker was at the desk.

"Looks like you don't know McKinnon as well as

you thought. He's got another address. An apartment, right here in Winnipeg."

Reid didn't say anything. He was always tempted to explain things, but it made him look weak, and Croker didn't listen anyway. Without another word, the two men left. Reid restrained himself from locking the door behind them.

So, he didn't know Jack had kept his apartment. As if that was going to make a difference. Did Croker really think a second address would lead him to a copy of the algorithm? You didn't have to know about his real estate holdings to know Jack. He wouldn't leave something valuable in a place he hardly ever went. If he cared about something, he liked to be able to put his hands on it. He liked to look at it and think, "That's mine." Croker wouldn't find anything. Nothing but dust and a nice view of the Assiniboine River.

Then what? He'd be back, crabbier than ever. And Reid would have nothing to give him. Because they were dead in the water. Nothing could be rescued from Jack's disk. Croker would see that as evidence of Reid's incompetence. Try explaining to a micromanaging Type A sociopath that there's a difference between being incompetent and having a strong adversary.

ALL THE FAMILY BUT ELEANOR and Liz had gone to Brian's for a blizzard party. Eleanor wanted to stay home and rest, and Liz wanted to work at something calm, a mundane job that would keep her mind occupied.

She sat on the floor in one of the spare bedrooms beside a 1950's steamer trunk, lifting out odds and ends. There was a Chinese checkers game with a handful of mismatched marbles. A tattered Pin the Tail on the Donkey poster. A plush cat that had lost its button eyes and most of its fur. Things that should have been thrown away a long time ago, but were tucked in this trunk instead.

She unfolded the checkers board, and arranged the marbles she had on the six-pointed star. Four blues in one point. Two yellows. One green. Three orange. And that was all. She rolled the last marble over and over in its spot. She used to pull the game out when the grown-ups were visiting, when they talked and talked longer than she could imagine anyone being able to talk. Her grandfather always saw her putting the marbles in place, and he always left the loud, laughing group of parents and aunts and uncles to play with her. She loved snaking her marbles across the board so she could jump all the way from one side to the other. Getting them right into the point was the problem. She never had patience for that.

Liz swallowed. Her throat felt tight. She took a deep breath, but it didn't help, it just spread the tightness to her chest. She leaned forward and breathed again. Deep breaths always did the trick, didn't they? Deep breath in, and slowly blow out, and the tightness goes away. It was foolproof. Not this time. She could breath in, but not out. She was going to burst. She leaned on the trunk to push herself up and hurried on unsteady legs out of the room and down the stairs.

''Grandma?'' Not in the kitchen, and not by the phone.

Eleanor's voice came from behind her. ''Elizabeth? I'm in the living room.'' She was sitting forward on the sofa, a finger keeping her place in her book. ''Oh, my dear.''

Tears flowed down Liz's cheeks. ''I'm so sorry, Grandma.''

"That's all right. A good cry may be just what you need."

Liz shook her head. That wasn't it. She managed to say, "I didn't come for Grandpa's funeral."

Eleanor set her book on the coffee table. "Sit down. Here, beside me."

Liz could barely see her grandmother patting the sofa.

"Shh. There now." Eleanor stroked Liz's arm. Her hand kept stroking and quiet words kept coming like a lullaby. Finally she spoke more firmly. "Now, my dear girl. Your grandfather wouldn't like to see you so upset. Would he? No, of course not." She reached into her pocket and brought out a handkerchief. "Here, see what you can do with that streaming nose."

Liz blinked to clear her vision. Irish linen, with a narrow lace edging. Like her dresses, Eleanor's hankies hadn't changed. Starched and ironed and folded in quarters, big enough for one good blow. Maybe. She sniffed and wiped her cheeks with her hand. "It's too pretty, Grandma." Still sniffing, she searched her own pockets. In one, she found a long strip of toilet paper.

"That should last you a week. I'll just put on the kettle. It'll boil before you're mopped up."

Liz followed her grandmother into the kitchen. She watched her lift the kettle, shake it, place it over the fire. Something in the familiar action made the tears start again. Bella and Dora came closer, their noses at her knees. She bent to pat them and cried harder.

"I understood why you didn't come to the funeral, Elizabeth, and your grandfather would have, too. Goodness knows there were more than enough people around who thought they were helping me...and many who really were, to be fair. I wish you had come for your own sake. Still, it's not the first time someone has said goodbye from a distance. Did you think he didn't hear you? Of course he heard you."

She hadn't said goodbye at all. That was the thing. There was nothing for him to hear. She had sent flowers. Why would he care about a bouquet of flowers? An assortment of Okanagan apples, maybe, all the unusual varieties he'd wished he could grow on the prairies.

"Your grandfather loved you. And he knew you, through and through. You were such a sweet child, but I remember him saying he wouldn't want to cross you. Even when you banged your knee on a door you'd look at it so fiercely, as if it had got in your way on purpose. He wondered what you'd do if someone really hurt you."

The strip of paper had lasted five minutes, not a week. Liz reached for a paper napkin in the holder Eleanor kept on the table and shook it open. After dabbing and blowing until it was saturated, she said, "I never thought of Grandpa knowing me. I just thought of him as someone who did nice things. He always had humbugs in his pocket."

Eleanor smiled. "The ones with the chewy centers."

"I'm so angry with him, Grandma." Her voice came out in a near whisper.

Eleanor looked startled. "With your grandfather?"

"With Andy." The words sat in the air in front of her, as solid as rocks. Lightning didn't strike.

"That's not such a surprise. He did a foolish thing, with disastrous results."

Still no lightning.

"You've spent so much energy not facing this, Elizabeth. A person could build a pyramid with that determination. You weren't so fearful when you were a child. You always waded into a situation, doing whatever you thought was right—''

''Whatever I *thought* was right,'' Liz repeated. ''I was wrong half the time.''

''Still, it was a side of you I liked.''

Liz felt a twinge of pain at her grandmother's use of the past tense.

''Do you remember when you were quite small—Jennifer's age—you told me about some boys you saw tormenting a snake in the school yard. They were older than you, but you weren't afraid of them and you weren't afraid of the snake. You just gave them what-for and carried the snake to safety in the woods.''

''Good thing it wasn't poisonous.''

''We don't have any poisonous snakes around here. But you didn't know that, and you didn't give it a moment's thought.''

''I should have.''

Eleanor's voice grew impatient. ''I'm trying to show you something with a parable or whatever, and all you can do is argue.''

Liz stared at the table, ashamed of herself but unable to cooperate.

''Look at that face. Exactly the same face you made when you were three and in the wrong and knew it and were determined to stay there. Sometimes I wonder if we ever grow up at all. We get bigger and pretend to be wiser...''

Liz managed a smile. ''I did understand your parable.''

''Well, that's a start.''

She'd made such a mess of things. Hugging anger

to herself like a prize. What had she thought? That time wasn't passing? That her life had a reset button? Her grandmother was right. It was time to get over it. Maybe that was the real reason she'd come home.

CHAPTER ELEVEN

LIZ WASN'T SURE WHAT GETTING over it entailed, but during the next few days she tried. Each morning, regardless of what the illuminated dial of her wind-up clock told her, she jumped right up, feet warm in the socks she'd worn all night, and dressed quickly, pulling on one of the thick sweaters she'd found in boxes under the eaves. So many sweaters, mostly hand-knitted, cardigans and pullovers, adults' and children's, a history almost as expressive as the family photo albums. She got to the kitchen long before her grandmother, turned on a soft light that made the outside even blacker and started a fire in the woodstove. Before making breakfast, she had a hot drink. She was developing a taste for Eleanor's instant coffee.

She liked being up and productive in the dark morning, in the gradually warming kitchen, with only the dogs for company. The first day she made eggs and sausages and pan fried potatoes, just like Jack, only she was up early enough to cook it from scratch. The next, she dug around in the pantry and freezer and served Eleanor's home canned peaches and warmed biscuits, a dense, sweet kind she remembered from when she was little, flavored with sour cream and nutmeg. The third morning she made porridge with chopped apple and cinnamon.

"Here you are again, my dear. How long have you been awake?"

"I didn't look at the clock. Not long." Liz moved the simmering kettle back onto the heat. The table was already set, including a bowl of brown sugar and jugs of milk and cream. Three baskets from a collection she'd found in the pantry sat in a row in the middle of the table, lined with white cotton napkins and filled with apples and oranges. She whipped the kettle off the stove at the first suggestion of a whistle.

Eleanor took a deep, appreciative sniff when Liz put a bowl of hot cereal in front of her. "It smells like apple crisp. And the table looks lovely. You found my baskets."

Liz carried her bowl of oatmeal to the table. "There was a whole collection on one of the lower shelves in the pantry. Fifteen or twenty of them, all different sizes."

Eleanor moved the napkin so she could feel the edge of the basket closest to her. "Still solid. We made them, you know. My sisters and I."

"You made these baskets?"

"Hats, too. From straw during harvest."

"Did you really?" Liz took a closer look at the weave. "How?"

"It's quite simple. Time consuming, although nothing really seemed time consuming then. Things just took as long as they took. We soaked the stalks in water so they'd be pliable, then we split them lengthways and pressed them flat. When they were dry, we wove them together."

She made the steps sound easy. Liz looked at the row of baskets, thinking of all the others in the cupboard. "That's a lot of straw stalks." Eleanor had a whole world of experience tucked away inside. Who knew how many generations before her had prepared and woven straw? No one else in the family could do it now.

"Elizabeth?"

"Yes, Grandma?"

Eleanor looked at her steadily for a moment. "Are you managing, dear?"

Liz nodded vigorously. Her grandmother had worried about her long enough. "I'm putting things in perspective."

"Are you really? I only see the same strained face I've seen all week."

"This is what I look like. This is me on a good day."

Eleanor smiled. "I wish I could advise you better than I have."

"Grandma, you've been wonderful."

Both women concentrated on their porridge. Heart to heart talks weren't a usual part of the Robb repertoire, and they'd had several. Eleanor seemed embarrassed whenever another one loomed. "I'm sure you know about the importance of sufficient sleep and fresh air, good food and exercise."

"All things you've been trying to make me do since I got here." Liz hesitated. If she couldn't convince her grandmother she was doing fine, she might as well say what was bothering her.

"My problem is taking that step, the one where you move from being furious with people to being not furious. I just can't do it."

Eleanor added a little more cream and brown sugar to her cereal. "My father would have applauded you. Once someone earned his distrust, he believed in keeping an eye on that person for life."

"So I come by the impulse honestly."

"My mother didn't agree with him, though. Not completely. She believed in keeping an eye on people who gave her a reason, but she also thought she should give them another chance."

It was a smaller step, one Liz might be able to take.

"Of course, that calls for time and a certain amount of togetherness. It's difficult to do long distance."

Liz almost laughed. Her grandmother was more subtle than her uncle, but she was beginning to wonder if they had the same goal. They seemed so sure home and family could fix whatever ailed you. Where did they find that certainty? She wasn't sure of anything. Every time she got her feet under her, something spun out of control again. It was like playing Blind Man's Bluff or Pin the Tail on the Donkey…she was always dizzy and in the dark and unsure where she was going. The oddest thing now was how content she was to be here. Her visit had passed the two week mark a few days ago, but leaving for Vancouver was the last thing on her mind.

JACK HADN'T SAID anything outright about fresh air, exercise or keeping busy, but he came by to take Liz out each afternoon. He didn't mention Andy or ask why in the world she was hanging on to something that had happened so long ago. She was aware that he felt more for her than compassion and that it might be unfair to lean on him, but she couldn't deny herself the comfort he offered.

They went skating on the creek one day and to Pam's classroom to see the children's finished books the next. Today they were going to visit the Christmas tree field. Of course, it looked exactly the same as it had the last time they'd seen it, but now that he was the renter, and not a suspected trespasser, Jack wanted to show it to Liz again.

They drove, even though it was walking distance,

continuing north on the road that followed Eleanor's property line. Bella and Dora lay on a pile of burlap sacks in the back of the truck, sensibly keeping their heads down, out of the cold. The municipality hadn't scattered salt or sand, so the snow looked as clean as it had the day it fell. Rows of tracks wound in and out of the ditches, proof that deer were still in the area.

Jack turned onto the access bridging the ditch and stopped at a barbed wire fence. The concern Liz saw in his face whenever he looked at her disappeared when he turned to the parcel of land that Eleanor had said was his for as long as he wanted. She hadn't offered to sell it to him yet, but Liz thought she was close.

"You can see why this is such a good location."

"I'm not sure I can."

"There's a bit of a slope facing north—balsams like that. It means the field would warm up slowly in the spring, so new growth wouldn't start before the last frost."

"It's close to the big creek, too."

"That might not be good in a really wet year, but it'll give the trees some protection from drought. The surrounding woods will provide a windbreak. This road stays in good shape in all weather, so it should support the traffic for a choose and cut operation."

He pointed out a protected spot near the creek. "I'm planning to build a shack down there, with a wood-stove, and keep a pot of cocoa simmering. People could go in to warm up, discuss which tree they want to cut. I thought I'd keep a section of the creek cleared so they could go skating, too."

"You could sell homemade decorations, get local craftspeople involved," Liz said, catching his enthu-siasm. "Oh! You could sell baking, the traditional treats a lot of people don't have time to make any-more. Gingerbread men and plum pudding and mince tarts.''

''That's getting a little cuter than I envisioned. I'm seeing an outdoor experience.''

''More shooting your own goose while you get your tree?''

''Hm,'' he said doubtfully. ''More hide in a blind and take pictures of them.''

''Oh, *real* he-man stuff. But Jack...an eight year wait.'' Far into a future where she didn't fit.

''It's not that long, Liz. Not with the other crops to see to in the meantime. The next six months will be hard, though. I want to see my field without snow. I want to start digging.'' He backed up onto the road. ''How about a hot drink at my place?''

''Sounds good.''

He checked the dogs through the cab's rear window, then accelerated, heading south. Bella and Dora stood up when the truck turned down Jack's driveway and jumped out as soon as it came to a stop. They rushed around the back of the house, following a set of foot-prints.

''Company?'' Liz asked.

''I hope not. I think those are just my tracks.''

They followed the dogs and found them sniffing around some foundation shrubs.

''Mice?''

''Probably. And other intruders.'' Jack held back a few branches so Liz could see a plywood door. ''That friend of mine who made you so uncomfortable the day I was in Brandon? This is how he got in. Under the addition and into the cellar, then up through the trapdoor in the kitchen.''

She had assumed the friend had found a key. ''What

an odd thing to do. Most people would leave a note. 'Sorry I missed you. Catch you next time.'''

Jack's face showed a mix of affection and aggravation. ''Reid loves games. They're a passion for him, to the extent that most people would say they're not games anymore. Coming to my house when I'm not here, finding some convoluted way in, making sure I notice he did it...that's all vintage Reid.''

''And is that the game in itself? Or is there more to it?''

Jack indicated the dogs, darting toward them, then leaping away. Dora used her nose to toss snow into the air, then bit the flakes as they came back down. ''Think of Reid scampering around out there. He's trying to interest me in playing.''

Liz smiled at the picture. ''Are you going to play?''

''Reluctantly. I've prepared something that should keep him busy for a while.''

She was curious about what that might be, but Jack didn't elaborate. ''He must have been poking around your place for a while to have found this way in.''

''That bothers me, too.'' He touched a gloved hand to her nose. ''Let's go in, Rudolph.''

''What about the second man?'' she asked on the way to the door. ''You haven't mentioned him.''

He'd stiffened. It was hardly noticeable, but she always seemed to catch his changes of mood. ''I don't know who Reid brought with him.''

''Well, that's just plain rude. If I were you I wouldn't go along with it.''

''I've almost changed my mind several times.'' He shrugged. ''I guess I have a soft spot for Reid.''

She hung her coat beside his on the hat stand. Jack added a couple of logs to the embers smoldering in the Franklin stove, then stood with his hands near the heat. He wouldn't offer her coffee this late in the day. It was his contribution to solving her sleep problems. Liz went to the cupboard herself. ''Do you have cocoa?''

''How about warm milk?''

''It's not that late!''

''I can froth it with the cappuccino machine, add a drop of vanilla and a sprinkle of nutmeg. Not so shabby. Sit by the stove and I'll get it for you.''

The dogs had already claimed the hearth, so Liz moved a chair as close to the stove as she could without disturbing them. As usual, the table was full of paperwork. Not just work this time. Handwritten music, too. ''Do you write your own songs, Jack?''

''If you're using the word 'songs,' I'd have to say no.''

She picked up one of the sheets. Enforced piano lessons were a murky part of her childhood. Mentally, she ran through a few bars of the music. ''I guess I don't remember how the notes should sound—this doesn't seem all that tuneful.''

He glanced at the paper she held. ''That one's an unfortunate experiment. A friend of mine told me that algebra is the basis of some modern compositions. I thought I'd give it a whirl.'' He handed her a mug of steamed milk, fragrant with nutmeg. He'd made some for himself, too.

The kitchen chairs were too close together. Liz's body was still on a low hum from that light-hearted touch on the nose. It wasn't right. Not for him, when her mind was half with Andy, and not for Andy. ''Let's sit in the living room.''

She led the way. He'd started painting the week before and he'd already done nearly the whole downstairs, the same off-white everywhere. He said he liked the simplicity, and the way the shade changed in different light. ''It's really coming along in here, Jack. No nail holes is a good look for the room.''

Jack pretended to throw a cushion at her.

''Now all you need is a vacuum. Maybe I'll get you one for Christmas.''

''Will you be here at Christmas?''

The question caught her by surprise. It shouldn't have—there shouldn't be any doubt that she'd be in her apartment or visiting her parents in White Rock. ''I suppose not. I'll have to leave your present with Grandma to put under your tree.'' She chose the armchair so there was no chance of him ending up beside her. ''When I called my landlord he asked how much longer I'd be away, and I couldn't tell him. But I'll have to go back eventually, won't I?''

''Not necessarily.''

''Grandma and I will never finish going through her things. We haven't even looked in the garage or the storehouse or the garden shed or the barn. There's a limit to how much her life can be tidied up. I can either stop helping at some point, or I can stay forever, packing boxes and drinking tea.''

''That sounds all right. As long as it's herbal in the afternoon.'' Jack smiled. ''So, within reason, you've done all you came to do.''

''There's one thing I haven't done.''

''What's that?''

''I've never heard you play your guitar.''

Jack put his mug on the coffee table. ''At last, something I can fix!'' He brushed past her to pick up the instrument and took it to the sofa, where he had lots of room for knees and elbows and the guitar's long neck. As soon as he settled it over his leg and felt for the strings, she could see he played often. He ran his fingertips up and down, strumming variations on the scale.

"It already sounds pretty, even when it's just notes."

"I got my first guitar from a secondhand store off Henderson Highway. Fifteen dollars. That was a big chunk of my newspaper delivery earnings, so I thought my uncle would be mad. Luckily for me, it turned out he liked the sound, too."

A moment later Liz recognized "Silent Night." It was beautiful on guitar, the instrument it had been written for originally, when the organ in a German church broke down for Christmas Eve. Jack played three verses, then moved without pausing to music that sounded Spanish, then to a sixties folk song. The music stopped her thinking. It was a relief to have her mind quiet.

A few bars into a new piece, she realized he was playing a simplified Beethoven sonata. "Pathetique." She only knew what it was because she had tried to learn it in the last year of her piano lessons. Even then, botched and clumsy, it had touched her. Funny how some music made you feel the worst and the best at once, the saddest of possibilities and the most hopeful. His long fingers brushed the strings, and the notes fell one by one on the air, peaceful and sorrowful at the same time.

When it stopped, Liz heard herself say, "I didn't tell you everything about the night Andy died."

"Oh?" Jack sat still, the guitar quiet on his leg.

Now she couldn't say it. It was the one thing she'd never admitted. She'd always known it was there, the monster at the back of the closet, but she'd refused to look at it all this time. It made the whole story a lie.

"Liz?"

"I should go home." Taking care not to spill her milk, she put her mug on the table. Bella and Dora watched her stand, their dark eyes showing what seemed to be endless depths of worry.

Liz smiled shakily. "Look at them. Do they really know, or are they just mood rings?"

"They know." Jack stood a comfortable distance away. "You don't have to run off just because you're upset. We're better friends than that."

"Maybe not if I told you everything."

"About Andy? I think you need to tell somebody. You're bursting."

She wanted to stay. This wasn't a confessional, though. It wasn't a therapist's office. The problem didn't have a solution. There was no point. She sat down and Jack went back to the sofa. The dogs sat, too, still watching.

"Andy didn't stand up for himself," she began.

"When Wayne provoked him?"

"He just stood there, listening. Everybody knew not to listen to Wayne, especially at parties or dances when he was drinking, but Andy listened. As if he believed what he was hearing."

Jack didn't say anything.

"Do you see?" The picture was clear as could be in her mind. "He was standing at the top of the hill, looking into the gravel pit and he hesitated. He didn't smile or laugh, he wasn't playing. Maybe he saw how far away the water was, how shallow. Maybe he was thinking it wasn't such a good idea. So they said, *'He's afraid.'* And he didn't stand up for himself. So I said, *'He's not afraid.'*"

"You mean he had to prove he wasn't afraid."

"For me." Her voice was unsteady. "I wanted my

outsider boy of a husband to prove himself. He didn't have a choice."

"Sure he did."

"You don't get it—"

"I get it." Jack sat forward. "You were young and a little unsure of yourself and your judgment left something to be desired."

"And he died."

He didn't absolve her. "That must be very hard to live with."

Her eyes closed.

"Liz." He spoke softly. She couldn't believe how kind he sounded. "It would be nice if we never did anything wrong. No regrets, no mistakes. Unfortunately that isn't possible. So, it would be nice if our mistakes never hurt anyone. But that isn't possible either. Emotions were high that night. A series of bad judgments were made, by a lot of people. Including you and Wayne and Andy. My parents made a bad judgment years ago. They went out for groceries during a blizzard. The next week I spent my sixth birthday with my uncle, wondering where they were."

"Jack—"

"Do you think I was never mad at them, or never found a way to blame myself? Bad things happen. The point isn't to blame yourself to the end of days, the point is to find a way out of it."

"I can't see any way out of it. Grandma says I should let it go. Move on."

Again Jack was silent.

"You don't agree?"

"How can I? The only acceptable thing would be to undo what happened. Repair the mistake. I can't undo it."

"No, you can't."

He made it sound even more final than it already did in her own mind. "I don't feel like part of the modern world, sometimes. People are always talking about forgiveness and healing. It's so..." Her voice trailed off.

"Restful?"

"Trite."

His eyebrows went up. "Well...that sounds very tough, but I don't like where it leaves you."

She almost smiled. "Me, neither."

"Your grandmother told me what happened after the accident."

"You mean that nobody cared?"

"That you left because you blamed the whole town."

"I shouldn't have. Except for Wayne. And what I did was worse."

"Ah, you're into the self-flagellation stage. If I hadn't complained that there wasn't any peanut butter..." Jack picked up the guitar and played a few bars of "Pathétique." "When I first heard this on the radio—I was fifteen, I think—it blew me away. Even now it's one of my favorite pieces. You know why?"

She shook her head.

"It reminds me that we're capable of so much more than most of us ever bother to reach for. Do you find that? Some music makes you feel like a better person."

"Or like you should be a better person."

Jack stopped playing. "There's an idea people used to have—I mean, a long time ago, 1500s—that we're all on a ladder balanced between the animals and the angels. We yearn to reach higher, climb higher, but something always pulls us down."

"You're telling me to climb the ladder."

"Don't you want to?"

More than anything, she wanted to. Her throat felt too tight to say so. She nodded.

"Then let go of what's pulling you down and climb."

"It's not that simple!"

"When you're ready, it's exactly that simple."

"When you're ready. That's the hard part, then. Climbing up to Beethoven's angels is easy. Being ready is hard."

"They weren't Beethoven's angels—"

"It's like one of Grandma's cookbooks."

Jack almost laughed. "What does cooking have to do with angels?"

"I don't remember which book it is, I just remember Grandma reading this part to me, years ago. You know how the recipe for rabbit stew starts? *First catch your rabbit.*"

They both smiled.

"Liz, you've built your life in a certain way and all of a sudden it doesn't fit. You need to build something else."

"So that's it? That's how I climb. I just say, The End."

"And then you turn the page."

Closing the book on Andy.

LIZ PULLED A CARDIGAN OVER the turtleneck she already wore and moved her worktable and chair away from the cold zone around the window. It had been an unsettling afternoon. She could hardly wait to open her sketchbook and start drawing.

Her mind was so full, images seemed to run from it to her hand and out the pencil. The woodland fairies first. She decided to give Jack the battle he wanted. A gargoyleish Wayne Cooper appeared in front of him and without wasting a second, Jack's character ran him through with a very sharp stick. Right away, she felt guilty. The least she could do was handle Wayne herself. She erased Jack's weapon, then sketched her character swooping down from a nearby tree on a drooping branch, stick-sword poised to pierce through Wayne's nonexistent heart. *Take that, you beast of the mud burrows!* Liz smiled at the satisfying, cartoonish thought, then quickly drew a healing fairy to patch him up.

Next, Andy's mallard appeared, uninjured and floating in the creek, then flying. In the middle of some woods, a deer, and behind it, the cabin with ants in the logs and mice in the corner and the tree growing from the roof. Finally, Andy. Even though she had the photograph now, she couldn't get him right. She was drawing the memory of a memory.

She retrieved the photo from the bedside table and brought it over to the light so she could compare it to her sketch. Andy, standing in front of his house in town. Tall, but gangly, his chest and shoulders not yet filled out. Hair longer than the grown-ups liked, and so blond you'd think he was always in the sun. The corners of his mouth were just beginning to curve. She'd clicked too soon.

She remembered the day, she took the picture. It was a hot, still afternoon near the end of July. Later, hail as big as crab apples had fallen, breaking windows and wiping out the north wheat field. She and her mother had stopped by Andy's place with an ice cream pail full of fresh-picked strawberries, as a welcome. It was just after he and his parents and his little sister had moved to Three Creeks. Someone had broken into their house in the city, and even though they hadn't been aware of other straws, that was the last one. They wanted to live in a place where they would know their neighbors, where people still smiled when they saw each other and said hello.

She'd never met anyone like him. He'd been to art show openings in Winnipeg's warehouse district, where she wasn't allowed to go without an adult. With some friends, he'd gone on a road trip to Toronto to see six Van Gogh paintings…all that way to see six paintings. He'd never played baseball or hockey in his life and didn't care if anyone found that strange. He wanted to be a wildlife artist. When she'd heard that she'd invited him home to see her drawings. He'd leafed through the sketches of family horses and dogs, and then he'd asked where she planned to study.

"Study drawing, you mean?"

"Yeah. I'm going to the Emily Carr school in Vancouver."

Liz didn't have any idea what she wanted to do after high school. Susannah planned to be a paleontologist—she'd settled on that when she was ten. Pam was going to be an elementary schoolteacher, so she wouldn't have to move away when it was time to get a job. Emily vacillated between the two options. Liz liked baseball and swimming, so when people asked she always said she was going to be a gym teacher, and they always said it was a good choice. "Can you make money drawing?"

"Probably not." Andy had grinned, as if making money was the last thing that mattered. Later, curled up on her bed with a polite distance and her stack of drawings between them, he had suggested they could go to Vancouver together after graduation in June. Find an apartment with a view of the ocean—get as many roommates as they needed to afford the rent—

and buy fresh fish at Granville Market every day. They could watch ships come in from all over the world. Maybe they'd even see whales. Everything about him had surprised her. Falling for him was easy.

She wouldn't ever say it out loud, not to anyone, but sometimes she wondered if it would have lasted. They'd known each other for less than a year. They never would have come to dislike each other, but they might have grown apart as they grew up. How would they have handled it? Not with anger and recriminations, she was sure of that. She could see Andy studying the problem with that frown he'd always got in physics class and saying something casual like, "Think we should forget about it, Liz?" He'd have some story to tell her, something about an artist who'd wandered the world in search of life, but who never stopped loving the woman he'd left behind.

Was she wrong to hold people responsible for what happened? That day on the swing, when they'd all crowded on, she had been calling for even more kids to join them when the adults had intervened. If the branch or the rope had broken, if someone had been hurt, would she have been blamed? When you knew what you were doing was risky, were the consequences still an accident? The two incidents weren't the same, though. There was no hostility on the swing.

She couldn't sit, she couldn't keep still. Liz paced to the window. How could you turn the page if you were at the end of the book? If you turned the page at the end of the book you didn't get more story, you got an index or the author's acknowledgments or advertisements for books to come.

There was a poem—she couldn't remember the title—that told the story of the Norse Gods. They'd all died after a shattering final battle, and the world died with them. The very end of the poem was unexpected. After reams of death and defeat, the earth reemerged, all fresh and sunlit green. It had been such a relief to read that.

Liz didn't know how long she stood at the window remembering Andy, letting each day they'd spent together sift through her mind. It was the middle of the night when she brought lamps and tables from the other upstairs bedrooms and began sketching, her hand moving so fast she kept dropping the pencil.

At the end of the week she spread the finished paintings across the bedroom floor. Twenty in all, on watercolor paper, eleven inches by seventeen. Each held more detail than she'd ever managed to record before, a close-up of some aspect of woodlands life. The leafy canopy of poplar, maple, elm and oak with variations of shape and shade, full of the life it sustains. The forest floor, with layered grasses hiding rodent holes. A funnel spiderweb, glistening after rain. In each painting, a boy stood or sat or crouched, watching, or drawing what he saw.

She could almost feel Andy beside her, focused, interested, telling her how much her technique had improved. His drawing from the school library would be the cover, and the text would be his, too, as much as she could remember of his eager spilling of nature facts. "Did you know prairie dogs keep separate rooms down there, Liz? It's like an underground house. Nurseries, pantries, bathrooms. They're very clean, very social..."

The paintings blurred. It was the best she could do. All she could do.

She went to her worktable. Flipping past drawings of her grandmother and Tom and Jack and the view outside, she found a blank page and tore it from her sketchbook. She pressed the top of the paper down toward the middle, and the bottom up to meet it, then folded in the sides. After one last look at Andy's photo, she tucked it into the makeshift envelope and placed it at the bottom of her overnight bag.

CHAPTER TWELVE

AT LAST, THINGS WERE LOOKING UP. That morning, two weeks to the day after it hit, the virus deleted itself. No explanation, no goodbyes. The cracker program was zipping along, breaking each password in seconds. *Baseball. Summer. Home Run. You're Out.* It was pathetic. Jack was using stream of consciousness passwords, backed up by a time-limited, and therefore toothless, virus.

Despite their intriguing names, like *myprogram.doc* and *secure.exe,* most of the files Reid had managed to open so far were empty. Others contained pages of elementary computer code. It looked as if Jack had just pasted in old school assignments. Maybe he had. Along with the couple hundred easy passwords and the short-lived virus, it might have been protection enough from some people.

Reid, on the other hand, was determined to see this through. If there was a valuable file guarded by a real password somewhere on this crowded diskette, he would find it. And when he opened that file, Croker would have to swallow all the things he'd never quite said over the past two weeks. That would almost be reward enough. Almost. He'd also like to hear an admission that it didn't matter one bit whether or not he'd known about Jack's Winnipeg apartment. A dust mite by dust mite search hadn't turned up a thing.

Reid leaned in to look at the monitor more closely.

After ripping along through about a hundred and fifty passwords, the cracker program had slowed down. The password on a file called *xn.210.exe* was offering a challenge. He waited, trying to talk himself out of the anticipation he was starting to feel.

It took nearly an hour, but the password fell. This one was a little different: *319-B_mnr.* Jack's address on Munroe Avenue growing up, with the vowels removed and the underscore symbol thrown in. It was stronger than most of the passwords Jack had chosen. Even more interesting were the numerals and letters on the screen when Reid opened the file.

The human radar lurking in the next room appeared in the doorway. "Got something?"

Reid kept his tone noncommittal. "Something."

Croker strode to the desk and stared at the unreadable text. "It's encrypted? Run the program. Break it."

Reid worked to avoid any trace of sarcasm. "Decrypt the algorithm with the password cracking software?"

"How do you handle it then?"

Reid took a few seconds to enjoy Croker's uncertainty. "We brute-force it, with a different program. You get the idea? We basically take a battering ram to the code." An idea struck him, and he laughed quietly.

"What now?"

"I'm just wondering if I've underestimated Jack."

"And that's funny?"

Reid laughed again. "The virus was frustrating, but other than that he applied virtually no security. What if everything we've seen so far is window dressing? What if he didn't need an effective password because he used his algorithm to encrypt his algorithm?"

Croker swore. It was under his breath, but it was still an unusual display of emotion, and Reid enjoyed it.

"Use an unbreakable code to encrypt an unbreakable code," Reid continued. "Why didn't we think of that possibility? We'll never get it, if that's what he's done. Well, not until we run it through a supercomputer for a thousand years. You understand, that's an optimistic estimation."

Croker shook his head emphatically. "He wouldn't have done that. He needs to be able to access the code, too. If he recorded the key, what's to stop us from finding it? If he didn't record it, he couldn't be sure of remembering it. Unless there's something you're not telling me, like he's got a photographic memory."

"He's got a lousy memory."

"Then quit wasting time." Croker paced away. His voice was still quiet, but something in it made Reid take notice. He wasn't sure when he'd begun to realize he wasn't in charge of the operation, although he was the one who had approached Croker. At first they'd let him think he was calling the shots. It was a bit embarrassing to discover his ego was that strokable. Gradually, it had dawned on him that he wasn't even an equal partner. He was there because he knew Jack and he knew codes. He'd decided from the beginning not to think about who these people were, but they sure as hell weren't a charitable foundation. What would his status be once he'd given them what they wanted?

Croker must have been counting to ten. Now he said, "Have you started running the appropriate program?"

It was obvious he hadn't. "I'm thinking. It's an added tool we security experts sometimes use." Reid leaned away from the monitor, studying the contents of *xn.210.exe,* trying to see the collection of figures as a whole. It wasn't as random as it had looked at first. There was a pattern. "Huh." It was a short, disbelieving sound that brought Croker to heel.

"What is it?"

Reid didn't answer. He activated his code breaking program and entertained himself by watching the tic beside Croker's eye while they waited for the result. It came much faster than he expected.

"Got it!" Jack had used one of the oldest encryption methods in the book. A simple Caesar-shift substitution cipher. He had shifted three spaces down the alphabet—absolutely, predictably, textbook—using the letter *d* in place of the letter *a,* the letter *e* in place of *b,* and so on. Any Boy Scout could have broken through it.

"About time." Croker pushed a button on his cell phone.

Reid stared at the monitor. "Wait."

Croker looked at him, phone to his ear.

"You'd better hang up." He thought Croker would ignore him. The receiver was a couple of inches away from his ear, but his finger wasn't anywhere near the disconnect button. Reid put a little more force into his tone. "Whoever you keep reporting to doesn't want to hear about this. Hang up."

Croker disconnected. He'd gone perfectly still, the way he did when he was really and truly annoyed. His face was devoid of expression, but his eyes more than made up for it. Reid thought of Roman emperors who killed messengers as a way of managing tension. This guy needed to learn something about dealing with a man like Jack. You put brains and professional pride together with the idea that math was just plain fun, and you got somebody unpredictable. You could look like a coldhearted assassin all you wanted, it wasn't going to get you anywhere.

"What you see on the monitor is an algorithm," Reid told him, talking calmly, like you would to a growling dog. "Just not the right algorithm. It's telling me where to find his next clue."

Okay, Croker hadn't looked like a coldhearted assassin before. He looked like a coldhearted assassin now. "He's stringing us along?"

"He's stringing *me* along." As serious a setback as it was, Reid couldn't help smiling. "He thinks we're playing a game."

AFTER JUST ONE PRACTICE, Jack was about to play in his first old-timers' game. Eleanor and Liz made their way past a circle of girls hunched over cigarettes just outside the community center. Even though smoking wasn't allowed in the building anymore, the smell of old smoke was the first thing Liz noticed when she stepped inside. That, and hot dogs kept warm. And the noise. And the crowd.

Behind the glass, the teams were warming up. It took Liz a moment to spot Jack under all his padding and a helmet. He skated fast, and smoothly, turning and going backward with that easy crossover stroke she'd always seen the boys do, but had never mastered herself. He was smiling, grinning really, and calling across the ice to another player—Martin, she saw, when he glided by the window, looking as if he had never in his life entertained any suspicions of his grandmother's neighbor. Except for Jack, it was a Robb lineup. Tom, Brian and Uncle Will were on the ice, too.

"I'll take these mittens to the tree before we go in,"

Eleanor said. Every November the municipal office put a Christmas tree in the community center that people decked with mitts and toques for kids who didn't have everything they needed to stay warm through the winter. "Will you wait right here? I don't want to lose you."

"I won't budge," Liz promised.

She soon wished she hadn't. Already three ladies had stopped Eleanor on her way to the mitten tree. It would be a while before she returned. The 4-H club was having a bake sale, the Ladies Auxiliary was having a raffle, and a veteran in a blazer and beret was selling poppies for Remembrance Day, but Liz couldn't approach any of them.

"Liz, what a pleasure to see you!" A slender woman of about sixty, wearing a red turtleneck and an unzipped navy ski jacket, stepped through a knot of people Liz didn't know.

"Mrs. Bowen!" Liz reached out eagerly, and the handshake turned into a hug. Her old 4-H leader hadn't made it to the barbecue.

"Call me Jean, if you can bring yourself to do it. I know it's difficult. Don't tell me you knitted that sweater."

"It's my grandmother's handiwork. I found it while we were going through trunks of clothes. In fact, I found a whole new wardrobe!"

"You look wonderful. Vancouver must agree with you. My understanding was that you were only staying for a week or two, though. Did I get that wrong? I hope your grandmother's not having problems."

Daniel Rutherford joined them in time to interrupt. "Can't tear herself away now that she's here. I know the feeling. When I got out of the Service, after all the places I'd been, there was nowhere I'd rather settle down."

Liz jumped at the sound of a slapshot ricocheting off the boards. The teams were five minutes into the game, and she hadn't noticed. It was a shot off Jack's net. He and the other team's right-winger reached the puck at the same time. Jack leaned in, rubbing his opponent against the boards, then hooked the puck with his stick, wheeled and whipped a pass across the ice, straight to Tom.

"Knows what he's doing," Daniel said. "On the ice, anyway."

Jean had gone closer to the glass to watch the action, so Liz and Daniel were as alone as they could be in the crowded lobby.

"He's told you, has he?"

Liz stared at Daniel. Did he mean Jack? "Told me what?"

"No? Never mind, then." He began to move away.

"Daniel! You can't say something like that and then leave."

Some men Daniel knew were on their way to the bleachers. He hovered, clearly eager to go with them. "I spoke out of turn. Just..." He hesitated, an unusual thing for Daniel. "Be careful."

"Be careful of what?"

But Daniel had moved out of hearing.

"Miss Robb! Hey, Miss Robb." A very small boy was making his way toward her, dragging along an adult version of himself. It was Jeremy, from Pam's class. Once he reached her side, shyness struck. He looked at her boots, muttering, "This is my dad."

Jeremy's dad reached out to shake Liz's hand. "Scott," he said. "Jeremy's been talking about you and that book-making project for a couple of weeks now.''

''I'm glad he enjoyed it. He told me you've worked with my grandmother's neighbor. Jack McKinnon.''

''A little, in the summer.'' Scott stopped to cough, turning away to use a wad of tissue. Liz found herself taking a couple of steps back. Flu season had started. It was the last thing her grandmother needed.

Eleanor had almost worked her way back from the mitten tree, a couple of trays of cookies from the 4-H table in hand. In spite of the crush of people she looked at ease and happy. Was there a chance she wouldn't mind being in town, with a little more hustle and bustle? Liz said goodbye to Jeremy and his father. When she turned away from Jeremy she came face to face with Wayne Cooper.

''Finally!'' he said. ''You're really hard to connect with, considering how small this town is.'' He made a face, half smile, half grimace. ''Unless you've been avoiding me on purpose. I've been wanting to talk to you.''

''There you are!'' Eleanor said. ''Shall we find a seat in the bleachers, my dear? Jack and Thomas want to see us there looking impressed, I think, and of course William never tires of showing off for me. Excuse us, Wayne.''

Gratefully Liz followed her grandmother, exchanging the heat and smoke of the lobby for the chill and sweat of the rink. The stands were nearly full. There were real fans, ready to scream themselves hoarse at the slightest excuse, and there were those who were willing to shiver in the seats to show their support, but who much preferred talking about hairstyles and boyfriends and offspring. The Pine Point supporters were on the other side of the ice. On both sides, preschoolers climbed up the stands and down, and no one other than Liz seemed worried that they'd fall.

A man Liz didn't recognize tapped her on the shoulder. "Your fella's doing a great job out there."

Fella? Jack? "He's not my—"

"We needed another strong forward. Pine Point's got two guys who played a season in the NHL. They made mincemeat of us last year."

"We're holding our own this time," she said, as the man moved away.

"That we are," a new voice agreed. It was Wayne. Eleanor had moved to talk to Edith, so he sat in the place she'd vacated. "You and McKinnon are the hardest people to get hold of. Seems to me every time I see either of you, you end up going in the opposite direction."

Why would he expect otherwise? Even before the gravel pit, Liz had never stopped to chat with Wayne. If she'd so much as paused beside him she'd ended up with a sign on her back or gum in her hair or her bra strap snapped.

She couldn't speak to him. She couldn't even look at him. So much for climbing ladders.

"Maybe you could tell him for me, my kid had a great time making his jack-o'-lantern at school. His teacher said McKinnon donated all those pumpkins." Out of the corner of her eye, Liz saw Wayne's head nod up and down as he talked. "That was nice. Real nice."

Liz kept her eyes on the center line. Her choices were as clear as if they were written down in front of her. She could walk away. She could punch him in the face with every bit of strength she had. Or she could try to be polite.

"I'll tell him," she said.

"Liz?"

He'd lowered his voice. She could hardly hear him. "What is it, Wayne?"

"Do you still think about Andy?"

The crowd roared its approval of a developing rush. It was Jack and Martin and Tom, racing up the ice together. Even Eleanor called out excitedly.

"Liz?" Wayne's voice sounded urgent.

Her hand had made a fist all by itself. She kept it on her lap. "Of course I do."

"Me, too." He talked faster. "Stupidest thing I ever did. I almost told you I was sorry, but that didn't seem right. That's what you say when you bump into somebody. But I am sorry, Liz. If I could have backed up...I kept thinking that afterward. Just back up a few seconds..."

He exhaled heavily. "Well, that's what I wanted to say. God. For fifteen years, I've wanted to say that. Funny thing is, it doesn't help a bit."

And he was gone.

Funny, it didn't help her, either. Liz concentrated hard on the game. The Robb line must have scored. The ref was dropping the puck again. The Pine Point center got it that time, shot it to his right wing and after that she couldn't see to tell what happened next. There were cheers in the bleachers on the other side of the rink, then groans. Blurred figures swished by, skating fast toward the Pine Point goal.

Someone tucked a handkerchief into her hand. "Do you want to leave? I can take you home." It was Mrs. Bowen.

Liz shook her head. She just needed a moment to get sorted out. She used the hanky to mop her face. "Thank you."

"All right now?"

Liz nodded. "He's sorry."

"Of course he is."

"It doesn't make any difference." As soon as she said it, she knew it wasn't true. Wayne's apology had left a huge hole inside her. The place where she'd hated him for so long was empty.

JACK SKATED TO THE BOARDS after the game and waited for Liz to make her way through the crowd to join him. Other players were there, too, lining up along the Three Creeks side of the rink. She squeezed past Martin giving Nell a kiss and Pam and Jennifer talking to an elated Tom.

"Congratulations!" She'd never seen Jack grin before. His skates gave him a few extra inches, so she had to tilt her head back to get a good look at him.

"Thanks! What a great game." He leaned on the boards, bringing his face to her level. "Did you see your brother set up Brian?"

"I must have missed it."

"It was amazing. He had two guys on him and he still got the puck right to Brian's stick. I'm going to hang around here for a while. We all sit in the dressing room now in our underwear, reeking and drinking beer."

Liz smiled. "That sounds like a good time. I wish I could join you."

Pam reached over to hook her arm through Liz's. "Too bad. You're coming with me. Anyone who doesn't need a shower is invited to your grandmother's for a cold roast dinner."

Liz had smelled a roast cooking the day before and wondered how the two of them were going to get through it by themselves. Hadn't she learned from that huge plate of waffles?

A houseful of Robbs didn't seem like such a bad thing right now. There were times when her family's noise was comforting, the way mountains were comforting. She needed something to keep her from her own thoughts for a while. Wayne had left her with an odd, dangling feeling. No one but Mrs. Bowen had noticed the two of them talking, at least no one had mentioned it. She found herself wondering what people who'd lived here for the last fifteen years thought of Wayne. Had he changed? "Of course he's sorry," Mrs. Bowen had said. Liz wouldn't have assumed he was capable of remorse. What did you do when your enemy lost its teeth?

Between dinner and tea, most of the group found its way up to Liz's bedroom. Even Aunt Julia wanted to see the paintings of Andy in the woods. Liz had already called her editor about the pictures and was planning to send them to Vancouver by courier. If they were going to be in a book, in stores and libraries, on shelves in people's houses, it didn't make much sense to want to hide them. All kinds of protective urges went through Liz's mind anyway. She wanted to push the paintings under the bed or into a closet, or throw a sheet over them, or throw herself in front of the bedroom door.

"Right there, against the wall," she said, pointing.

Aunt Edith was first into the room. "How lovely! So green." She walked closer to the first picture. "Those are the woods north of here, aren't they? Yes, because that's the path to the cabin." She leaned even closer, her posture mirroring Andy's. "What's he looking at? Oh! Wild strawberries." The tiny red fruit was nearly hidden in grass and old leaves. "There's nothing sweeter than a wild strawberry. We'll have to go out there in the summer and pick some. It's years since I did that.''

Pam stopped beside the fifth painting, in which Andy balanced on a tree that had fallen over the little creek. ''Is that a real tree, the one we used to walk over?''

''Of course it's real,'' Emily said. ''It's all real.''

''All these things happened?'' Edith asked, walking slowly from one painting to the next. ''Andy found a fawn lying in the grass?''

Liz nodded. ''He nearly walked on top of it. Newborn fawns don't have a scent that would attract predators, so their mothers hide them and stay away except to feed them.'' Andy had explained it to her.

''And he got that close to a ruffed grouse?'' Edith said. ''I didn't know he liked the woods so much. What a very observant young man he must have been. And you, too, Liz, not a man, of course, but to have noticed all this. I know I wouldn't. Julia would. She notices details. And Sue does, but only about creatures that have been dead for a long time.''

Pat had wandered over to the table where Liz usually worked. She held up an open sketchbook. ''What's this, Liz? Some kind of insect?''

''Insect?'' Liz realized she sounded indignant and tried to tone it down. ''It's a fairy.''

Now everyone was looking. Five heads shook in disagreement. Pam cocked her head to study the figure at a different angle. ''That's not a fairy, Liz.''

''It's a stick with a face,'' Pat said.

Liz tried to explain. ''It's a very old kind of fairy.''

''Fairies don't age, do they?'' Aunt Edith asked.

''I mean ancient. Primeval. A spirit of the woods. *F-a-e-r-i-e.* That kind of fairy.''

Aunt Julia said, ''I suppose you mean a dryad.''

Dryad? The word gave Liz a jolt. Her sticklike fairies weren't her own invention?

"Tree spirits from Greek mythology," Julia went on, as if reciting. "Female and beautiful, immortal unless the tree they belong to is cut down."

Liz relaxed. "Well, these aren't female and beautiful. These are something else altogether. Don't you think Grandma must be missing us?" She started to the door, hoping the others would follow. When they didn't she said something about the tea being steeped by now, and next thing she knew she was last on the stairs.

A tea tray waited on the dining room table, but Eleanor was in the kitchen, with a box of photographs. She held it in the air when she saw Liz and Pam. "I have something to show you two while you're both here." She ran her hand over the table, checking for damp spots and crumbs, then put the box down. The photo of herself in the drapery dress was near the top. She handed it to Pam. "Liz has seen this, but I don't think you have, Pamela. I was sixteen when that was taken."

"You look older. And glamorous."

"I was on my way to a dance. They wouldn't have let me in if they'd known my age, and no doubt Albert wouldn't have taken me. He had just turned twenty-one, and he was feeling very adult."

"Albert?" Pam asked.

Eleanor smiled at the photo. Liz had the feeling she was seeing Albert rather than herself. "I remember thinking his eyes were as blue as the sky and his hair as gold as ripe wheat. It would take a sixteen-year-old to think that, wouldn't it?"

"He sounds gorgeous." Liz didn't want to hear any more. The story had an ill-fated sound. Maybe he had been killed at Dieppe. A number of local boys had been.

Pam had no such worries. ''What happened to him?''

Eleanor rummaged in the box again and pulled out another photograph. She put it down beside the first one.

''Is that him?'' Liz could see what had attracted her grandmother. He looked as if he'd spent his life in a wide-open sunny field.

''But that's…Eleanor. Did you date my grandfather?''

Eleanor looked so pleased to have surprised them. ''He came to town with a threshing gang during harvest and stayed. I'd never seen such a handsome man. And he could jitterbug, besides.''

Now that Liz knew, she could see the resemblance between the Albert of the 1930s and the one she'd always known. ''But how could he choose Pam's grandma over you? Sorry, Pam.''

''She was quite exotic—''

Pam snorted.

''Compared to the girls around here, Pamela, she was. Her family left Europe between the wars. She had an accent and seemed mysterious, from another world. She was closer to Albert in age, ready to marry. They were happy for a very long time. As your grandfather and I were, Elizabeth.''

''I thought maybe you went off to see the Prince of Wales in your curtain dress.''

''Not that year.'' Eleanor laughed at their startled expressions. ''I could tell you anything, couldn't I? It's a benefit of age.'' She tucked the two photographs back into the box and fit the lid over top.

''I'll put it away, Grandma.''

In the living room, Liz stepped over Emily's stretched-out legs and returned the box of pictures to its place in the hutch cupboard. She heard snippets of a few quiet conversations. Nell's reluctance to sleep through the night was being discussed again.

"She'll be fine," Aunt Edith said.

"I know *she'll* be fine," Pat replied, a bit tartly. "It's Martin and I who aren't fine."

Brian's wife, Sandy, sat across the room. "Imagine," she said, "our last Christmas in this house. Six weeks and it'll be over. We'll have to get a really special tree and give the place a proper send-off."

Six weeks. That wasn't too soon to start baking and shopping. Liz realized she had no intention of going back to Vancouver for the holidays. She wanted to be here helping her grandmother with the plum pudding and joining everyone to decorate the family tree. She'd have to let her parents know right away. Maybe they would come back, too.

It wasn't until the others had left and the house was quiet that Liz remembered Daniel's cryptic warning at the arena. She had forgotten to ask Jack if he knew why Daniel thought she should be careful.

CROKER HADN'T STUCK AROUND for an explanation of the mathematical game Reid and Jack had played during high school and university. He'd left the office with his entourage of goons, and stayed away for the rest of the day. Reid divided his time between deliberating the wisdom of smashing the Collected Garbage of Jack McKinnon, plus a serious here's mud in your eye infection, and listening for the sound of the door.

He'd gone to them, with promises. One of those friend of a friend of a friend situations. Or it might be more accurate to say a shadowy figure known to an acquaintance who worked at another computer security company. But he'd gone to them, that was the thing. He'd promised to deliver the encryption algorithm of their dreams. It was a gutsy move, even for him. Or a stupid one. That was the problem with taking a gamble—you never knew which it was until you saw the outcome. It would help if he could be sure brass knuckles wouldn't be part of the equation.

Jack had always been the careful one. The way he looked at it, gambling on your future could send it swirling down the drain. You just worked, step after step after step, until you had scholarships and degrees and a dream business.

And then, apparently, you threw it away. You got what everybody else wanted, then turned your back on it to be Johnny Appleseed, of all things.

Maybe Croker and his people would cut their losses. If they did, should he keep trying to find the code on his own? He didn't even know if he could market it safely without help. Whether or not he kept looking for it, should he play along with the game? If he didn't, Jack might get suspicious. The worst thing would be if he called to see what was happening. Then Reid would have to be a snake to his face, a much different proposition than being one behind his back.

They weren't friends. That was the thing to remember. They'd been classmates for years, since before junior high, competitors for marks and scholarships and theorem proofs. That didn't mean they were friends.

About seven o'clock, when Reid was about to go and grab a burger, Croker came back to the office. No goons. The tic beside his eye was gone. Reid wondered if he'd met with whoever was on the other side of his cell phone, or if he'd just gone for a long walk, kicking his way through the snowdrifts. It was a picture he liked, leather-clad Croker communing with nature.

Croker went to the window, hardly glancing at Reid as he went by the desk. After a few minutes of staring silently at the opposite rooftop, he turned, leaned against the sill and started talking, his voice and face as flat as cardboard.

"Here's where we stand. I've got you taking care of technical problems and offering insights on McKinnon's psychology. I've got Webb mingling with the locals in Three Creeks, picking up useless gossip and telling me when McKinnon's going shopping. After weeks of time and effort and investment, we don't know anything." Croker raised his hand, stopping his own listing of facts. "Let me correct myself. We know he knows we were in his house."

"He knows I was in his house. I tried to tell you, we played these math games all the time in the old days. Treasure hunts. Puzzles. You solve one, it leads you to another—"

Croker didn't want to hear about the old days. "If McKinnon had the code he would have hit the roof when he saw that someone had been in his house. He wouldn't start playing games. So he must have destroyed the code. You said he wouldn't do that. You were certain."

Abandoning his rule not to be first to break eye contact with Croker, Reid looked away. He held his fingers to his aching eyes, then rubbed his forehead and temples. He could probably get into the Guinness Book of World Records with this headache.

One more try. His neck muscles were so tight. Burning. "Jack saw that someone was in his house looking for something. What did he conclude? That it was me, starting a game, the way we used to do. He didn't conclude it was someone after the code. If he knows I was searching his house, and he isn't worried about me finding the code, then you're right, he doesn't have it with him. I see two possibilities. Either he destroyed it, which I still don't believe, or it's hidden somewhere else. Anywhere else. In a locker at the bus station. In a bank vault. At RCMP headquarters. In his neighbor's sewing basket. I don't know. And I don't know how we find it.'' There. He'd said it. He'd admitted he was of no further use to them.

Croker had stared at Reid without blinking during his whole speech. ''Or…maybe McKinnon knows exactly what we're doing. Maybe he knows you better than you know him. All this idiocy about games could just be distraction. We need to check for post offices boxes, safety deposit boxes, more hidden real estate. Places he might stash the code, people who might know about it. Colleagues, business partners. Who does he talk to? Who matters to him?''

CHAPTER THIRTEEN

THE BORDER COLLIE PICKED UP the puck and ran. Two small figures took off after the dog, but they didn't stand a chance of catching him. Laughing, Uncle Will turned as Jack's truck drew into the yard. He waved and started kicking the goal-marking stones out of the way. Jack eased ahead, stopping near the path to the back door.

"That dog has taken every ball and puck we have," Will said, when the truck's doors opened. "Don't know where he keeps them. Got something for me to carry?" He took a casserole from Eleanor, then helped her to the ground, nearly lifting her down. He put out a hand for Jack's pies.

"With apologies," Jack said. "It's not really the season for it anymore, but it was this or pumpkin soup."

"Any season's right for pumpkin pie," Will said.

"That's the last of them, I promise."

"Until next year," Tom said gloomily.

Jennifer sat on the back step, hunched up inside her parka. Two small fuzzy heads were just visible inside its folds. In the month since she had started her campaign to get the kittens into the house they'd grown enough that it was almost time to call them cats.

Eleanor, Liz and Jack stopped in front of her. Eleanor said, "You shouldn't sit on cold cement."

Jennifer nodded grimly. "No one should be on cold

cement. They won't listen, though. My opinion doesn't mean a thing around here. As if these little kittens can survive a whole winter outside. What about when it's forty below? It's cruel. I should report them to the Humane Society. I will." Tears welled up in her eyes, so she clamped her mouth shut and stared at her boots. Liz heard one loud sniff.

"Ah, sweetheart," she began, but then the back door opened, and Pam leaned outside.

"You're just in time! The game's about to start." It was Grey Cup Sunday, a good excuse for a potluck dinner.

Young Will and Anne raced for the door, edging past the grown-ups and kicking off their boots as they went inside. "We found his hiding place! Right in the middle of the caragana bushes. The branches were so sharp we could hardly get in. But we got 'em, three pucks and three tennis balls."

"You're bleeding!" Pam exclaimed.

Will ducked away from his mother. "The branches were sharp," he repeated. "So, who wants to play after dinner?"

"You could have poked your eye out!"

He wiped his mitt over the scratch, smearing blood. "Dad? Mr. McKinnon?"

"Maybe at half-time," Tom said. "Put away your sticks and get cleaned up. We're going to miss the kick-off. Never mind Jennifer, Liz. She's having a sit-in. Pouty, but peaceful, so we're ignoring her."

Eleanor stepped around her great-granddaughter. "I've brought ginger cookies. I hope you'll be in soon to enjoy some."

"I don't think I will be."

Jack and Liz told Pam they'd stay out for a while, too. They sat on the step, one of each side of Jennifer.

She wasn't just being pouty. Digging in her heels, yes. But the child was honestly upset.

"Did you hear that?" she asked. "Never mind Jennifer. I might as well not be here, 'cause that's their motto." She explained the whole story from the beginning for Jack, concluding, "And it's ridiculous because there's thousands of animals on this farm, hundreds anyway, and not a single one in the house. The dogs are watchdogs and the cats are barn cats. We eat the hens and their unborn children and we eat the cows. If we had horses I bet you anything we'd eat them, too. We're just a bunch of carnivores."

"It doesn't look as if you can win this fight," Jack said.

"Oh, I'll win it." She hunched down further, as if she had every intention of spending the winter right where she sat.

"What's the main point you want to make?"

"I want the kittens in the house."

Jack nodded. He looked so serious Liz wanted to hug him. How many men would care about a ten-year-old girl and her kittens? "Why?"

"So they'll be warm."

"Is that all?"

"And safe. And so I'll have a pet. To sleep on the end of my bed."

"From what I've seen, I don't think your parents will give on that last point, for whatever reason."

"For no reason. Just because they have power over me."

Jack was quiet for a minute. "What if we could keep the kittens warm and they could be your pets, just not in the house and not on your bed?"

Jennifer heaved a long, slow sigh. The part about the house and the bed was clearly important to her.

"Mom already gave them a box at the door, with a blanket in it." Liz hadn't noticed the box. It was just cardboard, but it offered protection from the wind.

"She's trying, isn't she?" Jack said.

"Not very hard."

He laughed. "C'mon. Let's go to the barn."

"The barn?" There was doubt and a trace of indignation in Jennifer's voice.

"The barn," Jack agreed. "Let's see what we can figure out."

They went single file on a hardened path through the snow, Jennifer still holding the kittens, who made themselves feel better about their bumpy ride by digging their claws into her coat. A Pacific air mass had come through, and the air felt almost warm on Liz's cheeks. If it got much warmer, the snow would start melting.

The calves crowded to the front of their enclosure when the three humans came in. Just as she had with Liz, Jennifer assured Jack they didn't need anything, not even attention. They had plenty of food, and they had each other. She got the lights, and Jack pushed the door almost shut, leaving enough room for them to go in and out easily.

"Why would we need to go in and out?" Liz asked. "What are you planning?"

Jack just smiled, and went ahead to look around the barn. He soon stopped at a center stall about five feet long and four feet wide, well away from the walls and windows. "What do you think, Jennifer? This seems just right."

She looked disappointed. "You mean for the kittens?"

"I mean for you and the kittens."

Jennifer looked from Jack to her aunt. "For me?"

"What, are you going to build Jennifer a bedroom in the barn?"

"Not a bedroom exactly—"

Liz had been joking. Jennifer jumped excitedly, and the kittens dug their claws deeper into her coat. "A bedroom? That's so cool! I can live out here, I can eat out here and do my homework!"

Liz saw a fundamental problem. "Shouldn't we ask Tom first?"

"No," Jennifer said at once. "I'll need a really warm sleeping bag. Do those tin can phones work, Auntie Liz? I could run a string between here and the house..."

Jack had gone off to explore other stalls and dark corners of the barn. There were blocks of livestock salt, bags of feed, small rectangular bales of straw, burlap sacks and coils of binder twine hanging from the hooks. Against the north wall, he found a pile of weathered boards. He lifted one, brushing off dirt and flecks of straw. "These look good, Jen. Solid, no rusty nails or splinters." He sneezed. "They could use a serious cleaning."

"Tom might have plans for the wood." Liz hated to be the practical one, but it seemed like an important point.

"If he does, they're plans he's had for a very long time. Dust like that doesn't build up in a month, or even a year. I should know."

"I can have sleep-overs," Jennifer said. "Maybe I could get a stove hooked up and a fridge..."

Jack leaned the first board lengthwise against the wall and continued sorting through the stack. He muttered to himself, "Twenty ten-foot boards, six inches wide, ten, four, sixteen feet of wall, five feet high...yup." Louder, he said, "We should have enough right here. Now we need hammers, a saw, nails.''

''I'll get them!'' Jennifer detached the kittens' claws from her coat. ''Down you go.'' There was a loud, protesting meow. ''It's okay, Charlotte. You'll be fine.'' She ran outside.

Liz watched Jack lift and inspect one board after another. ''You've made her very happy.''

''Ten year olds should be happy. Going to give me a hand?''

By the time Jennifer returned with the tools, they had brushed the worst of the dirt from the wood. Jennifer held the boards while Jack sawed them into shorter lengths, and again while he hammered the pieces in place. Liz doled out nails as he needed them. They enclosed the stall, making walls five feet high, with window openings on two sides. Jennifer couldn't contain her excitement when the peaked roof went up.

''It's so cool! Like a real house!''

They piled straw bales around the outside of the walls for insulation, and opened one bale to scatter straw on the floor. Without a word, Jennifer whipped out of the barn again. She came back hauling a child-size table. She repeated the trip three more times, bringing two matching chairs, then an armload of books and finally a flashlight, blanket and pillows.

''We can make a door eventually,'' Jack said. ''We'll need to get hinges and a latch.''

''We can make curtains,'' Liz said.

''And if a little fridge won't work, I could have a cooler. And what about one of those slow cookers?''

Jack started to laugh, but he stopped when they heard boots clamping against the barn's cement floor. Tom's lower half filled the playhouse doorway.

''What's going on out here?''

Liz, Jack and Jennifer looked at each other guiltily.

Tom bent over and peered inside. "Wow. Neat." He looked at the kittens sleeping on the blanket spread over a straw bale bed. "This is something else."

"I hope you didn't have plans for the wood," Jack said.

"Nothing beyond thinking it should come in useful. And it has." He smiled at his daughter, then at Jack. "It's half-time. Stew's hot. Beer's cold. Great-grandma's cookies are waiting."

No one moved.

"I see your point. If we could hook up a TV out here I'd stay, too."

Tom disappeared, but he soon returned with Pam and a box full of dishes and food. The five of them sat around the little house, on chairs and on bales, and tucked in.

"I've never tasted such good stew," Liz said.

Tom took a deep breath, sniffing the air. "Smell that—the straw and the cattle and the stew. This must be what it's like out on a range."

"I could get a harmonica," Jennifer said.

"It's hard to imagine," Tom went on, "but this playhouse isn't much smaller than the log cabin in the woods. Remember it, Liz?"

"I remember."

"Grandpa's grandparents lived in that cabin their first year here, through the winter, even. I don't know how they did it. I wonder if it's still standing? It can't be. It'd be, what, a hundred and twenty years old? It has to have fallen down."

"It must have." Liz didn't want to talk about the cabin with her brother. She wasn't comfortable thinking about it in such a casual way.

Jack packed his dish into the box. "Liz, what would

you prefer? The second half of the game, or a little stargazing?''

She hadn't told him about the cabin. How did he always know when she needed rescuing? ''Let's begin with stargazing and then catch some of the second half.''

They thanked Pam and Tom for dinner and wished Jennifer well with her house. After they'd squeezed through the doorway they clearly heard the voices inside.

''Isn't that great?'' Pam said. ''I've been hoping those two would get together from the beginning.''

Tom warned her not to jump to conclusions. ''Looking at stars doesn't have to be romantic, and football certainly isn't. Besides, Liz will be gone soon and Jack has a big investment in his farm. They're committed to different ways of life.''

Jack and Liz went past the calves and out of the barn. Liz looked up and saw Orion, the can't-miss winter constellation, her brother's words still playing in her mind.

They must have been playing in Jack's, too. ''It's not such a big investment, Liz.''

IT WAS HARDER TO GET TIME by himself now. Even if he walked to the corner store to buy gum somebody tagged along. He hoped it was just a sign of tension. It must be, because if it was suspicion, they were only suspicious during office hours. As far as he knew they ignored him at night, right up until he reached the office each morning.

Jack's game message, when unscrambled, had been pretty obvious—*Hedberg passes to Hull, Hull takes the shot.* On Sunday afternoon Reid headed out to East

Kildonan. Henderson Highway was nearly empty. Everybody must be holed up watching the Grey Cup.

A few kids were on the ice at the Elmwood Community Center, jostling for a puck. One of them got it free and took off, his body all bunched with that excitement you got when you were almost sure the other guys couldn't catch you. What were they thinking? *Messier passes to Gretzky, Gretzky takes the shot?*

Over the years, he and Jack had played a lot of pick-up games here. Hockey in the winter, basketball and 21 and Kick the Can the rest of the year. Jack didn't have much free time, so he didn't play as often as most of the kids. They'd never set foot on the ice without doing that commentary. *Nilsson gets the puck, brings it up the outside, passes to Hedberg, Hedberg to Hull, Hull takes the shot…*

If Jack had hidden another puzzle here, he must have found a spot where it wouldn't be disturbed between the time he planted it and the time Reid found it. He couldn't embed it under the ice, not without help from the management. He couldn't attach it to the boards without the snow and wind or some kid interfering with it.

Reid walked all the way around the rink to the shed where kids put on their skates. He was only wearing shoes, and his feet were already getting damp and cold. Not as cold as they got those January nights when he and Jack stayed on the ice until their feet were so sore they could have cried. He remembered easing his skate off, hoping his ice block of a foot wouldn't shatter, and sitting there on the bench with his hand wrapped around first one foot, then the other, until he could bear to put his boot on. Jack did the same.

There was nobody in the shed. It wasn't much—cement floor, plank walls and benches. Just shelter from the wind, really. No nooks and crannies here. He got on his knees and craned his head to see under the benches. Gum, lots of gum. Kids were as disgusting as ever. And an envelope. He pulled it away from the rough wood and stuffed it in his pocket. So far, this was too easy. Had Jack even tried? He went back to his car and turned the key in the ignition to get the heater going before he opened the envelope.

No code this time. Just a problem.

If Gretzky has the puck two meters behind the red line on a regulation hockey rink, and begins skating straight toward the goal at a constant acceleration of one point two meters per second squared, and Hull is along the boards, halfway between the red line and his opponent's blue line, how fast must he be skating to bodycheck Gretzky at the blue line, assuming that his velocity is constant.

Right. Like his velocity could be constant.

Reid stared into midair, calculating, sometimes writing in the frost on his window with his fingernail. He couldn't help smiling, couldn't help enjoying this. He was almost embarrassed that Jack really believed he wanted to play just like the old days, that he'd drive an hour and a half from the city and break into somebody's house, go to all that trouble, to play a ridiculous game, like some overgrown kid...but it was a good problem.

There wasn't enough frost for all the calculations he needed to do. Reid rummaged in the glove compartment for paper and a pen. He started with a sketch of a regulation rink and figured out each player's trajectory. Using geometry and calculus, he found the answer. It nearly went on forever. He rounded it off to 3.31 meters per second.

Okay. What are you trying to tell me, Jack?

LIZ HELPED ELEANOR OUT OF THE TRUCK. "I'll just be a minute, Grandma."

"Take your time."

She climbed back into the cab. She wasn't sure what she wanted to say or do, she just knew she wasn't ready to leave Jack. "It was a good day, wasn't it? What was your favorite part?"

He sat with his gloved hands on the steering wheel. "I don't know if I can chose. I liked it all. The house-building, the stars, the football game, the company."

They hadn't stayed outside long. "Those five or ten minutes, when the two of us were in the field and we saw the nebula in Orion…that was my favorite part."

"Oh? I liked it when you were looking up and the moonlight was on your throat."

Liz stared at him. He hadn't said it suggestively or jokingly, just in his usual tone. It reminded her of the night they'd sat on the porch talking. His voice sounded warm in the dark, and being close to him felt comforting and stirring at the same time.

Jack went on, "The night we met, I couldn't sleep. I thought it was the cold. I burrowed under the blankets, waiting for my body heat to do something about the icy sheets, and finally I noticed I had something on my mind. I couldn't figure out what."

"The car speeding out of your driveway," Liz suggested.

"That was part of it. Not all, though. So, instead of counting sheep, I counted possible problems, things that might need my attention. There was nothing—nothing that should keep me awake. No forgotten birthdays, no unpaid bills. I had arranged to get the last load of pumpkins into Winnipeg, the iron wasn't plugged in—it hadn't been for weeks, to tell the truth."

"Was it the trouble you were having finding an evergreen field?"

"You know it wasn't. It was you."

"Oh." Should she apologize? It would be hypocritical, when she was so pleased.

"It was the first time thinking about a woman ever kept me awake."

"I've thought about you a lot, too. In spite of everything else. You've been such a help to me, Jack." She wished she'd phrased that differently. It was so much less than she'd meant to say.

"I'm glad. This has been a tough few weeks for you."

"I think Grandma's been pushing us together."

"She wouldn't do that, would she? Not with all you've had on your mind."

"I think she thinks we'd be good together."

"I think she's right. This isn't the time for it—you need to go home and take care of your life, think about what comes next. I've wondered if you'd like to visit again at some point and see what we've got here. If you feel ready for that later, just let me know."

"I do want to see what we've got here. I'm ready now."

His voice softened. "You're not just trying to be nice, are you? Because Christmas is coming?"

"Christmas is a whole month away."

His gloved hand came up to her face, barely touching her skin. "We'll take it slow. I'll ask your grandmother's permission to see you and we'll sit in the parlor the proper distance apart—"

"No, we won't."

"I saw the shape you were in at the gravel pit, the worries you've had since then. You can't jump from that to—'' He stopped, leaving her with a very clear picture of where they'd left off the night he'd come to dinner. He was determined to be patient. A laudable instinct that she would bypass as soon as possible.

''All right. My grandmother's parlor. Tomorrow?''

''If she agrees.''

Liz began to think he wasn't joking. He really intended to behave like an old-time suitor. Giving him no chance to take his role too far she helped herself to a good-night kiss, then scooted back to her side of the truck. As soon as she opened the door, the dogs had their front feet on the running board. Liz stepped down carefully, avoiding their paws. They twitched their noses in her direction, then Jack's, uncertain on which human to lavish their attention.

''Down, Bella. Dora, get down. Good girls.''

Liz swung the door shut and headed for the house, her path lit by Jack's headlights. After a longing look at the truck, the dogs followed her. She waited on the porch before going in, watching the lights back down the driveway and swivel, highlighting the road. The tires crunched on the hard-packed snow as the truck rolled away.

Already, she knew him so well. The details might take years, but she knew him through and through. And she knew he fit her perfectly.

Eleanor was waiting in the kitchen. ''That was a nice long talk.''

''It's official, Grandma. He plans to come calling.''

''Oh, good,'' Eleanor said, with the satisfaction of someone who has been waiting for the pieces to fall together as they should. ''That calls for a cup of tea.''

CHAPTER FOURTEEN

"JACK? DICK GRAHAM HERE."

His bank manager. His bank manager never called.

"I'm just letting people know someone tried to hack into our system last night. We've got all kinds of protection, of course. It was very professional, though—not some high school geek trying to prove his manhood. This guy nearly got through." His unruffled tone faltered a little at that, but Graham went on, trying to spread a message of calm. "He didn't seem to be trying to get into our accounts. He was interested in our records—who has accounts here, who keeps safety deposit boxes, that kind of thing. We think he got the list of customers, but I can assure you he didn't get into your accounts, business or personal. We're in the middle of shoring up our firewalls. It won't happen again."

Jack expressed his confidence in the bank's staff and hung up, frowning. He felt like he'd been punched in the stomach. There was a big difference between wondering if your friend had betrayed you and finding out that, yes, he probably had.

It was years since he and Reid had played the game. They'd never included other people, they'd never broken into each other's homes. What if, when they'd searched the house the first time, they'd found the disk at the bottom of the bin? They could have opened the Linux partition that night. The algorithm, the implementation program and the key, all in the same place. At least he had them separate now, and he'd taken steps to protect the key. They wouldn't get anywhere without it.

Jack stood at the kitchen window for a few minutes, his mind stuck on the videotaped image of Reid waiting calmly at the door to be let in. Then he retrieved the disk from the bin in the cellar and slipped it into a padded envelope along with a note. He scrawled a name and address on the front. *Ned Hardy. Brandon University.*

DANIEL BALANCED NEAR THE TOP of a ladder stringing Christmas lights along the eaves of his house. When he saw Jack, he called, "Hang on. I'll be right down."

"Need a hand?"

"No, no. I've got it." He left the remaining section of lights dangling, put his tools in his pocket and came down the ladder, feeling for each rung as he went. "Think I'll leave 'em up this year," he said, when he was safely on the ground. "Wasn't going to do it at all, but once the season rolled around and I started seeing the lights everywhere, I couldn't help myself. Never liked ladders, though. Like 'em less now. Catch your punks?"

"I found out who they are." Jack paused. His next question was bound to arouse Daniel's curiosity. "Do you have anything that can check for listening devices and cameras?"

Daniel leaned against the ladder. "How do you mean?"

Jack thought his meaning was clear. "I mean I want to find out if there are any cameras or listening devices hidden in my house."

Daniel looked at him with what Jack had come to

think of as his Special Branch gaze. Knowing, but not cynical. "These are high-tech kids you've got poking around." He waited, but Jack didn't answer. "You in some kind of trouble, Jack?"

"Not really. I can handle the problem."

"Can you, now?" Daniel straightened up and strode to his back door, all business. "I won't be a minute. I'll get a few things together, come and do a sweep myself."

The more Jack thought about Reid and his friends listening to his conversations, or watching him, the itchier and angrier it made him. It wasn't just his privacy. Liz had been in his house, talking about things no one else was meant to hear.

If they'd planted a camera, that would explain how they'd known they had time to search his house the day he went to Brandon. They could have seen him get the boot disk ready to send to Ned this morning.

On the other hand, if a camera had been in place all this time, they would have watched while he encoded the key and hid the algorithm, too. They wouldn't have felt any need to search for a safe deposit box.

He was relieved when Daniel told him the house was clean, upstairs and down. No bugs, no cameras. Of course, that wasn't the end of it for Daniel. He made himself comfortable at the kitchen table. "Now suppose you tell me the whole story."

"Coffee?"

"No, thanks."

"That's all I've got to offer."

"You know folks around here think you're into drugs." Ignoring Jack's startled expression, Daniel went on, "Doesn't seem too likely to me. Far more likely it's to do with your computer business. Not a lot of industrial espionage with Christmas trees, as far as I know, but computers—that's another story. Programs, codes, takeovers, identify theft—well, the list goes on and on. You know, don't you, the RCMP has a whole department that deals with that kind of thing, if a guy was in a jam and needed help."

Jack wondered how long it would be before Daniel decided to call whoever he still knew in the Mounties. "A friend of mine is behaving strangely. That's all. He broke in here a while ago, just fooling around. He seems to know what I'm doing all the time, when I'm going to be away. It made me think he might have planted a bug of some kind."

Daniel stared at him. Finally he said, "You see, friends don't usually behave that way. Spying. Breaking and entering. When they do, I've got to ask myself why."

Jack shrugged. "It's easy to get hold of that kind of technology now. Some people are fascinated by it. Like playing soldier when you're a kid."

The thought of boyhood games didn't distract Daniel. "Out here, keeping somebody under surveillance isn't easy. Unless you've got access to a satellite. Your friend got access to a satellite?"

"Of course not."

"Then you'd need a receiver nearby. In the city, you'd rent the neighboring apartment, or park on the street outside the house and nobody would notice. Van parks by *your* driveway, everybody's going to ask about it."

Jack looked out the window to the garage, the tumbledown barn, the woods. He needed a dog.

Daniel reached for his coat. "All right. Let's leave it at that." At the door, he gave Jack another Special

Branch stare. "I'm not as past it as I look. You ever need a hand, you call me."

ELEANOR SAT BY THE WOODSTOVE, with a big bowl on her lap, combining butter and sugar by hand. Liz had forgotten she did that. Watching the gooey mixture squeeze through her grandmother's fingers had always fascinated her, but she'd never wanted to touch it herself. Eleanor did it that way because that was the way her mother had done it. Good shortbread depended on body heat.

When the flour was thoroughly mixed in and the dough was as light as she wanted it, Eleanor moved to the table to roll it out. She smiled at Liz. "Are you going to put on the colored sugar?"

Green-tinged sugar for the trees, red for the sleighs and bells and Santas, yellow for stars and angels. She had always loved the job.

Eleanor pushed a box of cookie cutters toward her. "Which shape shall we use first?"

Liz handed her an angel. In practiced movements, Eleanor cut and lifted angel after angel, sliding them onto the cookie sheet without tearing a single one. When the first cookie sheet was full, Liz chose the sleigh cutter. This one had more curves and corners where the dough could stick, so Eleanor went more slowly. "I might as well tell you, I called Mrs. Anderson first thing this morning."

The news surprised Liz. It shouldn't have. "You're ready to list the property now?" Calling it "the property" felt better.

"There's no point putting it off. We have to do what's needed. Satisfaction and self-respect come from that." Eleanor pointed at the bowls of sugar. "Sprinkle the angels, won't you? Everyone keeps repeating this will be the last Christmas. As if it really is the last, not just the last in this house."

"It feels a bit like the end of an era. That's all they mean."

"Not everything will change. I'll still make shortbread."

"And I'll still come to help."

Eleanor looked up with a smile. "Will you?"

"I'm planning to make a pest of myself. A visit per season."

"How extravagant! I don't suppose you'd stay a few months each time?" Eleanor broke off. Abruptly, she sat in the nearest chair, the rolling pin clutched in one hand.

"Grandma?" Eleanor's face was unnaturally pale. "Are you all right?"

"I need to get off my feet for a bit," she said. "Just for a few minutes."

Liz touched the back of her hand to her grandmother's cheek, then to her forehead. Her skin didn't feel cold or hot. Not clammy, either. "For a few minutes? Grandma, if you're supposed to do what's needed, you'll stay off your feet for the rest of the day. I'll finish the shortbread." She wasn't sure if she was imagining what she wanted to see, or if Eleanor's color was already improving. "Do you have a pain?"

"My energy went out of me, that's all. It happens sometimes. Goes with the territory, I'm afraid." Eleanor sat up straighter and brushed her hands over the hair combed back from her forehead, as if sitting so suddenly might have messed it. "Why don't you roll and cut, Elizabeth? I'll choose the cutters."

As she worked, Liz kept glancing from the shortbread dough to her grandmother's face. No one in the family seemed worried about her health. She needed to rest often and she took pills of some kind each morning. Not unexpected at her age.

‘‘Are you sick, Grandma?’’

‘‘You’re rolling the dough too thin. You need to be gentle with it, or the cookies will be tough.’’

Liz tried not to press the rolling pin so hard. ‘‘Like that?’’

‘‘Much better. Remember, you’re not tanning leather.’’

She cut a row of bells and still her grandmother hadn’t answered her question. ‘‘Grandma?’’

‘‘You won’t fuss?’’

‘‘It depends what you call fussing.’’

‘‘I’m not sick. My heart is putting significantly less effort into its job than it used to, that’s all.’’ She said it calmly and went right on talking. ‘‘You’ll be able to take Jack a tin of shortbread when you go over this afternoon. Tell him it’ll be a couple of weeks before they have much flavor. They have to ripen. Isn’t it nice that we can send him baking for a change?’’

‘‘He can have the cookies another day, Grandma. I’m not going to visit him this afternoon, not after—’’

‘‘Elizabeth. Look at me.’’ Eleanor waited until she had her granddaughter’s full attention. ‘‘Jack’s expecting you, and you’re going.’’ From her tone, it was safe to say her strength was back.

THREE POINT THREE ONE…3.31—no matter how he looked at it, it was days before Reid got an inkling of where Jack might be pointing him. He looked up revolutions of planets, half-lives of elements, statistics about family size in the fifties…then, it finally occurred to him. The Dewey Decimal system. He was looking for a book, a library book. If he discounted the decimal, three-three-one was the classification for books on labor economics.

First he checked the downtown library, then the East Kildonan branch where they'd gone when they were kids. "Yes, we do have a book reserved for you," the librarian said, sounding pleased with herself. What, had she found and solved Jack's next problem?

Labor Economics, An Analysis. Reid sat at a long, empty table and started flipping through the pages. Why was he doing this? He could quit. Maybe he would. He'd take one look at the problem and if he didn't like it, that's what he'd do. He'd quit running around at Jack's bidding.

There. He'd almost missed it. A folded paper. Reid opened it and found a message in Jack's handwriting.

Hey, Reid

I was going to come up with something that would keep you busy till your fortieth birthday, but I just don't feel like it. Sorry to bail on you. Why don't we skip the rest of the work and go straight to the beer? You know where to find me.

The note wasn't signed.

He didn't *feel* like it? Until Reid remembered he wasn't really playing the game, he was indignant, even annoyed. Still, what did Jack mean? That he was bored, or that he couldn't be bothered with his old friend, or that he was a little bit busy setting up a sting operation with the police? *Who loses and who wins…* He couldn't quite get that out of his head.

Reid pocketed the note and left the book on the table. When he got back to his office, he found an extra person hanging around with Croker's regular bunch. Webb and his constant throat clearing had come to visit. He looked relieved to see Reid. Croker's goons had a very low social IQ.

Webb accepted a cup of coffee, but waited until Croker arrived to say what was on his mind. A telephone call was considered good enough for most news, so he must have picked up something bigger than usual to rush into the city like this.

"Well?" Croker said, as soon as he saw Webb sitting by Reid's desk. "What is it?"

"He knows." Webb treated them to a half-coughing, half-throat clearing sound that made Reid want to beg his doctor for preventative antibiotics. He'd have to remember to put a little bleach in that coffee mug. "At least I think he knows. He got a guy in town to check his house for bugs. A retired Mountie."

Reid's heart pounded. He'd only been joking about the sting operation.

Croker wasn't jumping to any conclusions. "He's a step ahead of us this time." He started pacing. "Maybe we've been going at this all wrong. It's been two months, and we've got nothing. I can't waste any more time. Why are we looking for a disk or a CD or a computer or a printout? We could have McKinnon easily. The code came out of his brain, didn't it? It's got to be in there still. You said he has a bad memory, but if he invented it once, can't he invent it again?"

Sure he could. Knowing Jack, he could invent three or four unbreakable codes, all before breakfast. Unlike other people, who couldn't invent any. He'd tried. Ever since Jack did it in grad school, he'd tried. No luck yet. Maybe tomorrow.

Reid kept his voice calm. "Those are valid questions." They weren't, but it was always a good thing to say. "We're talking about, I don't know, a page and half or so of equations for the algorithm, maybe five pages for an implementation program. The algorithm is the most important thing to get our hands on. I can guarantee you Jack doesn't remember it. He'll recall roughly what he did, but figuring out the details again could take three, four, five weeks. That's a whole lot of kidnapping and unlawful confinement. You say you don't want to waste any more time on this. How do feel about ten to twenty years?''

LIZ COULD TELL RIGHT AWAY that Jack had bought a vacuum. ''No dust, Jack.''

''No nail holes, no dust,'' he agreed. ''No insulation, either.'' He was warmly dressed in the navy fleece top he'd worn the night they met, with a turtleneck of almost the same color underneath. He handed her a large mug of coffee.

There had been no sudden rush to romance since they'd talked about courting after the Grey Cup game, but right now he barely seemed to notice she'd arrived. ''Is something wrong, Jack? You seem distracted.''

He looked ready to issue an automatic denial. Instead, he apologized. ''A problem's cropped up. I had a busy morning dealing with it. I guess I'm still a bit worried.''

Liz sat beside the table. ''Can I help?'' He hesitated, so she added, ''I know you don't like to talk about yourself, but you've listened to me for days. Come to think of it, for enough days to make it weeks!''

''It's not the same. This isn't a personal problem.''

''That should make it easier, shouldn't it?''

He downed half his mug of coffee before he joined her at the table. ''You're not going to like it.''

''All right.'' A cash flow problem would be manageable. She might even be able to help. If it was a health problem, bad news from a doctor, she didn't know what she'd do.

"I'll need to give you some background first. I told you I used to develop computer programs. In grad school, I specialized in encryption. So did Reid."

Liz relaxed a little. This didn't sound so bad. "You mean you're the guys who make it possible for me to use my credit card on the Internet?"

"That's one application of encryption techniques. If you can't encrypt and decrypt information safely and efficiently, you can't do business online whether it's retail, banking or government. Reid and I both started our own companies when we got out of school. I focused on programming and he went into computer security."

"Okay." She was a long way from seeing what was bothering him now.

"I told you about the game we used to play."

"You told me there was a game, but not how you played it."

"It started in high school and got more elaborate as we learned more. It was sort of a mathematical treasure hunt. You had to find the first clue, work out a solution to a problem and figure out what the solution was telling you, so you could find the next clue, and so on. It could take weeks to prepare and weeks more to solve."

They did this for fun? It sounded like a nightmare. "What kind of prizes did you have?"

"Whoever won bought the other one a beer. And whoever lost bought the other one a beer."

Liz laughed.

He sat forward, tense again. "So, here's the problem. While I was still at school, I came up with a method of encryption. It was kind of a fluke. My method was stronger than the RSA code most people use today. Strong enough that in some countries it couldn't be used legally.''

Liz didn't know the first thing about encryption, but it sounded like something he shouldn't have been able to do without years of research and help from other mathematicians. ''I'm impressed.''

''So was Reid, I think. He seems to be trying to steal it.''

Liz stared at Jack while she put the rest of the pieces in place. ''So when I saw those men outside your house and my instincts went into overdrive—''

''It may not have been your imagination.''

''And the car that whizzed out of your driveway?''

''Reid, in a hurry for a good reason.''

''The creep!''

Jack gave an unamused laugh. ''My thoughts exactly…if that's what he's doing. I don't have absolute proof. Just a series of odd events. Maybe I'm worried about nothing.''

He didn't strike Liz as a man who worried about nothing.

''The night the car nearly ran into you,'' he said grimly, ''I saw signs that someone had been in the house. When I decided it must be Reid letting me know he wanted to start the game again, I made a disk for him to find. It had an encrypted message that would lead him to another clue. It also had a virus that would temporarily disable his machine and delete the message on the disk.''

''You made a virus?''

''It wasn't much of a virus. I thought he deserved it. He broke into my house, he ran you off the road.'' Jack sounded a bit defensive. ''I wanted to know how he got in, so I bought some surveillance equipment from Daniel Rutherford—''

"Oh! That must be what he meant."

"Daniel?"

"At the first hockey game he wondered if you'd told me something and then said I should be careful. I meant to ask you about it, but I forgot."

"He was fishing. Anyway, maybe I'm wrong about Reid. I've added more protection for the algorithm, just in case."

Liz's mind was racing. "So you have this code, but it's a secret? You don't use it? No one uses it?"

"That's right. You can use any code you want in Canada, at least for now. The world is still adjusting to online business and all its repercussions, so there's disagreement about what the laws should be. Even if I could use the code here, or sell it here, businesses don't operate within borders. I don't want to break another country's laws. I also don't want to upset the balance between security, personal privacy and crime fighting."

"I don't understand."

"If the wrong people got hold of it, they'd have an encryption system police couldn't break."

The wrong people. He meant organized crime, or terrorists.

"On the other hand, if the government had it, I'd be concerned about how its use could affect citizens. If a corporation used it, how might that affect consumers or stockholders? They could collect and store personal information with no safeguards, no way for anyone to oversee what they're doing. The codes we have now are strong enough. Usually they develop slowly. People who make codes respond to people who break them, and so on. If you have a code that can't be broken, that process is ended."

It was like listening to a stranger. Jack's tension, his

expression, his outlook all were so different from what she'd come to expect.

"Only a couple of people knew about my algorithm," he went on. "Reid and another friend who works in Brandon now. I told them I'd destroyed it."

"Told them?"

"I was going to do it. But it's a beautiful thing, Liz."

"The code?"

"I told them I'd wiped the hard drive of my computer clean, then I smashed a diskette right in front of them. It was blank, but they didn't know that. Reid must have realized I kept it."

"But, Jack…why? It seems risky. And that's an understatement."

"A code, a code this strong, is like a work of art. Would you burn a manuscript or a set of paintings? Most likely, I'd never use it—"

"Most likely?" He'd just explained all the reasons he shouldn't use it.

"Definitely, I wouldn't. Of course I wouldn't. And if I wait long enough, someone will come up with a stronger algorithm, or with a decryption method that'll make my code useless. Sometimes, though…" He stopped.

"Sometimes what?"

"Sometimes I like the thought that I *could* use it. Can you imagine the power and wealth an unbreakable code would give you?"

Liz shook her head.

"Me, neither. It's fun to try, though."

She stared at him, at the dreamy look on his face. He was tempted. Jack was a pirate. Her mysterious otherworld hero was a pirate.

CHAPTER FIFTEEN

LIZ HAD SPENT THE MORNING visiting, first at Pam's, and then at Aunt Julia's. Christmas preparations were well underway in both households. For Pam that meant plum pudding and mincemeat and nineteen varieties of perfectly shaped and decorated cookies, handmade Christmas crackers stuffed full of little gifts and jokes, and cards addressed to everyone she'd ever met. For Aunt Julia it meant reading about the origin of Christmas traditions while Emily filled the freezer with holiday baking. In between houses, Liz had dropped in on Jennifer and found her stretched out across a bed of bales with the kittens, reading while they slept.

As soon as she stepped into the kitchen, Eleanor came to greet her. "Jack called. He'd like you to go to dinner tonight."

Liz unwound her scarf. "Just me?"

"Just you. He said to dress warmly."

"Why, has his furnace quit?"

"All he said was to dress warmly and to arrive around six o'clock."

More mystery. She was still uncomfortable with Jack's revelations about his code. It wasn't just that he'd kept it and was tempted to use in spite of any problems it might cause. It was that he'd made it. That he could make it.

At five minutes to six, wearing a long winter coat

Eleanor had dug out from the back of a closet, thermal underwear and two pairs of socks inside her boots, Liz turned down Jack's driveway. She slowed her grandmother's car, a twenty-year-old Buick that Uncle Will called a sofa on wheels, and took in the scene before her.

The oak grove sparkled. White fairy lights wound through the trees' bare branches, and under the biggest oak stood a table covered with a snowy-white cloth and set with silver and crystal that caught the light and held it. She didn't see Jack at first, but then she noticed movement, and he appeared as if from the oak's trunk.

Liz got out of the car and hurried to meet him. "Jack? This is magical!" Votive candles nestled in the snow, with little melted circles around them. Paper snowflakes seemed to drift from the trees, moving on air currents. She cupped her hand around one. "Did you make these? Or did you commandeer Pam's class?"

"It was my favorite craft in grade one. I'd forgotten all about it until Halloween, watching the snow fall while I waited for kids to come. It took me a whole morning to figure out how to fold the paper."

Pirates didn't make snowflakes.

Jack pulled out a chair for her. As she sat, she noticed a second table deeper in the grove, filled with serving dishes and insulated carafes. Music came from a small CD player out of the way of the dishes. Spanish guitar. The sultry, hot-weather sound made her smile.

They had mulled wine to start, then shrimp and scallops tasting of lemon and dill, served on ice. Chilled tomato soup with a touch of mint followed, then tandoori chicken, kept hot in a slow cooker.

"You didn't make all this, did you?"

"There's more to me than pumpkin pie, Liz."

"How did you learn to cook so well? I know you're an independent single guy, but this goes way beyond what I'd expect. You didn't just make the food. You made it wonderfully."

Jack smiled at her enthusiastic response. "I started cooking when I was eight or nine. I got home a couple of hours before my uncle, so it seemed reasonable to have his dinner ready. After a few years, we got tired of macaroni and cheese and tinned beans."

They finished with homemade lemon ice cream, fluffy and almost as white as the snowbank in which Jack had packed the serving container. Each spoonful melted in her mouth, creamy and tart at the same time. "You are the kindest, most thoughtful man in the world. All this work to make something so special. Thank you."

Jack looked embarrassed. "I'm glad you've enjoyed it. Want to go in and get warm?"

"Please." The ice cream had undone the good of thermal underwear. "I'll help you clean up."

"Tomorrow's soon enough for that." He whipped out a white cotton sheet and let it float down to cover the table. The mess was gone, blended into the snow.

Inside, a fire burned in the Franklin stove. Jack had cranked the oil furnace higher than usual, but Liz still kept her coat on in the kitchen.

"Are you that cold?"

She peered at Jack over her turned-up collar and nodded.

"Maybe I'm not so kind and thoughtful." He rubbed her arms briskly, then her back. "Espresso to warm up, or brandy?"

"Brandy, please." She waited for her glass, then

carried it into the living room. Another surprise waited for her there. "Jack!"

The books and newspapers had been tidied away, and instead the tables were full of flowers and fruit. He'd arranged bare branches inside and decked them with the same miniature lights he'd used on the oaks. The drapes were open so they could see the outside lights outside, too.

"I wish I had my sketchbook. This would be perfect for the woodland fairies!"

"I was thinking about that, too."

She had shown him her sketches. The characters and plot were continuing to have an undeniable similarity to her own experiences since coming back to Three Creeks. The female fairy had an old score to settle, and there was a knight and a wise old woman who helped her. There was an evil thorn-tipped character who, it turned out, didn't sleep well and wished only to undo all the harm he'd done in the past. "Imagine the woods after the battle, when they feast and celebrate. It could look like this, only the lights would be low to the ground, high for them, of course."

"Fireflies?"

Even Jack had trouble understanding there was nothing cute about her fairies. She'd have to think of a different name for them. "They'd use torches. Thousands of little torches. Heads of wild barley, maybe, doused in oil and set on fire the way we do with cattails."

Jack brought a blanket downstairs, so Liz could get rid of her coat. They sat on the floor under it, leaning against the sofa, close enough that she could feel his arm move every time he inhaled. A different sort of warmth built inside her. She watched the lights, inside and out, through half-closed eyes, letting her impressions of the evening drift through her mind, and a sense of anticipation build.

There was still something in the way. "You really wrote a code that's better than anything being used now?" She was afraid he was an Einstein. Could she handle that, even if he was an Einstein who preferred to grow pumpkins?

"It was mostly luck. I was fooling around with work other people had already done and just happened on it." He smiled at her skeptical expression. "Really. A lot of inventions happen that way."

"I'm no good at math. Sometimes I count dots to add. When I shop I forget that $6.99 means $7.00. I always think it means $6.00. So by the time I get to the till, thinking I owe twenty dollars, and I'm told it's thirty, I can't believe it. Then there's the sales tax. Don't even ask me to calculate the tax."

"Well, that's it, then. I always said I'd never get involved with a woman who couldn't write a better algorithm than I could."

That was exactly what concerned her. Could he care, in the long run, about someone who knew nothing, absolutely nothing, about a subject he loved, work that had once been a vocation, by his own description?

"Tell you what," Jack said. "You try to write an algorithm and I'll try to write a children's book. I bet we'd come out even."

"Maybe not. At least you know what a children's book is."

"Don't let algorithms intimidate you, Liz. An algorithm is just a list of instructions. Steps to accomplish an objective."

He slipped an arm around her shoulders. She'd been wanting him to do that ever since they got under the blanket, and if he hadn't done it soon she would have taken matters into her own hands. She'd had more than enough of Jack's kindness and consideration. In an urgent undertone, she said, "I made a rather embarrassing stop at the drugstore in Pine Point."

"Did you? Sounds like a stop I made in Winnipeg when I was planting clues for Reid to find."

"Oh. Well, the more the merrier." She felt him smile.

"Still cold?"

She shook her head. She didn't know if she was, or not. It was the last thing on her mind. He ran his hand along her face, then cupped her chin, his fingertips brushing the soft skin behind her ear. It was enough to send a shiver of feeling throughout her body. With the back of his hand he stroked the warm curve from her chin to her collar bone.

When she moved against him, he pulled her sweater over her head, then drew the blanket higher over them. His hand went to her blouse. Slowly and methodically, as if counting, he unfastened each button. He slipped his hands underneath her thermal undershirt, fingers cold against her heated skin. When they reached her breasts, she couldn't wait any longer. She tugged off the shirt, then reached around his neck and pulled him closer, feeling the wool of his sweater against her skin.

A little breathlessly, he said, "And that, more or less, is an algorithm."

Her laughter was muffled against his lips.

A FOR SALE SIGN STOOD near the road, almost hidden by bare lilac bushes. Eleanor had taken the step. A touch ambivalently, maybe. Without the help of a real estate agent, an unmotivated buyer might drive by without seeing the sign.

House and 640 acres. That was short and to the

point. You couldn't say, "For Sale: Five Generations of Family History." Eleanor was taking the position that she was selling boards and cement and whatever else had gone into building the place, that you took your past with you wherever you went. Jack wasn't so sure. He didn't have a segment of his brain or heart reserved for family history. Not even a trunk in the attic. That wasn't quite true. He did have one thing that tied him to the past. A box of Christmas decorations.

There were moments when he visited Eleanor that he got a feeling that was almost creepy, an impression that other times and other lives were soaked into the walls of the house, waiting to be sensed by each generation. That sort of thing was more Liz's territory. It was a fanciful thought for an ex-mathematician.

Or maybe not. Numbers could be fanciful when you thought about it, whether you were trying to explain the universe with hyperbolic curves or writing a complicated computer program. Liz had asked him if growing Christmas trees and pumpkins meant he wanted to make things magical for children. If only she could see how ones and zeros were turned into animated movies and the pages of books and graphs of how someone's business was doing. Most people would never understand how those transformations happened.

Liz was smiling when she opened the door. "Look at you! You've come prepared."

"I hope you're not laughing at my hat."

"I wouldn't! It's just that you look as if you're dressed for forty below. It's a nice day!"

"You think I'm dressed like this for the woods? I'm dressed for my living room."

They were going to find a Christmas tree for Jack

this afternoon. It was a little early to put up a real tree, but he didn't want to wait. Later in the week, Tom planned to get one for Eleanor. Everyone was demanding a giant of a tree, one that would reach all the way to her ten-foot ceiling.

"Now you two wait just a minute. You should have a hot drink with you." Eleanor hurried to the cupboard, found a tall, black insulated jar and filled it with strong tea from the pot on the stove. "There's a second cup inside the lid. You've got a hat, Elizabeth?"

"In my pocket."

"Well, your pocket doesn't need it." Eleanor felt in both pockets, found a green toque and pulled it over Liz's curls. "Fashion," she said dismissively. "Think about warmth. Besides, it looks pretty. Don't you think so, Jack? The green brings out the reddishness in her hair."

"Brings out her freckles, too. Better keep the girls with you, Eleanor. They'd exhaust themselves where we're going. It's uncharted territory."

"Uncharted?" Liz asked, once she was in the truck.

"No snowmobile or ski trail, no farm machinery. Just deep snow. We'll be okay." Jack backed out to the road. "Eleanor got down to listing the place, I see."

"Everyone's been mentioning the sign. It's almost as if nobody really thought it would happen. Uncle Will's been telling Martin and Brian one of them should sell their place and move in here."

"That must have gone over well. Your family doesn't like change—whether it's losing old houses or gaining new people."

"They're warming to you."

He nodded. "They've decided to give me a chance. For your sake, I think."

"For my sake? It's for the sake of the hockey team."

Jack laughed. "Maybe."

"I'm sure they don't know about us. All the little comments don't mean anything. They've been making those since I got here."

"Dream away, Liz." He pulled off the road beside a field that bordered thick woods. It was a quarter section to the north of the original Robb homestead, and it had never been touched. From the first William on, nature had been left alone. The trees were bigger here than they were for miles around. Even the poplars soared. Shrubs grew beneath them, hazelnut, high bush cranberry and saskatoon. Bright red cranberries still clung to the branches here and there, flash frozen where they grew.

"We never cut from this parcel, Jack."

"I don't think you'll mind when you see the tree, but we won't cut it if you're not willing." He pressed his foot down on one strand of the barbed wire fence and lifted the other, so Liz could get through safely, then she did the same for him. Clean, bright snow, untouched since it fell, lay deep on the ground, swept by the wind into hardened waves and peaks. "The trees were easier to reach the last time I came. You should be all right if you step into my tracks."

"Snow will get in my boots whatever I do. I might as well walk beside you." Her tone changed. "In fact, now that I think about it, I might as well knock you down and roll around with you and get snow on your tummy—"

Jack backed away, laughing. "No, you don't—not until we've got the tree." Then, as far as he was concerned, anything could go. "Make sure you give me a chance to get rid of the saw, before you do anything rash.''

She advanced, the snow well over her boots. One mittened hand reached under his coat and under his sweater. His muscles tightened at her touch. He pulled her to him, trapping her hand between them. It was wonderful to see her back from all the sadness and self-doubt. Not just back. She was more than back. There was color in her face, a sparkle in her eye. She was more ready to laugh, more open to other people's good intentions.

She still hadn't said how long she would stay in Three Creeks. Sometimes he got the impression she didn't want to go back to Vancouver, but then she would talk about her apartment or her next book or fresh seafood and his heart would sink. It was a new feeling for him. He'd been close to a few women, but he'd always kept his sense of independence. Lately he'd begun to worry that his happiness was caught up in Liz's plans, and that it always would be.

''Would we get hypothermia?'' she whispered.

''Almost certainly.''

''Would it matter?''

''Maybe not.'' He kissed her lightly. ''Maybe just a little hypothermia would be all right. But not until we've got the tree.''

He took Liz's hand as they crossed the creek, the one the kids played hockey on closer to town, and he kept holding it after they reached the other side. They worked their way past some low-growing willows. He didn't want to tell her what was around the corner. He wanted her to be as surprised, as impressed, as he had been.

''Oh!'' The word was soft, almost a sigh.

A spruce tree grew alone in a small clearing, far

enough from shrubs and poplars that nothing impinged on its shape. Seven feet tall, maybe four feet across its widest, without a bare spot or brown needle to be seen.

"It's too beautiful to cut, Jack."

He smiled at her intensity. "I'm with you there. This one's just to admire. No one's pruned this tree, or sprayed it to look greener. It's come to this all by itself."

"I wonder if anyone's seen it before. It's off the main path, away from the meadow. People aren't supposed to hunt here. Maybe we're the first."

He nearly said they should come every year, every Christmas season, just the two of them. He had to remind himself how unlikely it was that she would ever stay in Three Creeks, given how determinedly she had avoided the place. For all he knew, this was a healing interlude for her. *He* was a healing interlude.

Jack started walking. "Further in, some spruce are growing close together. Taking one out will be good for the rest. Want to help me pick?"

He led her to an area of dense bush, so protected wind couldn't reach inside. The snow lay flat, with mouse tracks etched across the surface. All around, branches seemed to move, full of chickadees that fluttered from spot to spot, feathers fluffed for warmth.

They chose a spruce that wouldn't have room to grow healthily for much longer. Jack started cutting just above the snow line, accompanied by supportive comments from Liz. Just when she was issuing her third offer to take a turn, the tree began to tremble. He checked to be sure Liz was no where near its trajectory, then gave it a push, guiding it past the branches of the remaining trees.

JACK HAD UNWRAPPED EACH of the bells and baubles in the box with infinite care. They had belonged to his mother. Liz's opinion of his uncle had taken an upward slide. Anyone who saved his sister-in-law's paper thin Christmas ornaments for more than twenty years and never broke one had to be okay.

They walked back and forth, checking the three sides of the tree that showed for burnt-out bulbs and empty spots.

"What do you think?"

"I think it's beautiful. The most beautiful tree ever."

Jack stood behind Liz, his arms around her. "Jerry always got us a spruce. Not as nice as this one."

She folded her arms over his. "That's the kind we always had, too. That's what grows wild around here."

"We got them because they were the least expensive tree in the Dairy Queen lot. I never knew when Jerry would turn up with it. It could be two weeks before Christmas, or two days, whatever evening after work he had money in his pocket and time to look through the lot. I got so excited when the apartment door swung open, wide-open, not just a little bit to let a person in."

Liz knew just what he meant. Wide open, and nobody making a fuss about letting cold air in or warm air out. The tree was always too big, and it always scratched the door frame, but nobody minded that, either.

"Jerry would walk in beaming, as excited as I was, with a scrawny tree over his shoulder. I guess it was a Charlie Brown tree. Not to me, though."

"Kids are never disappointed with Christmas trees. They're always magic."

"Exactly. It was magic." Jack's voice slowed and softened as he remembered. "That woodsy smell filled the apartment, and the lights made everything glow. I could believe there were forests full of bears and cougars, not just on TV, but in real life. And if that was true, who knew what else might be? Maybe there really was a grandfatherly old man at the North Pole who wanted to give me toys."

"And did he?"

"Oh, yeah. Somehow he always managed." Liz felt Jack take a deep breath, his chest rising against her back. "You're going to stay, aren't you, Liz?"

"Here?" She couldn't stay here, no matter how much comfort she was finding with Eleanor and Jack.

"With me. Here, Winnipeg, Vancouver, the Gobi Desert…"

She nodded. Even if he was a pirate, she'd stay with him somehow.

AFTER DARK THEY'D MADE LOVE in front of the tree, their skin colored blue and yellow and red and green by the lights. Eventually impatient with the living room floor, they had gone up to Jack's bedroom, the coldest place in the world. Liz lay in the dark, listening to his even breathing. She didn't know how long she'd slept, her head on his shoulder, his arm around her. She felt boneless, every trace of muscle tension gone.

"Liz?" He turned on his side, his hand over her stomach, more rounded now than it had been when she first came home and saw all that whole milk and butter in her grandmother's fridge. "You're nice to wake up to."

"Jack."

"Hmm?"

She ran her hand along his arm, from shoulder to

elbow. She didn't want to hurt him. "You know I can't give you my whole heart."

His hand on her stomach went still. After a moment he said, "Of course you can't. And that's how it should be. If it were me, I wouldn't want to be forgotten."

She raised herself on one elbow, peering where she knew his face must be. Gradually, shapes materialized out of the darkness. The line of his forehead, the curve of his cheek. She felt his chest rising and falling under her. This time, cocooned under the quilt, she took control. She needed to show him how much of her heart she could give.

ANNE HELD THE CRANBERRY and the needle a few inches from her face. Her hand wavered as she aimed the point of the needle at the exact middle of the fruit's stem end. For the past hour she had patiently sifted through the big bowl in the middle of Eleanor's kitchen table, looking for cranberries that were perfectly oval and evenly red. Her chain wasn't very long, but Liz had never seen one more carefully made. Young Will's, on the other hand, was more than five feet long, and growing, and some of the berries were in danger of falling off the thread. Every now and then he popped one into his mouth, screwing up his face at the bitter taste.

The two children had already helped roll out and cut the gingerbread men destined for the tree, using cutters as small as an inch high and as tall as six inches. Anne had arranged hers on the baking sheet as a family, rounded hands touching so they would fuse together in the oven. When the cookies were cool, Eleanor would help them trace the edges with white icing and draw on icing faces and vests. She had done exactly the same thing with Liz and Tom and their cousins at that age.

"Do you ever get tired of making gingerbread men, Grandma?"

"What? Never!"

Will said, "Never get tired of eating them, either, eh, Great-grandma."

Anne looked at Liz with quiet curiosity. Liz smiled, intending to reassure her, but Anne immediately stopped staring. Was she wondering who this person was who claimed to be her aunt, who wrote books and never came home and put the phrases "tired of" and "gingerbread men" in the same sentence?

"You should come to a rehearsal," Pam told Liz. Her students had adapted some of their stories as skits for the school Christmas concert. "You'll be so pleased when you see the kids. Even Jeremy is getting into it. He's a hockey player."

Liz paused while threading a cranberry. She was trying to be as careful as her niece. "Not in Stephen's skit?"

"Oh, no. Jocks only for Stephen. Jeremy is playing one of Dave's friends in the creek hockey skit."

"Has Jennifer found anyone willing to play Charlotte and Smoke?"

Anne raised her hand and bounced lightly in her chair. "I'm Charlotte. I have a long, long tail and whiskers. I have to crawl and meow and follow Jen everywhere."

"Just like normal, eh," Will said. He stood, holding one end of his chain high above his head. "How's that, Great-grandma?"

Eleanor wiped icing sugar from her hands before coming to Will's side. "That's perfect. Let's lay it out in the hallway so it doesn't get tangled."

Liz glanced at the clock. They were all waiting for Tom and Jennifer to return with Eleanor's tree. Tom had refused to tell anyone where he'd found it. All he would say was that it was the best tree ever, and growing in a spot so hard to reach the two younger children wouldn't be able to manage the hike. Of course Will and Anne were indignant about that. Liz suspected Tom wanted to have a bit of an adventure with his oldest daughter, after all the weeks of conflict about the kittens. They had left a few hours ago, with sandwiches and reindeer-shaped shortbread and a big carafe of cocoa. From the length of time they were taking she thought Tom must be following their father's tradition. His excursions for Christmas trees had always turned into a day in the woods, with a snow fort and a campfire.

Pam lowered her voice and leaned close to Liz. "I'm glad you're not mad at me anymore."

Liz glanced at Anne. "I wasn't mad at you, Pam."

"You were. Not just at me."

Anne's cranberry chain rested on the table. She would hear the whole story some day. Maybe it wouldn't be a bad thing if she heard the apology.

"We've been friends all our lives, Pam. When you and Tom got married, I was so happy that we'd be family, as well." There was a wobble in Liz's voice. She stopped to get control of it. "I'm sorry you got caught up in all the blame I threw around."

Pam's eyes were damp. That was something that almost never happened. "I can't believe we've never talked about this. Maybe you'd rather not now. Liz...I'll always wish I'd tried to stop it. We could have just gone up there and got him, dragged him home. Tom and I talk about that sometimes."

Brian had been too old to go to the party at the

gravel pit, and Emily was too young. Liz hadn't ever thought, not even for a second, about how that night might have touched the others. "We all made mistakes, a whole slew of them." She didn't know what else to say.

Will bounced in from the living room and slid all the way to the kitchen door. "They're here! The tree's here!"

Tom and Jennifer came in red-faced and laughing, hair full of static from wearing wool hats. Anne and Will watched quietly, clearly aware they'd missed a big adventure. The tree was huge. It reached right up to the ceiling, but the spaces between its unpruned branches made it look almost lacy.

Fortunately Martin arrived with Pat and Nell in time to help Tom settle the tree into its usual corner. The stand wasn't up to the job on its own, so they tied the top of the tree to a hook screwed into a rafter. They needed a ladder to attach the lights and drape the cranberry chains from branch to branch.

"The star will hide the hook and the rope," Pat said. She looked through boxes until she found it, wrapped in layers of tissue paper. It was just cardboard, painted gold. Liz's grandfather had made it when his children were small.

Liz blinked back sudden tears. This was the last, the last of more than a hundred trees and a hundred Christmases.

Pam's arm came around her. "We'll just have to remember, that's all."

Remembering wasn't enough. Memory distorted things. It made them better or worse or cockeyed. It made her ache. She wanted real things happening. She wanted to be part of them, not watching from a hazy distance.

She couldn't stay. It was a crazy idea. She'd have to sleep on it, and then sleep on it again. The ghosts were receding, though, and most of her memories were happy ones. It was just that the worst one was such a bad one.

She wasn't sure any more if she had run away from Three Creeks or to Vancouver. Whichever it was, it might have been the right thing to do at the time. She just had to figure out if it was the right thing now.

CHAPTER SIXTEEN

ANGLE PARKING WAS STILL ALLOWED on the main street in Pine Point, and it was free. Liz pulled in between a minivan and a pickup truck, almost directly in front of the drugstore. Thinking of all the packages she hoped to be carrying by the time she finished shopping, she slipped her wallet into her coat pocket and her purse under the driver's seat.

As soon as she stepped out of the car, she heard singing. Not the words, just the tune. "Away in the Manger." Down the road she could see a choir in front of the Town Hall. Must be the Brownies and Cubs and 4-H clubs. She used to wonder which of her uniforms to wear. Even during the coldest of winters all the children's groups got together for carolling and then crowded into the bakery for free hot chocolate. She remembered stirring hers with a candy cane, the peppermint flavor melting in.

She stood beside the car, half smiling, until the last notes of the song died away, then headed into Pommerue's drugstore to pick up her grandmother's prescription. When she turned to leave, she bumped into a man standing solidly in her way.

"Oh!"

"Sorry." He was about her height, but broad, and he had a pleasant voice. Almost too pleasant, if there was such a thing. "My fault," he said. He didn't move, though. "Have we met? You look familiar."

"I don't think so." Sometimes people had seen her picture in the back of one of her books. She waited for him to move, and finally he did, with a sudden apology as if he hadn't realized he was between her and the door.

Now the carollers were singing "The Holly and the Ivy." Liz went into the stationer's beside the drugstore, and the carol faded. When she came out with a new set of charcoal pencils for herself and a box of watercolors for Jennifer, they'd moved on to "O Little Town of Bethlehem." It was one of her favorites, so she strolled along the sidewalk and didn't go into the toy store until they were done.

By the time she reached the Town Hall she was loaded with packages. She spotted Jennifer and Will in the group and hoped the bags holding their gifts were hidden in the mound she carried. Jennifer saw her and stopped singing to whisper to the girl beside her. They both waved.

In front of the choir, a hollow bell for donations hung on a pole that looked like a shepherd's crook. A few words scrawled on the accompanying sign said, "Five turkeys still needed." Rearranging her parcels, Liz managed to pull a twenty dollar bill from her pocket. She folded it twice so it would fit into the slot. As her hand came away it collided with someone else's hand.

It was the man from the drugstore. He smiled. "Small street." He pushed his money into the bell. "Between us that's three turkeys. Oh, what the heck." He slipped some more bills from his wallet. "There. And a little extra for cranberry sauce."

"That's very generous."

"I'm usually a miser. Must be the kids' singing." He looked at her with an interest she couldn't interpret. "I don't suppose you'd like to go into the bakery with me for coffee? I need to warm up."

Liz didn't particularly want to have coffee with a strange man. This wasn't Vancouver, though, as her grandmother often reminded her. It was Pine Point. And the bakery was a public place. "A quick cup would be nice," she said, hoping she hadn't hesitated long enough to make him uncomfortable. "I'm afraid I don't have much time."

The bakery was busy, but they found a small table and hung their coats on the backs of their chairs. Because she'd watched him empty his wallet, she insisted on paying for their drinks. Every now and then while she waited at the self-serve counter she glanced his way, telling herself she wasn't really keeping a distrustful eye on him. Each time she looked he was reading a flyer that had been stuck between the napkin dispenser and the salt and pepper shakers. He didn't seem at all interested in making off with her Christmas shopping.

When she finally got through the line, she set a tray with two coffee cups and a plate of cookies on their table. "Sorry for the wait."

"We're not the only ones wanting to warm up today. Thank you—for the drink and for agreeing to have one with me. I don't know many people around here yet."

His name was John Findlay, and he was new in town. He'd transferred from Winnipeg. Hardware, he said. His company wanted to start some rural branches. Envisioning bins of nails and bolts and other things she didn't know how to fit into the conversation, she left it at that. She resisted an impulse to invite him to meet Jack. Just because they'd both moved to the area from the city didn't mean they'd get along.

After a few minutes, she decided not asking him was the right choice. Like Jack, he was reserved, but in a different way. As she found out more about Jack's life with his uncle she realized he'd learned to keep to himself, not as a form of protection, but simply because he'd spent so much time alone. John Findlay was polite, even talkative, but he gave no hint what he was really thinking.

When their coffee was done he gripped her hand warmly, her left hand as if they were Boy Scouts, and held it tightly while he told her how pleased he'd been to meet her. She was glad to get out onto the street, into the fresh air. Next time, Pine Point or not, she wouldn't have coffee with a stranger.

REID COULDN'T BELIEVE IT when Croker told him. He'd bumped into Elizabeth Robb on purpose, introduced himself using a fake name and had coffee with her. At the end of the meeting he'd given her one of those overly sincere two-armed handshakes and committed an amazingly dim-witted act. He'd applied a tiny listening device to her watch. His reasoning was that with Jack now having the old guy over twice a week to check for bugs, they'd never be able to listen in at his house. But if the woman carried a bug with her it was unlikely to be uncovered, and they just might hear something. Croker acknowledged they'd mostly hear her talking to her grandmother. Still, it was a chance. That Croker. Always an optimist.

It was going to be Reid's job to camp out nearby with a receiver. "The idea is, it won't fall off her watch, she won't notice it, and we can get close enough to receive the signal? It just doesn't sound likely."

"It's a state-of-the-art bug."

Reid couldn't keep his tongue bitten. "That'll be a big help later, when we're all standing in a lineup behind glass. She can point you out. 'That one, Officer. That's the oddball who waylaid me just before the whole thing blew up in his face. Yes, the one with access to state-of-the-art surveillance devices.'"

Croker didn't take well to the criticism. "I don't recall the part of our contract that deals with you questioning my judgment."

Reid had to grind his teeth together to keep from saying the rest of what was on his mind. "Fine."

"Fine?" Croker repeated, way too quietly.

"You're right. It's your plan. You're the only one who can judge the best course of action." Croker looked disappointed at how thoroughly he'd backed off. Maybe he was just as frustrated as Reid was. Maybe he was itching for a good, cathartic fight. *Itch away, buddy. Just find another scratching post.*

To get closer to the action Croker had checked into a Pine Point hotel, and no goons had been invited on the trip. *Now* he was keeping a low profile.

LIZ TUCKED HER PARCELS into the bedroom closet and went downstairs to find her grandmother. Eleanor had been spending a lot of time by the tree, so Liz looked in the living room first. She was there, with the lamps turned off and the tree lights plugged in. Lines of tears ran down her face.

"Grandma? What's wrong?"

Eleanor wiped a hand over her cheeks. "Nothing at all."

Somehow, Liz hadn't expected that people cried any more after a certain age. Wasn't it all wisdom and peace and calm detachment once every hair on your head was truly white? She wasn't sure what to do.

"It's nothing," Eleanor repeated. She managed a smile. "Vanity, maybe."

"There's not a vain bone in your body."

"You don't think so? I'll tell you what's bothering me, then, so you can change your mind. It's that ridiculous photograph. Me, sixteen, a dress of curtains."

"I love that photo."

"Oh, so do I." It was out of its box, on the table beside the sofa. Eleanor held it out to Liz. "Look at that skin. It's not just the lack of wrinkles. It's the fullness, the texture."

"My skin doesn't look like that anymore, either, Grandma."

"It's hardly fair, is it? I sometimes wonder where it went. All that time. The Depression. A World War. A man on the moon. People living in space now, for months at a time. But where did this girl go?" She tapped the photograph. "I'm being greedy, I suppose. You see what a hypocrite I am? After treating you to a fine lecture about responsibility and self-respect, I'm still hanging on with all my might to my house and my dining-room table."

"Of course you are!" Liz wrapped her arms around her grandma, carefully, because she felt so fragile. "I have a surprise."

"Well, it's the season for surprises."

"I've decided to stay. To move back to Three Creeks."

Eleanor pulled away. "No, you haven't."

"I have."

"You cannot give up your life in Vancouver to be my caretaker. I won't allow it—"

"And I wouldn't dream of it. You don't need a caretaker."

"Then it's Jack?" Eleanor sounded hopeful.

"It's both of you. But it's me, too. I need to come home. I'll call Mrs. Andersen tomorrow. This house is the heart of the family, Grandma. This house, and you. And neither of you are going anywhere."

SEVERAL DAYS AFTER REID started listening in on Liz Robb's life, Croker told him to come to his hotel room to give a report. He had a sunken-eyed look, as if sleep had been in short supply. Reid couldn't keep his thoughts to himself, no matter how wise it would be to do so. He was the one moving from an old, stinky barn to a nice, cozy snowdrift and back again, receiver in hand. Croker had room service from morning to night.

"I've heard paper rustling and tape tearing," he said, feeling reckless. "I've heard five hundred cups of tea being poured, some rather tuneless carol humming, and I know what she's giving the whole family for Christmas. She's found just the right balance. Thoughtful, but not so much that anyone will feel beholden."

Croker just looked at him.

"Jack hasn't discussed the code with her," Reid went on. "He hasn't mentioned in passing where he keeps it. He hasn't recited his algorithm on bended knee."

Croker rubbed his hand over his eyes, hard, pulling the skin. "This has to be over. You understand? It isn't some game. You started this, you called me. Now we're both *beholden.* And that's not a good thing."

This was a different Croker. He was supposed to be a scary guy, not a scared guy. It made Reid's stomach queasy. "I don't know if it does us any good…he's picking her and her grandmother up for some concert tonight. A Christmas concert at the school."

AN ARTIFICIAL TREE stood in the lobby, not quite straight in its stand, its branches disappearing under gold and silver garlands. All Liz could think of was an aging, tipsy vaudeville queen with too much rouge and too many feather boas.

When she was a student at the old gym-less, stage-less Three Creeks Elementary, the Christmas concert was held at the community center. Each year a real tree had welcomed people at the door, and someone, she'd never learned who, had whisked by in a sleigh, metal runners gliding over the snow, bells jingled by a team of trotting Clydesdales. If they weren't on stage performing, they could see the sleigh go past the windows. They'd never thought, "Oh, but it should be reindeer." They'd just looked at each other, eyes full of unsayable things, enjoying the shivers that went through them, listening as the sound of the bells died away.

The whole town still came, though, and the children, performing in skits they wrote themselves, were as sweet and excited as ever. When Anne crawled cat-like around Jennifer's feet, and young Will tripped over Jeremy's hockey stick on Dave's imaginary creek, Liz wished her parents had been able to come. It was odd to think that this was the first of many concerts she would attend. Next year she might even help with the backdrops. Maybe one day she'd sit here watching her own children hang stockings by a cardboard fireplace, or gather around a plastic doll lying in a bed of hay.

As it had when she was six years old, in grade one, and thirteen in grade eight, and all the years in between, the concert ended with a medley of carols started on stage by the children and joined by the audience. They finished with "Silent Night." Liz reached for Jack's hand.

"All right?" he whispered.

A little blurry-eyed, she nodded. "I have something to tell you."

He raised his eyebrows in question.

"Later."

"Good or bad?"

"Good, I think."

The curtains closed on the stage full of children, and after a long standing ovation, the lights came on. Everyone crowded into the school's lobby, finding coats and keys, and looking for ways around clusters of chatting people. As usual, the Robbs were meeting at Eleanor's so the children could put their letters to Santa up the chimney. A line of headlights wound their way from town, up Creek Road. Liz sat beside Jack in his truck, wondering when she should tell him her news. There were two things she wanted to say, but each time she got close, she changed her mind. It was a big step. Two big steps. What if they were bigger then he intended?

Jack braked, then turned into his driveway. They were stopping to pick up his cappuccino maker.

"Will you come in?"

"Just for a minute." Not that he needed her help, but she had something of her own to do.

Liz hung her coat on the rack and added her boots to the pile behind the door. As she straightened up, Jack's arms came around her, ribbed wool against tweed. He brushed her hair away from her neck and tried to find skin to kiss.

"Turtlenecks are a torment. I kept looking at you this evening, boots to your knee, tights and tweed, sweater to your chin, hair hiding your ears. It drove me nuts."

"You were supposed to be watching the concert."

"I was! I can prove it. There were skits and songs."

Liz laughed, enjoying how that felt when she was surrounded by chest and arms.

"I forget why we came to my house."

"To pick up your coffeemaker."

"Oh, right." He made no move to let go of her. "Can we take five minutes?"

"What self-respecting man would say such a thing?"

"Ten? Ten minutes now, and a hour or two after the party?"

"Done." She eased out of his grasp. "I'll meet you upstairs."

"You're looking mysterious. What are you up to?"

"No questions. No peeking. Not at this time of year."

When he was gone, she pulled a small package from her coat pocket. She glanced up the stairs to be sure he wasn't lurking, then went into the living room and tucked it deep into the branches. It wasn't much. A wooden guitar decoration, with real strings. She kept seeing little things that made her think of Jack, and each time she came to the house she hid something on the tree.

She hurried upstairs and out of her clothes and slid into bed beside him. As soon as she was there, she knew she wouldn't want to leave. It was getting harder to spend only part of her days with him. She wanted to go to sleep with him and wake up with him, have meals with him and read the paper with him…she pressed her hand against his chest, holding him back. "Wait a minute, Jack."

"One of our ten minutes?"

"There's something I have to tell you."

"I hear good things about nonverbal communication."

"It can't wait. If I don't tell you now, it'll be hours before I can."

He moved back, focusing on her face. "Is this what you mentioned at the concert? The good thing?"

She nodded. "I hope it's a good thing. You remember my attempt at math?" She wanted to keep things light. "About percentages of heart space available?"

There was a flash of his old caution. "Oh, that math."

"I was wrong." She patted her chest. "I have here an entire heart, just for you." Whatever she'd been expecting in response, it wasn't that worried frown.

"There's turning the page, Liz, and then there's tossing the book out. I never wanted that for Andy."

"I'm not tossing anything out. I'm done with tossing parts of my life away. He'll always be with me. I hope that's all right."

Jack nodded. "Of course."

"You, I love in a different way." There. The word was out. "It's more grown-up, more real than it ever got a chance to be with Andy. And, if you don't mind sharing my left ventricle, it's complete." Talk about throwing caution to the winds. He said she should take a risk. Now she needed to hear something back. It didn't have to be eloquent. *Me, too* would be all right.

"I've been checking out some property in British Columbia," he said. "There's nothing appropriate really close to Vancouver, but I found an existing Christmas tree farm that's not a bad commute."

Liz smiled, amused and relieved. Content, too. He'd grown up without a mother's hugs. As a declaration of his feelings, it was fine. "There's no need for you to move. I'm staying."

"Here?" He looked as if he didn't dare believe it. "You're moving back?"

"I'm buying Grandma's house. I'm going to get old in Three Creeks. I'm going to learn to make baskets from straw, cream butter with my bare hands, stuff like that. It's got the added benefit of averting a family crisis."

"You mean your grandmother won't have to move? Unless she wants to, of course."

"I mean I'll own the land, and you can rent your field forever. Grandma was going to sell it to you, you know."

"Oh, boy." Jack looked surprised at first, then touched, and finally, relieved. "I would have been thrown off the hockey team."

AS MUCH AS JACK LOOKED forward to experiencing one of the Robb's traditional pre-Christmas evenings, it was hard to pull himself away. He kissed Liz one last time, then flipped back the covers. "If we're any longer we won't be able to explain it to your family." He hurried into his clothes, jumbled on the chair. Liz still stretched across the bed, completely uncovered. "Aren't you freezing?"

"I'm seeing if I can entice you back."

"It's your Aunt Edith I'm thinking of right now."

"Oh!" She thumped him with a pillow.

"You know how she is. She'll say something embarrassing in that vague tone of hers. *'Oh look, it's Jack and Liz at last, we wondered what the two of you were up to on your own for so long…'*"

Liz had pulled the sheet over her head at the thought of what Edith might say, but she came out from under it to add, *"But oh, how becomingly pink your cheeks are, my dear."*

And laughter made them even pinker. It was good to see Liz light-hearted. What if living in Three Creeks turned out to be as bad for her as she used to think it was? "Are you sure about this? Because I can go to British Columbia, no problem. Growing balsams would be a breeze there. I don't have a lot of reason to stay in Manitoba, other than habit. My parents' roots were here, but I've never felt them."

"Both of our roots are here."

Jack shook his head. "Some days I think the land I bought is already in my blood. The rest of the time I wonder if I'm just trying to convince myself I can make a life here because I don't want to admit the whole thing is a huge, expensive mistake. An impulsive mistake, just like my old computer buddies say."

Liz got hold of his sweater and gave it a gentle shake. "Your old computer buddies are wrong. You haven't made a mistake. And I'm sure."

Jack kissed her hand, then pulled himself away. "I'll find a box for the coffeemaker. It'll be ready by the time you're down." When he got to the door, he looked back at her still sitting in bed, rumpled covers and bare skin and wild hair. "I love you, Liz."

Before she could answer, he kept going, out to the hall and down the stairs. Hard to believe he'd got this old without ever saying those words. He and Jerry knew how they felt but never mentioned it, and although he'd cared about other women, it was never like this.

He was in the kitchen packing the coffee machine and a few varieties of coffee into a box when the back door opened. He half expected it to be Edith. *Now, Jack, I realize you're from the city and people do things differently there, but this is no way to treat a young lady like Liz…*

It wasn't Edith.

It was Reid. And the two other men on the videotape.

CHAPTER SEVENTEEN

THEY STOOD JUST INSIDE THE DOORWAY, a man Jack didn't know, but remembered from the surveillance tape, with Scott Webb and Reid on either side. Scott was Legs? That was hard to grasp. They'd worked together in the spring and part of the summer. Somehow you didn't expect the worst from a guy who planted pumpkins with you.

He couldn't take all three of them. Jack forced his muscles to relax. His plan, such as it was, had never included an all-out fight. Behind them on the hat stand, he could see the sleeve of Liz's coat. What if she'd heard them come in? She would race from the bedroom, expecting relatives, looking guilty and embarrassed, blurting some cover story about searching for coffee filters upstairs.

Hoping she would hear and know to stay where she was, he spoke as loudly as he dared. "Reid, I've been meaning to talk to you about this. You've got to learn to call before you drop in."

"Door was open, bud."

Jack hadn't got into the rural habit of not locking his door, but he and Liz had only meant to nip in for the coffeemaker. At least his old friend had trouble meeting his eyes. Reid looked haggard. Jack felt a moment of pity, but it disappeared fast.

His attention moved to the other man he'd trusted. "Found new employment, Scott?" Scott sniffed wetly, and mumbled an embarrassed greeting. He'd been barely visible on the videotape, but Jack was surprised he hadn't noticed anything familiar in the small figure. ''Or was the job always about keeping an eye on me?''

Scott shook his head and started to say something. He stopped at a sound from Leather Coat. The man who was clearly in charge came further into the room. Jack tensed when he approached the staircase, but he went past it, into the living room, straight to the VCR. A glowing green light showed the machine was on, and a red light that it was taping. Too bad he hadn't noticed that when he first came downstairs. The man hit the eject button and threw the tape to Reid. ''You have another tape, I believe. Where is it?''

''I took it to the police.''

From behind Jack, Reid said, ''He wouldn't involve the police, Croker.''

The man's eyes swiveled to Jack. The expression—or lack of it—in them stopped any idea Jack had of denying it further. He didn't want those eyes searching the house, coming to rest on Liz. ''Second shelf, in the Charlie Chaplin sleeve.''

Croker took the time to insert the tape into the VCR, checking to be sure it was the right one. ''Any copies?''

''No.''

The empty eyes flicked over him. Jack got the feeling no one could convince this guy of anything. He believed what he wanted. Did what he wanted.

''What does the tape show, anyway?'' Reid said. ''Couple of friends knocking at the door, someone letting them in. Nothing more than that.''

''Maybe.'' Croker headed back to the kitchen. He sat at the table and turned on Jack's laptop. ''Every day we've spent on this exercise has cost money. And here it is, the middle of December. I don't know about you, Jack, but I don't like to go into the New Year with old business hanging over me."

Jack was almost sure he'd heard a sound from upstairs. There was no sign that Croker had heard it, but he seemed like the kind of man who could file away a creaking floorboard and investigate it later. He had to get them out of the house. "You're looking for a code I made a number of years ago."

Croker smiled. "It's so much easier to accomplish things when everyone is straightforward. Yes, the code. You have it. I want it."

"Didn't Reid also mention that I destroyed it?"

The man's voice got softer. "I see. We're not quite done playing games."

"Jack," Reid said.

It was a warning. Remnants of loyalty, or a simple threat?

"I couldn't risk keeping it. There was always a chance someone would try to take it."

"Such a conundrum for you. Dangerous to keep, impossible to destroy."

Jack shrugged. "It had to be done. I burned my notes, wiped the hard drive and reformatted the disk. Even then, I worried about some hotshot rescuing the data, so I took a hammer to it and threw away the pieces. You saw me do it, Reid."

"I saw you destroy a diskette."

Croker rubbed his finger over the laptop's touch pad, highlighted one of the icons on the screen and double-clicked. A box appeared, requesting a password. "You know what I think? I think you keep your algorithm right here, close to you."

"On a laptop? Do you know how often these things are stolen?"

"All the time," Croker agreed. "We tried to hack into your machine. Couldn't do it. Eventually, we realized your computer wasn't hooked up to the Internet. Ever. An odd thing for a man like you. What possible reason could you have? Then I saw it. You don't want to risk anybody getting in, breaking through your firewall, finding your treasure. Tell me, Jack. What's the code worth to you?"

"Millions if I'd kept it—"

"Is it worth the old lady down the road?"

Jack went still.

"Or maybe the lovely Elizabeth. We had coffee the other day in Pine Point. Charming town. Like those little houses people put on their mantels at Christmas. You know the ones I mean, with the candles inside?"

This was the man Liz had met for coffee?

"Friendly woman, in a restrained way. And easy on the eyes, eh, Jack? Really quite an attractive combination, warmth and coolness at the same time. Tempting."

Scott cleared his throat the way he always did when he was nervous.

"But lovely young ladies are a dime a dozen, aren't they, for a man in your position? The old lady's special, though. Sort of a surrogate grandmother. Nice for both of you, I'm sure." Croker looked at his watch. "I can give you five minutes to think it over, Jack. The code, or the old lady. No, make it two minutes. Then I pay Grandmother a visit." He smiled. "Show her what big teeth I have."

LIZ WAS AFRAID TO MOVE AWAY from the grill. The floor was bound to squeak. When she'd first heard voices downstairs she'd started out of the bedroom, hoping she didn't look like someone who'd just had a very satisfying experience in bed. She was preparing an excuse for being upstairs—maybe she could say Jack needed a warmer sweater?—when she'd heard Jack say Reid's name.

She'd almost forgotten about the men who'd broken into the house. She'd almost forgotten about Jack's code. Unbreakable codes and traitorous friends didn't seem quite real, not as real as falling in love and deciding where to live and getting ready for Christmas.

This time, they weren't sneaking in. Jack's truck was in the driveway, lights were on in the house. They could see he was home. That meant the guessing games were over. One way or another, they intended to take the code tonight.

At first she'd thought keeping quiet and out of the way might be the best thing to do. Jack would know how to deal with them. Reid was a friend of his after all, though not a very good one, and Scott Webb… well, Scott was Jeremy's dad. She couldn't believe they meant much harm. Everything changed when the third man, the one she knew as John Findlay, threatened Eleanor. She had to make sure he didn't get any closer to her grandmother than he was at this minute.

At last there was movement in the kitchen, a chair scraping back, a door creaking—enough noise to cover any she would make. She went to the spare room, the one over the living room. Through the heating vent, she heard Scott say, "We looked there." He sounded defensive. "Three times."

Looked where? What had they found?

"Just what I complained about, isn't it? Old houses are a real pain when you're trying to find something important.'' It was Findlay, or Croker, again. His tone was almost conversational, except that it was so cold. ''All right, Jack. Do your stuff.''

Liz heard a beeping sound, the kind Jack's laptop made when he turned it on. Her heart twisted when she heard him speak, his voice so calm. ''We still have a problem.''

''I sincerely hope not.''

''The computer's hard drive is divided in two parts. Not equal parts, I set aside just a few gigabytes. Each section is run by a different operating system. It's not apparent when you boot up.''

''A hidden partition,'' Reid said. ''Nice.''

''Don't tell me about it. Just open it.'' It was Findlay, or Croker, whoever he was, sounding a little less conversational.

''I'm afraid I can't. I got rid of the boot disk.''

There was a silence. Liz found herself holding her breath.

Then Reid spoke. ''He's screwing with you, Croker. He can make another boot disk easily. Hang on—I've got Linux on my machine.''

More noise. From what she could tell, someone was going outside. Liz got her fingernails under the grill and lifted, tensing when dust caught under its frame rained down into the living room.

The ceiling was eight feet from the floor, not ten as it was at her grandmother's, so by the time she got through the grill's opening, she wouldn't have all that far to drop. Still, landing wouldn't just make noise. It would shake the floor.

Whoever had left the house was coming back. There was noise from the door again, louder voices. Liz sat so her feet went through the opening in the floor, then her legs, and, with another scattering of dust and her skirt pushing up to her waist, her hips. Tight fit. One more piece of pumpkin pie, and she'd be stuck.

Now her shoulders. She was through, dangling from the living room ceiling. And still, they didn't seem to have heard her. She stretched her leg toward the armchair. Too far. She hooked her foot under the end table, and pulled. It slid, protestingly, a few inches across the carpeted floor, a pile of books on top tilting. She tugged again, moving it a few more inches, and again, until it was right under her. By then the books had had enough, but she caught them with her foot before they fell. The table was so full it was hard to find anywhere to stand. Balancing her weight on either side, she eased herself down, then stepped onto the floor.

Now to get out. She was reluctant to leave Jack alone. She reminded herself what his priorities would be: the code, and Eleanor's safety. Getting out and finding help was the best thing she could do.

Liz's heart, already thudding, found a way to beat harder. When she got to the front door she would be almost in line with the path to the kitchen. If they moved backward, they would see her. If she'd heard them open the back door, what would happen when she opened the front?

She moved as lightly as she could, past the armchair where she usually sat and past the Christmas tree, over the very spot where they had laid together. Through the kitchen doorway, she could more clearly hear them browbeating Jack. He was staying calm, sounding as if he really wanted to help them, if only he could. She recognized an artificial quality in his tone. Did Reid? Did Scott? A feeling of dread filled her, the fear that when she went out the door she would never hear that quiet, strong voice again.

She turned the deadbolt with a little click, then the doorknob. At that moment Scott Webb moved a few steps back, steps that brought him into view.

He blinked rapidly when he saw her. And then looked away, clearing his throat loudly. A moment later he was seized by a prolonged coughing spell.

Liz went outside.

AFTER HIS BANK MANAGER'S CALL, Jack had bought a second laptop, identical to the one Reid and the others had already tried to hack. He'd copied all his files, all but the code, onto the new machine, wrapped the original in a dustcover and secreted it in the crawl space under the kitchen floor—difficult to find, especially if the searcher wasn't familiar with the idiosyncrasies of old houses. He hadn't counted on a situation developing that would end with him telling thieves where to find it.

He could kick himself. Why had he ever thought he could keep the algorithm safely hidden? His precautions so far were useless, worse than a game. Everything had hinged on Reid. On Reid believing the code no longer existed, on Reid's loyalty. It was a given that if information about the code got out someone would come looking for it. Someone with the means and the will to get it.

Using his own laptop, Reid easily made a new boot disk to open the Linux partition. Jack entered the password without being asked and his long-hidden files opened.

"Well?" Croker said.

Reid leaned over Jack's shoulder. "It's encrypted. As we expected."

Croker's hand landed heavily on Jack's shoulder. "You can save us some time, get us out of here sooner. Whatever code you've used, one we can break, or your own, you've got the key. Just get this gibberish into a state I can use, and I'll be gone."

Webb had started pacing. Barely raising his voice, Croker told him to settle down. He turned back to Jack. "The key, McKinnon. Now."

Jack had taken particular pleasure in hiding the key. He'd hoped to keep it safe for itself, regardless of its use. He leafed through his sheet music and found the piece Liz couldn't hum. He'd decrypt the files, and they'd open. Reid and Croker would see the algorithm for a few seconds, and so would he, one last look. Then his final precaution would activate.

SHE RAN FROM THE LIGHTS of the house into the yard, slipping on the path. She couldn't believe she'd got out, that Scott hadn't stopped her, that the others hadn't been aware of something, noise or fear or her brain rushing from one thought to another. She looked longingly at Jack's truck. If only she had the keys.

Keeping one eye on the house, she eased her way to the truck. She placed her hands on the ice-cold metal and heaved herself up to stand on a tire. She couldn't see a thing, but she knew there was a pile of burlap sacks inside. She leaned in, feeling around. There. She pulled an armload of burlap toward her and jumped to the ground.

The road or the woods? The road would be easier going, but if Scott changed his mind, and they came after her, they would find her in a minute. She headed down her usual path to the woods, the hard packed snow painful against her stockinged feet. She was thankful to reach the shelter of the trees. It was darker there. The path curved, hidden by crisscrossing branches. After all her trips back and forth, she could remember the twists and turns, but if they followed they'd have a challenge. She paused to tie some sacks over her feet, then tore a hole in the bottom of a few more and layered them over her head. It wasn't much, but it helped.

Already, she was shivering. The snow reflected enough moonlight that she could see where she was going, just barely. Shuffling awkwardly in the layers of loose burlap, she tried to run, only once going straight ahead when she should have turned. Whenever she heard a crackling sound deeper in the woods, she refused to let herself think about wildlife and instead replayed Croker's voice and pictured those two traitors, Reid and Scott.

Now she was in her grandmother's woods. She hurried on, her breath coming in shuddering gasps, shooting cold air deep into her lungs. Light shone from the house, and from the colored lights on the evergreens in the yard. What if they'd followed? What if she'd led them to Eleanor?

She heard barking. Two dark shapes barreled toward her. Liz bent to get hold of the dogs. They whined and sniffed her face anxiously. If only they were like Lassie and would go tell the humans what was wrong.

The kitchen door swung open. Uncle Will was silhouetted against the light inside. "Who's there?" His booming voice gave her the energy she needed. She was halfway to the door when he recognized her. "It's Liz!" Figures streamed outside. Brian and Tom, Pam and Martin, Emily and Jennifer. And Daniel. Why Daniel?

"Jack—"

"Don't worry," Tom said. "We'll take care of it."

"We've figured it out," Martin said. "We've figured something out, anyway.'' He went on, talking about computers and bugs and suspicious cars and a strange man asking questions in Pine Point. Tom tried to lift her, but she wouldn't let him, so he got an arm around her and helped her into the house. Voices all around exclaimed that she had no coat, no shoes. Eleanor called for blankets. It was hard to form words with her teeth banging together. Then she saw the guns. Shotguns and hunting rifles. No one got a gun out at all unless it was hunting season or coyotes were bothering the cattle. They were always locked up. Now they were out, and they were meant to deal with people.

JACK HEARD A SMALL SOUND from Croker when the program opened. The fulfillment of his quest. Lucky guy. Not everyone got to see their personal Holy Grail. He counted the seconds. Five, four, three…

Without warning or fanfare, the symbols on the screen dissolved.

''What?'' Croker wasn't mad yet. ''What happened?''

Jack looked at the empty screen. At least Liz had stayed quiet upstairs after that first squeak of the floorboards. They had no reason to go up. No reason to go to Eleanor's.

Croker gripped the back of Jack's chair. ''I asked you a question.''

Jack got up slowly, moving so his back was to the kitchen counter. He wanted to be able to see all three men. Scott's heart wasn't in this. Reid…he had no idea how far Reid would go. Croker was the one to watch if things got wild. ''The files are gone, Croker. They deleted themselves.''

''Deleted themselves?'' Croker repeated.

"I programmed the files so that if they were opened and I didn't enter a specific pattern of keystrokes within a certain time, they would self-delete."

At first, Croker's face was as blank as the monitor, then rage flowed in. Out of the corner of his eye Jack saw Scott back toward the door and out of it.

Reid spoke urgently. "He'll have a copy! Jack, tell him. Where is it? Did you burn a CD? That's what I'd do."

There had been a couple of tough streets between Jack and his school when he was a boy, so Jerry had taught him how to defend himself. He'd only needed to use his lessons once, when a couple of older kids had tried to relieve him of the money he'd collected from his paper route, so he hadn't built up much expertise. Watching Croker's anger build, he reviewed the basics of a solid punch, and when Croker came at him, he let go, sending all the power he could from his shoulder and down his arm to his fist. He felt the impact in his elbow. His hand was going to hurt when the adrenaline left his body.

Croker crumbled onto the floor.

Both surprised, Jack and Reid stared at each other.

"Was it just the three of you?"

"Croker has guys of the faceless goon variety working with him. I don't know where they are. I don't even know who he works for." Reid seemed shaken. Or angry. Jack wasn't sure which. If he said the whole thing had gotten away on him, that he never would have allowed any harm to come to Liz or Eleanor, Jack could forgive the rest.

Croker moaned and tried to move. He didn't look ready to function, but to be on the safe side Jack tied his hands behind his back with a tea towel. The leather coat came open, exposing a shoulder holster. Jack had never seen anyone but a cop carry a handgun. Should he remove it, in which case a gun would be floating around in the same room as Reid, or leave it snapped in place?

There was a clicking sound. Jack looked up. Reid didn't need Croker's gun. He had his own.

"Come off it, Reid."

"You come off it." Barely suppressed anger filled Reid's voice. "Off your high horse. Off your pedestal. You think this is a game?"

"I haven't thought that for a while."

"Sure you have. Right up to now. You were ready to pop a couple of Labatt's a minute ago, if I looked sheepish and chagrined enough. You're going to have to take me more seriously."

"Okay."

"Okay?" The word was like a small explosion. "Don't patronize me, Jack. I know my brain isn't quite up to your high standard—"

"Reid."

"—but it's managed to turn your life upside down and it's going to keep on doing that. You have a code and I have a gun. Q.E.D." He gave a tight smile. "Where's the other copy, Jack?"

Muscle memory. Jack saw his uncle in the apartment living room lunging toward him with a spoon to simulate a weapon. Lift, swing from the hip, release. The kick worked just the way Jerry had told him it would. The gun flew across the room and Reid cried out, clutching his hand. Jack dived for him, and they both landed hard on the kitchen floor.

"That was well done," someone said.

Figures appeared at the back door and in the doorway to the living room. Jack couldn't get a good look. Even though he could hardly use his right hand, Reid was putting up a fight. It seemed to be the entire Robb family, cradling guns pointed at the floor.

Will said, "Looks like you have everything under control, Jack."

A knee colliding with his stomach kept Jack from answering. He was trying to subdue Reid without hurting him. "Would you check on Liz?" he gasped. "She's upstairs."

"Liz is fine. Chilly, but fine. Likely having tea with her grandma by now."

Daniel picked up Reid's gun and showed it to Brian. "What do you want to bet that's not registered?"

"Need a hand, Jack?" Tom asked.

"Nope." This was his friend, and he was going to deal with him. Jack grabbed hold of Reid's shirt. "Can't you keep still? Look at all the people in this room. You're not going anywhere. I don't want to hit you again."

That reinforcements had arrived seemed to be news to Reid. He stopped struggling and looked around the kitchen. He gave a half smile. "I guess I lose, you win."

REID AND CROKER HAD ALREADY been transferred to Ottawa, where people from CSIS and the RCMP Technical Security Branch were lining up to talk to them. Scott was under lock and key in Pine Point. He was low in the pecking order, hired because Croker believed he could keep an eye on Jack's comings and goings. It was a few days before the police finished asking questions and everyone settled down enough to get together again for the pre-Christmas visit at Eleanor's.

The table was set for eighteen. Jack hadn't arrived yet. Everyone else was there, noisy by the tree and in the kitchen. They were still talking about Liz's stocking-foot trek through the woods and the Robb men's descent on Jack's house. It was the best kind of story, because everyone felt like a hero.

Liz went to the kitchen when she saw Bella and Dora trot to the door with that puppyish enthusiasm they only showed for one person. There was a figure in the yard, standing still, staring at the house. She grabbed a coat without checking to see if it was hers and hurried outside. Light snow had started to fall, big, soft, slow flakes.

"Jack? We're waiting for you."

"I know. Sorry."

"What's wrong?"

He shook his head. She wasn't sure if that meant he didn't know or he didn't plan to tell her. He put his hands on her shoulders, gently, as if she were breakable, then kissed her forehead. "You came so close to getting hurt. It never entered my mind that anything I did could harm another person. I'm sorry, Liz. You and Eleanor…"

"We're fine, Jack."

"I didn't take the risk seriously enough. I put you in danger."

"You took care of everything. You safeguarded the code. When it needed to be done, you destroyed it."

He wasn't reassured. "You see couples all over the place. It seems so easy. But look at my father—he was driving the night they died."

"And look at me, the night Andy died."

"No—"

"Yes. We'll just muck along as best we can, two despicably imperfect people."

Jack smiled at the description. Snowflakes rested unmelting on his hair, their patterns as clear as paper cutouts. Her mind's eye filed the image away, then zoomed in on the light gray eyes full of purpose, on the gloved hand reaching out, then touching her face. She closed her eyes and rubbed her cheek against his woolen palm.

"Are you two coming in?" Tom was in the doorway. "The kids are waiting with their letters."

They hurried to the house and hung up their coats before joining the others in the living room. In the corner by the front window the tree Tom and Jennifer had found stood tall, the star Grandpa had made brushing the ceiling. Nell stared, transfixed, her hair multicolored. Anne and young Will looked for the gingerbread men they'd made earlier. Tonight, they were allowed to eat them.

Uncle Will raised his voice. "Who's got letters for Santa?"

Nell turned, uncertain. Her eyes searched the darkened room. "Here, sweetie," Pat said. Her hand stretched out, holding a paper covered in crayon scribble.

Jennifer bent over so her face was near Nell's. "Want some help, Nellie girl?" No amount of cajoling could get the toddler close to the fireplace, though, and she refused to give up her letter. Finally, she ran crying to Martin, who retreated to the sofa with her, quietly singing "Jingle Bells."

When Jennifer and young Will had sent their letters up the chimney, Jack approached the fireplace with a thick wad of paper, a number of sheets folded many times.

"Whoa," Tom said. "That's quite a list. What are you asking for, Jack?"

"Never you mind."

Anne said, "Grown-ups don't put lists up the chimney."

Jack caught Liz's eye before dropping the paper into the flames. She came to his side, and leaned close enough to speak into his ear. "Another copy? A paper copy?"

"I'm an old-fashioned guy. That's the last one. It was in a safety deposit box in Pine Point."

"I'm sorry you had to do that. Did it hurt?"

"Not a bit."

"Jack."

"Hmm?"

"Will you marry me?"

His arms came around her, hands locked over the small of her back. "You know I will."

"Whispering is rude," Anne said. "That's what I've always been told."

"I'm not sure what we'll do with two big old houses."

"I think we'll keep the slightly warmer one."

"And we'll keep the transplant bed."

"Land and insulation. That's what matters." Jack's expression became serious, and a bit uncertain, the way she'd learned it did when he was about to get personal. His mouth was right beside her ear, and his breath tickled her as he talked. "And you. Knowing you makes my life so much richer. To spend it all with you…I can't believe my luck."

Jennifer jumped up and down near the tree. "Look, Liz and Mr. McKinnon are kissing."

"Jennifer, shush."

"In public," Anne said.

"Well," said Edith. "I had no idea things had gone this far. Of course, you people have said things, but you know how I am. I don't pay attention to gossip.

I wonder...do you suppose she'd let me make the cake?''

''Liz's mom will want to make the cake.''

''I don't know about that,'' Will said. ''Jack's a man of means, apparently. He'll likely want to hire one of those caterers that charges more than any sensible person pays for a house—''

''That's enough.'' Eleanor's voice was firm. ''Leave them alone.''

''They won't, you know,'' Liz whispered.

Jack smiled. ''That's what I'm hoping.''